Praise for His Vision Of Her
by G. D. Dess

"Dess charts the cultural geography of New York's downtown art scene with care and arch wit."
—*Publishers Weekly*

❧

"...Mr. Dess considers art and authenticity, love and
exploitation, appearance and reality. It is a tribute to
Mr Dess' technical precision and to his compassion that,
even though the medium of Stephen's rarified vision of
Gilberte, we get an indelible and poignant vision of them
both."
—*New York Times Sunday Book Review*

Harold Hardscrabble

A NOVEL BY

G. D. DESS

AUTHOR OF HIS VISION OF HER

What follows is a novel in the classic mode, but one that in the words of Don DeLillo endeavors "to be equal to the complexities and excesses of the culture." The characters are fictional, but the literary and critical texts cited throughout are not. Footnotes referencing many of the works mentioned have been provided so readers can locate them if they choose.

Harold Hardscrabble
Copyright © 2017 by G. D. Dess
Lone Wolf Books
All rights reserved
Printed in the United States of America
First United States edition, 2017
desswrites.com

Library of Congress Control Number: 2017901633
ISBN 978-0-9985589-0-5 Hardback
ISBN 978-0-9985589-1-2 Paperback
ISBN 978-0-9985589-2-9 ebook

Cover design by Andy Moore
Book design by Ashley Ruggirello, www.CardboardMonet.com

In memory of my father

H. M. Dess

1929 - 2010

But there comes a day,
there always comes a day of tears and madness.
—Saul Bellow

The great American substitute for social
revolution is murder.
—Walter Dean Burnham

Harold Hardscrabble

We all know people whose lives didn't work out the way they appeared destined to unfold ... people who drifted off in a direction that could not have been foretold.
Harold Hardscrabble was one of these people.

Harold met his future wife during his junior year in college. Her name was Carol. She was in his English class and although they often exchanged glances during class, they didn't speak to each other before or after.

Then one day when Harold was studying in the library, Carol appeared and sat down across from him. She lazily draped one leg over the empty chair next to her and flicked a pencil back and forth in her hand. She stared at him, sizing him up as it were, and smiled at him.

—Which authors are you going to write about for your term paper? she asked when she finally spoke.

—I'm not sure yet. Maybe Hemingway and Henry James, Harold said.

—Why is it always Hemingway? Why doesn't anyone ever use his first name?

Harold had no answer.

—Well, it's probably not important, Carol said.

—How about you? Which authors are you going to write about?

—I haven't given it much thought yet, she said, at least not as much as you.

—I haven't thought about it at all, he said. I mean, I have the names, and.....

—That's more thought than I've given it.

There was an awkward pause in the conversation, such that it was.

—I think they have different aesthetic outlooks, he offered.

—Who?

—The authors I'm going to write about.

—Oh, well, maybe, Carol said. I wouldn't know anything about that.

She got up as abruptly as she had sat down.

—See ya, she threw over her shoulder as she walked away.

That was the beginning.

In the coming days, Carol visited Harold in the library when he was studying. She showed up in the cafeteria when he was eating, and on the quad when he was relaxing between classes. He was flattered by Carol's attention. Due to her persistent continuing attentions, he began to notice her pleasing physical attributes. For Carol had beautiful strawberry-blond hair that framed an angular face, and a glowing, flawless complexion. She had a perfectly proportioned figure and carried herself with a self-assured cockiness he found sexy. She also appeared to possess more intellectual prowess than any of the girls with whom he had previously had relations, which was, to Harold, an added attraction.

Carol was majoring in the social sciences because, as she explained, they had practical applications in the real world. Harold's interest was literature, the lessons of which could be applied to any world.

—I don't read a lot of fiction. I don't study stories like you do. I read for fun, Carol said. I just like a decent plot line.

She didn't study stories, but like Harold, she was devoted to her schoolwork and took learning seriously, believing, as he did, that you only got out of learning what you put in. Since she wanted a lot, and was ambitious, and had plans to *make it* someday, she worked hard. He was drawn to her industriousness and her diligence. That she could hold an intelligent conversation about myriad topics gave her an additional charm that was hard to resist.

And then there was the sex.

They had been going out for weeks and had kissed and canoodled in all the local bars and on the quad and in quiet, deserted aisles in the library before they went to her apartment and had sex. Only then did she inform him that the delay was caused by a former boyfriend, or roommate who had been a sometime boyfriend, and now was not. It didn't seem right, Carol said, that she should be sleeping with two men at the same time.

〜

Carol lived off campus in a cramped apartment that had formerly been the attic of an old Victorian-style house. The ceilings were sloped so low Harold had to duck to move around. Carol had lived in the apartment since her sophomore year. She had furnished it herself, mostly from Goodwill, the Salvation Army, and secondhand furniture shops. Beads hung from the ceiling and separated the so-called living area from the sleeping space. Rope rugs were scattered on the floor. There was bric-a-brac everywhere: candles and beaded picture frames and ceramic flower pots and wicker baskets, Chinese fans, earth-mother figurines, crystals, Navajo rock sculptures. Chimes dangled from all the windows. Leaves from potted plants poked out of corners. It was cluttered but cozy.

Harold preferred spending time at Carol's apartment because he didn't have his own. His housing situation entitled him to an incommodious bedroom in a three-bedroom apartment he shared with two roommates who kept irregular hours and exhibited unpredictable behavior. Carol visited him there once and pointed out that his bedroom was dirty, the kitchen filthy, the bathroom revolting. Harold didn't disagree. But after passing several consecutive days at Carol's, he became agitated and anxious. While at first he attributed these sensations to the miniature doll-house proportions of Carol's apartment, which sometimes did make him think he was suffocating, he soon concluded that the cause of his unease was not the apartment, but his continual physical and psychological exposure to Carol.

〰

Harold had never dated a girl who had her own apartment. All the girls he had gone out with prior to Carol had either lived in the university dorms or shared an apartment with roommates as he did. Communal living had limited the amount of time he and a girlfriend could spend alone. It made sex a rushed or hushed exercise. Moreover, at some point, you were expected to return to your own place. At Carol's they had all the time in the world. They had sex, cuddled in bed for hours, took a shower, ate a snack, walked around naked, and had more sex, all without worrying about someone barging through the door and interrupting their private pleasures.

Harold complied with Carol's desire for him to spend his days and nights at her place. It was so much nicer than his. But there were those times when he felt smothered by Carol and needed to be by himself. At the beginning of their relationship, it was easy to slip away without giving Carol an explanation of where he was going or what he intended to do. A simple *I'll be back later* sufficed.

Then, one day when he announced he was heading back to his apartment Carol asked: *Why do you have to go?* He didn't comprehend how fraught with issues this innocuous-sounding question was. Only after a long and excruciating exchange did he learn that there was no satisfactory answer to Carol's inquiry, at least none that would free him from the dialectical terror to which she subjected him. For while on the surface, *why do you have to go?* appeared to be a straightforward question, he discovered multiple meanings were concealed in the phrase, and they were revealed only when it was closely and painfully analyzed.

Close parsing of the words revealed, for example, the word *have* in Carol's interpretation of the phrase was a colloquial substitute for the more formal construction *it is necessary*. Another problematic term turned out to be the infinitive *to go*, which is a timeless verb tense, as well as an imperative. So when Harold said he had to go, and she asked *why do you have to* go, her words implied she understood him to mean that he had no choice except to leave and that his departure was necessary, and time had no bearing on his behavior. He was saying, in other words, *it is necessary that I leave you*. How could that possibly be? Clearly, Carol pointed out, there was no necessary reason for his departure. If he was planning to study at his place or in the library, he could just as easily choose to study at her place, couldn't he? Thus, he had no legitimate reason for leaving. She wouldn't bother him. She had to study as well. So why did he have to go? Looked at in this light, it was indisputably true that he didn't *have to go*.

The amazing conclusion Carol drew from this analysis was not only that Harold did not *have to go*, but that the locution *it is necessary that I leave you* was equivalent to him saying, *I want to leave you*.

—You want to get away from me for a little bit, she said. You don't have to deny it. I understand.

He did his best to explain he didn't want to get away *from her*. There were times when he needed to study alone, to be in his own head, by himself.

—Sometimes I need to work without witnesses, he said.

—No, no. You need breathing room. That's what it is. I can be suffocating, she admitted, because I don't like not knowing. I don't like mystery. That's why I like to know what you're doing all the time. I'm sorry.

Confessing she was at fault for his behavior, along with her explanation of her motives and her apology, had the uncanny effect of making her obsessive, irrational demand appear rational. Harold recognized he was being manipulated. Nevertheless, he felt obliged to comply with her request, even if it meant becoming a captive of her desire for certainty.

He knew it was wrong of her to be so controlling. He came to understand that she was a person who needed to be in control of every situation and was only trying to keep order in her world, of which he was now an intimate part. She became dependent on him and couldn't bear to be without him or have his whereabouts and the hour of his return unknown. While her possessiveness was unsettling and annoying in the beginning, he convinced himself it was an endearing quality that demonstrated her vulnerability. He told himself her outsized demands were indicative of the depth of her feeling for him. She was crazy about him to a degree that no one else he had dated had been.

⟨∿⟩

Harold was normally a placid and peaceful person. Carol was brash, energetic, and volatile. He had a lively mind and imagination, but was laconic. He had been raised by parents who were emotionally reserved but kind, doting, yet slightly distant. His mother and father loved each other, but they didn't, for example, use pet names. They didn't call each other *dear* or *honey* or *darling*. And Harold was always *Harold*, never *Harry*.

Harold's parents had focused their efforts on bringing their son up correctly, which included having him accompany them to church every Sunday. However, the behavioral principles upon which they based their precepts for raising him to become a good person were in reality more profane than religious. They instilled in him an appreciation of the rules of proper etiquette, which, in their broadest sense, are no more than a guide to appropriate behavior under any circumstance. Thus, he generally knew what to do in every social situation.

Lacking siblings, he lived an interior life that was dream-like and rich with images. He wasn't in the habit of having long discussions with people. He was the quiet one on the cross-country track team. When playing chess with his friends, he remained as silent as the pieces on the board, only infrequently uttering a few words, mostly having to do with the playability of a position, or pointing out an obvious blunder. At school, he spoke only when called upon. The few discussions he had with his college professors were limited to questions and answers about specific topics concerning assignments. He had a dry sense of humor, and was often witty in conversation, but he was too introverted to engage in idle social banter. He liked silence, and it was silence he sometimes sought when he left Carol.

Silence depressed Carol. She thrived on sound. She had to have music playing or the television squawking in the background. Unlike Harold, she had the gift of gab. She thought nothing of speaking her mind. She came from a family of four and was the youngest child and the only girl. All her brothers at one time or another were suspected of having behavioral disorders. Mealtime at her house was like a riot, with each of her brothers speaking at the top of his voice, trying to be heard over whichever person was speaking. The cacophony was unending. Carol's mother had encouraged Carol to speak up as loudly as she could and to voice her opinion—otherwise, her mother said, people would think she didn't have one.

Carol was capable of talking for hours. She could carry on a conversation with herself. It was exhilarating for Harold to listen to her articulate every thought that came into her head.

They would lie in bed and she would go on and on and on. She spoke extemporaneously and fluidly on any topic having to do with her major areas of study, sociology and political science. Like many people who are comfortable talking out loud and eager to demonstrate their mastery in an area, she sometimes mixed a bit of exaggeration or misinformation in with her disquisitions. When Harold, who was no slouch when it came to analysis, indicated a logical inconsistency or that she had reached an invalid conclusion, she redirected her arguments with alarming rapidity, often changing the subject under discussion altogether. She moved from one topic to the next in the blink of an eye. It was an amazing talent, one she encouraged him to cultivate.

—You're such a smart man. It's surprising you don't have more to say. I mean, you could talk about so many different things. Yet, you listen more than you talk, Carol observed.

—Everything happens in my head, he said.

—Well, we're going to work on that. If you don't talk about things and discuss and analyze things out loud, they begin to clutter up your mind. That's what your mouth is for, to empty your head.

Carol analyzed and verbalized almost everything. She was temperamentally a practical and rational person. She tried to uncover the reason why they were feeling this way or that, and she could demolish any emotional state with endless questions. She drove him insane by insisting they dissect the health of their relationship, or by trying to analyze why they were happy after sex. Yet despite her compulsive psychological analytics and her scary possessive nature, he was drawn to her.

⌇

By the end of their senior year, they had forged that vast entanglement of habits and shared emotional experiences that comprises a loving relationship. Having never been in love, Harold was a little surprised at its topsy-turvy nature. The demands Carol made on his time were the most annoying part of love, to be sure. That she cared about him so deeply and desired his constant presence made him feel good. He felt needed and important. She stimulated within him the desire to reciprocate and make her feel good even if, from time to time, he had doubts whether she was the right one for him. And though he loved her, he couldn't stop wondering if their union would ultimately cause him more pain than pleasure.

〜

Two months after their classic June wedding, the Hardscrabbles moved to New York City and took up residence in a rundown tenement building on East Ninth Street, between Second and First Avenues. Ninth Street was one of the main thoroughfares from the East to West Village, and the parade of people walking up and down it day and night was endless. All the old railroad-flat buildings, such as the one they lived in, had been divided up into studios or small one- or two-bedroom apartments. The nearby streets were packed with these same low-rise but high-occupancy dwellings out of which people poured, filling the sidewalks with a maelstrom of humanity no matter what the hour.

Using the money they had received as wedding presents, they furnished their one-bedroom apartment, which had none of the charm of Carol's former bachelorette pad but was as dank and dark and cramped and uncomfortable as Harold's former living quarters. The bathroom was so small it was impossible for them both to be in it together. They lived on top of each other. Between their bodies and their egos, there was hardly room to breathe.

While their immediate neighborhood was relatively safe, the surrounding areas were perilous. That first winter, on cold days, when Harold had nothing to do and he imagined the risk of an adverse encounter was low, he explored the nearby streets and avenues. Just to the east of where they lived was Tompkins Square Park. At that time, it was inhabited by the homeless, crazies, and drug addicts. Some of them camped in the park, others in and among the skeletal remains of the destroyed buildings that surrounded the park. A little farther to the east, in Alphabet City, there were entire city blocks of nothing but rubble from the torched tenements that had collapsed. The avenues and streets were oddly desolate. On some streets, there were piles of bricks and cement slabs with gutted, charred cars resting on top of them like monuments to the devastation. There were acres of wasted, blasted, burned-out buildings. Wild dogs and feral cats roamed freely or napped in doorways. There were no trees anywhere. The people were dirty, destitute, dangerous. All of this was a stone's throw away from where they lived.

—It's a totally different world, Harold told Carol.

It wasn't one she wished to visit, she informed him.

⟨∿⟩

Harold and Carol had known each other for eighteen months before marrying. After moving to New York, it sometimes seemed as if they were starting their relationship over. The cloistered campus life they had enjoyed for four years while undergraduates left them unprepared to confront the stark reality of living in the city that never sleeps. Having to rise every morning and try to find work every day to pay the rent and buy food was very different from luxuriating between classes in the quad or repairing to Carol's apartment for an afternoon quickie, after which they would lie in bed in bliss until it was time for their next class. At school, they had often discussed their hopes and dreams for the future as they roused themselves out of their postcoital torpor, but now they were in the middle of all the madness and mayhem that was New York, and they discovered that mapping out a plan for life was not the same as choosing courses for the fall semester. It made their college days seem like a dream and the future more obscure than ever.

Since they were both academically inclined but had no clear idea what career path they intended to follow, they began investigating the possibility of continuing their education and attending graduate school. And, instead of looking for entry-level jobs, they signed up at temporary employment agencies and took any assignments that came their way.

The temp agencies sent them to work in offices all over town. They never stayed at any one place for more than a week or so. This nomadic approach to the labor market appealed to Harold because after a week on the job he became bored with the work he had to perform and looked forward to a new assignment to break the monotony. Carol found the constant resettlement trying because no sooner was she comfortable in one environment than she was uprooted and moved to another.

Before the end of their first year in the city, Carol decided to apply to graduate school. She planned to earn a master's degree in communications and then go into public relations. She would continue to work part-time. Harold didn't have an ultimate plan, but shortly after Carol was accepted into the program at NYU, he too applied there with the thought of obtaining a master's degree in English literature. What would he do after he received his degree? He had no idea.

↜∿↝

After they settled into a routine of school and work, they began to patronize the Kiev, which was a Ukrainian café of sorts, on the corner of Second Avenue and Seventh Street. The Kiev was open twenty-four hours a day, seven days a week. It was a ramshackle, down-at-the-heels place but served the best challah in New York. It had a crisp brown crust and a yellow, textured, cake-like inside. A couple of bucks secured a cup of one of their fabulous soups and two gigantic slices of the buttered bread. When Harold was very hungry, he opted for the French toast, made with the same challah, or the blintzes. As the Kiev fit their budget and was close to their apartment, they dined there often, though Carol was not enamored of the eatery, especially when no booths were available and they had to sit at the counter.

The place was always crowded at night. The activity level was frenetic. The atmosphere was raucous, with many conversations carried on in drug- or alcohol-induced high-pitched voices. Everyone talked at the top of his or her lungs. All the downtown night owls and freaks frequented the Kiev: leather-clad Hell's Angels whose headquarters were only a few blocks away, drag queens who paraded about as if they were on stage, hard-edged, stoned-out CBGB patrons with Mohawk haircuts, band members who had just ended their set at CBGB's, gays wending their way back to Brooklyn after a visit to the Mineshaft or the Eagle's Nest, actors who had finished performing at La MaMa, art students who couldn't afford to eat any place else, the homeless who had scavenged enough money for a cup of coffee and held down seats at the counter while bumming cigarettes from those around them.

—I don't know why we have to come here, Carol complained.

—Because it's close and cheap, Harold explained.

—It makes me uncomfortable, Carol said.

—It's loud, he conceded. But I like the food.

—Maybe, but I always have the feeling anything could happen. It's like riding on the subway. Any of these people might act out or do something weird.

—They scare you.

—Some of them, yes.

—I think a lot of the people in here are doing what we're doing.

—What do you mean?

—They're trying to figure out how to put their life in some kind of order to realize their dreams. Just like us.

—To look at them you'd never guess that, Carol said. Most of them are dressed like they're going to a costume party. Do you think you could ever be that outrageous?

—I guess it depends upon the circumstances.

—I can't think of any circumstance in which you would act outrageously. You play by the rules. That's why I love you. The world is crazy, and I like rational. I don't like spontaneity.

—Spontaneity is not the opposite of rational.

—To me, they're linked. Anyway, most of the people in here are weird, she whispered. I mean, in case you hadn't noticed.

—Are we normal?

—Of course we're normal. I mean, in comparison. Don't you think? she asked.

She appeared concerned.

—I don't know, Harold said. I'm sure we're as unique as any of the people in here, in our own way.

—Maybe. But most of the people here are strange.

—It's hard to judge.

—It's not hard to judge. Just look at them. And I've heard enough to know most of these people are not like us. Anyway, why can't I judge if I want to?

—Nobody said you couldn't.

Carol clarified that she meant to say judging from their conversations, the people around them appeared to live lives fraught with risk and uncertainty.

—You know I don't like that, she said.

—Like what?

—Not knowing what will happen.

—How do we know what will happen? How does anybody ever know?

—That's why we plan.

—These people have plans. We just don't know them.

—I'm guessing for a lot of them the plan is to get lucky.

—Luck often appears to be spontaneous, but it's often the culmination of a long series of planned moves, as in chess, he pointed out.

—Harold, I'm not trying to start a fight. All I'm trying to say is that I want to do something with my life. I want to be someone. To make that happen, I need a plan. And by the way, so do you.

&

In the summer of 1984 Harold came to the conclusion, *I'm not happy.*

He was floundering, unsure about what to do. He had recognized creative abilities and had often thought about pursuing some sort of a career in the arts, of becoming a writer or an editor or an art critic, since he had, he believed, a good eye. Throughout his years as an undergraduate, he'd discussed with his parents the possibility of majoring in art, and each time he did so he'd had to battle their insistence that he do something sensible and practical with his life. The Hardscrabbles were not of the mind that the arts, or anything having to do with art, represented a wise career choice. His parents' constant, mundane admonitions to think long and hard about how he would earn a livelihood after graduation did make Harold wonder how he would support himself if he did go into the arts.

The question became ever more acute as graduation approached, but he had refused to confront it. The knowledge that he would be thrown off his parents' payroll, as they put it, after he earned his diploma frightened him but didn't help him to decide what to do. Whenever he and Carol engaged in talks about *the future,* she, unlike his parents, didn't try to discourage him from pursuing something in the arts. She did, however, remind him that if he chose to take a flier, as she called it, and spend time working in a nontraditional job, one day or another he was going to have to start thinking about a real career choice. She told him if he was serious about becoming a writer or an editor, that was okay, but in the meantime he would have to make money somehow. She couldn't support the two of them. The arts were a long game, she said, and unpredictable. He came to understand that she, like his parents, wanted him to seek out something stable and steady that had a discernable pathway to success. Neither his parents nor Carol overtly denigrated his yearning to do something creative. But that they didn't encourage him to follow his avowed interest was sufficient to subtly weaken his resolve to pursue a livelihood that was meaningful to him.

〰

While Carol wasn't fond of the Kiev, sitting in the café lifted Harold's spirits, until he began wondering about what to do with his life. For in the Kiev, he came face to face with the people he wanted to be. People who gave off a fervent affirmation of their being. No matter what they were doing—blocking out scenes in a video that might never get made, or rehearsing lines for a part in a play that might be given to someone else, or writing poetry that might never be published—they were who they were. And because they so fully embodied whatever it was they were, Harold knew they had faith in themselves and believed in their mission, regardless that the outcome was uncertain. They were authentic, and he admired them. He felt fake and cowardly in their presence.

He knew Carol's critical comments and snide remarks about the people who frequented the Kiev were a defense mechanism that helped her define herself in contrast to the *other* they represented. It allowed her to put distance between her and them and affirm her own being. She was not one of them.

Who exactly was Carol? Harold began to wonder. The question troubled him. Prior to moving to New York, he had thought of her as possessive, smart, sexy, and intellectually inclined. Now, while she was less possessive, she had become more concerned with improving their material circumstances and *making it,* as she said. The talks they used to have when they were students, about the books they were reading and reports they were writing, were superseded by talks about a future in which they would have real jobs, an ever-increasing income, and a higher standard of living. Harold's anxiety increased in proportion to Carol's expectation of living the good life.

⟨∿⟩

Sometimes the employment agency sent Harold to a business that had no work for him to do but occupy the seat of an absent employee and answer his or her phone. So he would sit, filling the seat, killing the day, doing nothing but taking vague messages for the person for whom he was temporarily substituting, possibly helping a fellow worker by making copies of documents or putting documents into three-ring binders or sharpening pencils. If he was placed in an office instead of in a cube and no one was able to observe him, he would go through the drawers of the desk. They might contain a brush, a comb, a bottle of aspirin, some deodorant or mouthwash, a box of crackers or a box of sanitary napkins, a pack of gum or breath mints. Oddly, nothing that gave away any indication of the worker's personality. Once, hidden behind some manila envelopes in a filing cabinet, he discovered a half-empty bottle of Jack Daniel's. The boredom was often unbearable.

To break the tedium, he began to write. He scribbled imagined biographies of people whose names he randomly picked from the Rolodex. Then he started writing responses to articles he read in the *New York Times* and the *Wall Street Journal*. Writing rekindled his desire to find work in the arts. He made attempts to contact the editors at *Artforum*, *Art in America*, *Interview*, and the *Village Voice* about employment. He was either ignored or, if he managed to obtain a face-to-face meeting, he was ultimately, politely, rejected. He submitted a revised version of his senior thesis to *Salmagundi* and never received a response. The *New Yorker* didn't acknowledge him. The *New York Review of Books* was not accepting unsolicited manuscripts. *Harper's* turned down his essays. He accepted these rejections, viewing them as a sign he was most likely on the wrong path. So rather than continue to write and send out submissions, or try to find someone who might offer him some advice or encouragement on how to break into the world of arts and letters, he resigned himself to the fact *it* wasn't going to happen for him. He didn't have it, whatever that mysterious, elusive *it* was.

Eating lunch in the Kiev one afternoon while Carol was out on an interview, it struck him that talent was not simply being good at something. It was also convincing other people you were good at it. Somehow, he hadn't grasped that. Now, after a few years in New York, he understood that one of the essential ingredients needed to achieve artistic success was the ability to socialize, to make connections, to create advertisements for yourself, a talent he sorely lacked. Neither his upbringing nor his personality permitted him to say, *look at me, look at me.* While he had no trouble using forcing moves in chess to obligate opponents to do something that improved his strategic position, he was too shy and well-mannered to try to force his work, or himself, in front of people and make them take notice of him. He didn't have the mettle to move outside himself to win his part in the talent show that was New York. He had the facility but lacked the self-confidence. This was the gulf separating him from the people who surrounded him in the Kiev who had the inner strength of character, the will to power, that allowed them to stand up in front of anyone who would give them an audience, anyone who might buy what they were selling. It's not in me, he admitted to himself.

He came to this conclusion without much drama. In many ways, he was relieved he had uncovered the source of his incapacity since it made him less unhappy. He didn't become bitter about it. He shared his insights with Carol.

—I don't have the personality to make anything happen, he said. After I get my degree, I'm going to get a regular job like everybody else.

—You have a great personality, Carol commiserated. But you're being sensible. You can always write if that's what you want to do.

He did continue to write, although sporadically, and without ever managing to get anything in print. And while the art world wouldn't acknowledge him, he took full advantage of that world. For he believed art was something that gave the highest quality to the moments of your life, that it served a high-order social and psychological function. Moreover, in art there was solace.

He insisted upon taking Carol to see productions at La MaMa, the Performing Garage, and Judson Church. Whenever he could, he spent hours wandering in and out of the art galleries in SoHo. He frequented the Thalia and Theatre 80 St. Marks, where he would slump in a seat and watch foreign films. He attended the early new-wave French and Italian movie festivals when they included films by a director whose work he liked or an obscure film he had read about but hadn't seen. Once, when he was between jobs, he devoted the entire afternoon to watching Satyajit Ray's *The Apu Trilogy*.

On Saturdays, he and Carol would go their separate ways, he to the galleries, she to the shops. When they would reunite, she would show him what she bought, and he would try to explain what he had experienced.

Whenever possible, he would slip into 393 West Broadway and stare at Walter De Maria's *The Broken Kilometer*. The stillness and silence of the sanctuary that housed the beautiful five hundred illuminated brass rods granted him a serenity he couldn't find elsewhere in the city. It was his urban Walden Pond.

↞↠

Despite her overt materialism, Harold admired Carol's determination to achieve the goals she set for herself. She earned her master's degree in two years while managing to secure an internship during her second year that led to a full-time position in one of the most prestigious public relations firms in New York.

It took Harold a year longer than Carol to finish the course work for his degree. He wrote his thesis on manifestations of love, desire, and perversion, using *Romeo and Juliet* and *Lolita* as his source texts. Encouraged by his advisor, he explored the idea of remaining in school and working toward his doctorate, but the possibilities of university employment after graduation were dire in the mid-Eighties, and it didn't seem like a prudent investment of time and money. He continued to work at temporary jobs while he cast about, seeking a sign that would guide him in one direction or another.

He didn't know what he wanted to do.

Carol said what he had to do was find a full-time job. Something that would lead to *something*, something that would have a future.

—You're not getting any younger, and you've never had a full-time job. It's going to begin to look suspicious, she warned. Careers take a long time to build.

〰

Harold knew he had to work, he didn't know what kind of work would satisfy him. All those years of education and I'm at a loss about how to earn a livelihood, he thought. It was amazing. How did one build a career? His father's was atypical. He had worked in several different fields after college, beginning in the securities business, selling stocks and then bonds. He invested his bonuses in coin-operated laundries and car washes. Not very glamorous industries but they made money and were easy to understand and to keep running without very much effort. When these began to generate some income, his father quit the securities firm, leveraged his capital investment, and began buying commercial real estate. Once his properties began producing sufficient operating cash to maintain him and his family in the style to which they had become accustomed, he hired property managers and accountants to watch over his assets, and he stepped back and spent his time dabbling in the stock market, from which he also managed to extract a not insignificant revenue stream. He thought of himself as an entrepreneur. Self-employment was the best employment. Corporations and corporate life were evil, he told his son.

—Go into a business where the risk is calculable, the returns reasonable, and one from which you can earn money while you sleep. This is the sure path to success.

He encouraged his son to do the same.

Harold's aesthetic and artistic sensibilities were far more dominant in him than any drive to master the practical axioms of commerce. He had always been more interested in increasing his intellectual capacity than in pondering how to accumulate capital. He preferred to study famous chess games rather than analyze a company's free-cash flow. While he recognized the need to make money to pay the rent, chasing money as an end in itself, or going into business with the hope of becoming wealthy, was not something he considered to be a worthy enterprise.

In many ways, Harold considered himself a spiritual refugee from the late sixties and early seventies. While he had been too young to directly participate in the politics of those heady times, he had studied them, and felt nostalgic whenever he thought about them. He remained convinced that the most important political text of his generation, or perhaps of any generation, was *The Port Huron Statement*, a manifesto that had been finalized at the SDS convention in Port Huron, Michigan, in 1962.[1] This was years before Harold had come across it in a college class on contemporary literature and politics. The

---

1 Tom Hayden et al., *The Port Huron Statement* (New York: Students for a Democratic Society, 1962).

authors wanted to set the political agenda for their generation and, more ambitiously, reset the moral compass of America by *understanding and changing the conditions of humanity in the late twentieth century, an effort rooted in the ancient, still unfulfilled conception of man attaining determining influence over his circumstances of life.*

Harold was deeply moved by *The Statement.* But by the time he read it, and came to believe everything was political, the radical momentum of the sixties had dissipated. On his college campus, all that remained of the seventies was a hodgepodge of movements in constant flux, each one clamoring for the political limelight: the civil rights movement, the student rights movement, remnants of the antiwar movement, environmentalists, veterans' groups, feminist awareness parties, gay rights activists. Everyone wanted recognition and power. Unsure of which cause he should take up, he sat on the sidelines. His contribution to the counterculture consisted chiefly of smoking as much marijuana as he could get his hands on, which, at the time, was considered to be a gesture of sticking it to the man.

In reality, it was too late for Harold to participate in any of the seminal political movements. The Civil Rights Act and the Voting Rights Act and the marches on Washington and Selma were history by the time he arrived at college. The progressive leftist social movements had reached their apex in the sixties, and their philosophical flights of fancy had begun to stall. The Left had been unable to fulfill its dream of radically transforming life in America. The clarion call of *The Port Huron Statement* to form a participatory democracy and stop the growing concentration of wealth and power wasn't going to happen.

By 1978, the year Harold graduated high school, it was clear there would be no social revolution. By then the middle class had shown itself to be shrewder, more stable and united and, on the whole, more perceptive than the intellectuals on the radical Left who had been clamoring for revolutionary change for two decades. *The people* would not participate in overturning the establishment. As the decade drew to a close, it was evident that there would be no revolutionary changes to the status quo. There would be no mass uprising. There were, intermittently, guerilla attacks against *the establishment,* the government and corporations. But the sad thing everyone discovered during that decade was that structural inequities, economic predation, ecological destruction, and perpetual warfare could not be effectively undermined by either cultural radicalism or transcendent consciousness.

While Harold had hated the seventies, the questions raised in *The Port Huron Statement* remained troubling to him. How could he *attain determining influence over his circumstances of life? How should he live? What is the good life?* He worried the answers might never be revealed to him. Was that because he was a victim of his times, in which case any answer might be, a priori, filtered through a false consciousness and therefore suspect? How would he know? He was further troubled by the thought that if he were not actively searching for answers, it might mean he had in some way already sold out. Or, it might mean he had evolved into the next phase of his personal history and was doomed to remain ignorant. Either way, it was disturbing. He didn't have a clue how to live. He only knew his life wouldn't involve chasing money.

〜

For the most part, Carol was tolerant of Harold's quandary. She tried to get him out of his funk, as she referred to his depression, and stir him to action without badgering him.

—We don't have kids, so as long as you're working and we can pay the bills, I suppose for now it doesn't matter what you do, she said. You'll figure it out. And when you find something you like to do, your work will become your life. And your life will get easier.

Harold wasn't sure he agreed with her assessment.

↜↝

Throughout the next several years Harold held any number of different temp jobs at various corporations and small businesses. The longer he stayed in any one place, the more his employers came to recognize and appreciate his talents. Eventually he began to receive challenging and intellectually interesting assignments. His prime skill set, it turned out, was his ability to make order out of chaos. His finely honed critical faculties helped him see how to reduce the entropy quotient in any set of qualitative data and to see patterns or associations or gather disparate facts and package them in a conceptual framework. He brought order, logic, and clarity to each of his challenges. This was a rare and highly sought-after talent, one of his many supervisors told him. He was advised to exploit it for all it was worth.

The temp agency began sending him to market research firms and marketing services companies. Six months after leaving the employ of a direct-mail marketing firm, the supervisor he had worked for called him and offered him a three-month gig. Soon, other former employers began calling him. Over time he developed his own client list and began working for himself as a consultant. That he now made a living on his own thrilled him.

—I'm an independent contractor, he bragged to his father during one of their weekly phone calls.

—Son, that's the only way to go. I'm proud of you, his father said, which had the effect of making Harold feel proud of himself.

〰

While Carol had to trudge off to her job every morning, Harold often had a more relaxed schedule. Thus, sometimes in the summer he spent several hours in Washington Square Park playing chess with the hustlers. In the fall when it turned too cold to sit outside, he slipped into a movie theater to see a film. Sometimes he wandered through all the aisles of the Strand Book Store. And there was always *The Broken Kilometer*.

After a couple of years, he had six or seven steady clients he could depend on to keep him steadily employed. Not counting the perks that Carol got at her job, he was earning more than she was. Eventually, one of his clients was adamant in wanting to keep him, and offered him a substantially higher rate to keep him at his marketing consultancy indefinitely. Harold liked the work, so he explained to his other clients he was taking a long-term assignment.

He became a permalancer. Carol approved of his decision. She figured it reduced the uncertainty in their life and increased their income.

※

The work at the consultancy was interesting and often mentally challenging. Harold spent his days quietly pushing his pen across a piece of paper in his office, or comfortably ensconced in a deep-cushioned leather chair in a conference room surrounded by his colleagues, jotting notes on his pad while listening to a presentation, nodding his head, attentive to the political dynamics, trying to come up with solutions to the problem at hand. The people sitting around the table with him were well educated, well spoken, and polite, even if some of them were colossal egotists and insanely competitive.

※

Harold wasn't unhappy with his situation. He was treated with respect and remunerated handsomely. For the first time, he didn't want anything to change.

He was surprised when he received a call from a former supervisor, Charlie, who had promised to keep in touch. Charlie had left the company where Harold met him, and he and some partners had started their own consulting firm. We'd like to talk to you about coming on board, Charlie told him. We're growing fast and need somebody with the kind of conceptual and analytical expertise you have. Flattered he had been sought out, Harold was unsure if he wanted to join an organization, or *come on board*, as it had been put to him.

—You have to take the meeting, Carol commanded.

—I'm not sure I want to be hired.

—Who cares? Go see what they say.

Harold went. Charlie greeted him with a familiar, hail-fellow-well-met hug even though Harold didn't know him that well and they hadn't seen each other in over a year. He was introduced to the other partners, who were also very enthusiastic about securing his services. They had prepared a package outlining his compensation and responsibilities, his perks and vacation days, holidays and profit sharing. He went over the offer in detail with Carol.

—This is fabulous. I think you should accept. Only if you want to, she added, backing off. It is a generous offer, though. Getting in on the ground floor is a great opportunity.

—They said I would be coming on board.

—What?

—They were implying I would help sail their ship, and you're implying I'll help construct their building, metaphorically speaking.

—Well, we're not talking about metaphors. We're talking about a job offer.

—I can't help thinking that if this were a few years ago, I would say, no thank you, like I've always done. Why should I worry about having a staff job?

—Times have changed, she said. You're thirty-two. We should be building a life, and part of doing that means accepting responsibility.

—I'm responsible. I go to work almost every day.

—It's not the same.

—No, I guess it's not, Harold conceded.

—But it's up to you. I can't decide for you.

—But you think I should do it.

—Yes, I think you should do it.

After he signed and turned in the required paperwork and gave notice at his current place of employ, the idea that he had surrendered to the system began to haunt Harold. I've abandoned all my principles, he told himself. Why did I give up my freedom as an independent contractor? What would his father say? He admonished himself for buckling under the pressure of Carol's passive-aggressive push to make him accept the offer. She had guilted him into feeling he had no choice but to acquiesce for the greater good of their relationship. His self-recrimination focused on the fact that he knew he was doomed to accept the job offer the minute he had brought it to Carol's attention. He should have had the nerve, the willpower and self-restraint, to have never mentioned Charlie's call. Was it vanity that had got the better of him? Was he so insecure that he'd needed to use the offer to prove to Carol he had something of value to offer the world? And how ironic was it that while the world of arts and letters had ignored him, the business world had come calling? He felt horrible.

〰

During his week between jobs, Harold pondered his employment status over coffee in the Kiev. It was August. The heat was blistering and oppressive and added to his feeling of solitariness. I'm a traitor to my own cause, he admitted to himself. The customers in the café put him to shame. Bristling with their fuck-you attitudes, they were genuine, and he was fake, inauthentic. He had signed on to be a jacket-and-tie guy, another man in a gray flannel suit. He didn't want to be that man. But he had to entertain the possibility that maybe he was, because, after all, he had accepted a full-time position. Wasn't that tantamount to making him part of the corporate system? There was a riot raging in his head over the meaning of his decision.

He had further opportunity to reflect upon what he had done when he shared the news with his parents. He told them the deal he had been offered was too good to refuse. His mother was enthusiastic and proud that a firm would make him such a fine offer.

—You're a smart boy, and they should be glad to have you, she said.

As he feared, his father was not so sanguine.

—There are no deals when it comes to people, he warned. You're always trading labor for money. Before you made your own rules. Now you'll have to follow someone else's.

His father had voiced the unhappy truth: He was no longer his own man. He was now a company man. He was no longer an individual. He was an employee. Moreover, by signing the paperwork he'd completed his transformation from a bohemian to a bourgeois. Was this where history had led him? Why hadn't he continued to try to define himself as an individual? Perhaps he had suffered from a failure of imagination, or from an inability to see beyond where he was. Was this really how he wanted to live? He was at a loss.

⟨∿⟩

Despite his transformation, and his awareness that he had taken an ominous first step toward dehumanizing conformity by taking a staff job, Harold fit in at his new place of employ. He donned without complaint the socializing yoke of moral imperatives that guided the systematic performance of his duties. He despised being forced into a position in which he was made to concede the need for cooperation, but he recognized its necessity.

Fortunately, he possessed the ability to get along with others, an attribute all organizations cherish. He was able to master the firm's ruling assumption set, the normative behavioral codes, and the underlying structural logic that assured uninterrupted productivity and created the reality that ruled his life at work. Being on staff led to a different social dynamic from the one he had experienced as a freelancer. His position, with its attendant roles and responsibilities, fostered much closer camaraderie than he was used to, which was, he perceived, essential for productive output.

In time, Harold discovered he was linked in one way or another to everyone in the office through a series of alliances, fealty relationships, networks, cliques. There was an invisible, unspoken web of personal loyalties that kept the place running every bit as much as the standard operating procedures outlined in the workflow manuals. Everyone's function was interdependent. From the editors and the administrators and planners to the strategists and analysts, everyone took pride in performing their function to the best of their ability. No one could fuck up, or the whole operation would suffer. His internal drive to be successful at whatever he did therefore pardoned the concession he made to his individuality to help achieve the common goal.

❧

With two steady incomes, an ever-increasing savings account, and every sign of a bright future, the Hardscrabbles decided to move out of their hole in the wall on East Ninth Street and into more commodious quarters. Harold wanted to move to the Upper West Side, where he felt he would be more politically at home and the rents were reasonable, and Carol wanted to move to the Upper East Side, which she felt was safer and more stylish and was closer to her office, which was on Third Avenue. They looked at places on both sides of Central Park and fell in love with one or two, but there was always something that fell short of their expectations, or exceeded their budget, and every time a real estate agent pushed them to sign a lease, they balked.

Then someone in Harold's office suggested they look in Tribeca, in Lower Manhattan, which was still a relative bargain. The neighborhood was still undeveloped. The idea of making a home in a loft had only recently been pioneered by artists priced out of SoHo by a combination of creeping commercialization and gentrification. A loft was a wide-open space intended for industrial purposes, and most weren't zoned for residential occupancy.

This did not dissuade them from renting one of the very first places they were shown, on Vestry Street, between Greenwich and Hudson. Their new home was a huge, raw, open space, with double-sized dormer windows that let in more daylight than they had seen since moving to the city. At night, there was also light because there were no blinds or shades or drapes on any of the many windows, and refracted light from the street lamps and the general glow from the city seeped in, illuminating the space in a delicate chiaroscuro. Rows of overhead hanging halogen bulbs filled the room with light when needed. The floors were cement and painted light gray, the walls white. They were on the fifth floor, and had a view of both the West Side Highway and the Hudson River. Harold would sometimes sit outside on the fire escape and listen to the ever-present sound of pneumatic jackhammers eating their way through a piece of sidewalk or a road surface someplace in the vicinity. On Hudson Street, the cars and trucks inched their way forward, their horns beeping and engines revving as they struggled bumper to bumper from one traffic light to the next, headed toward the Holland Tunnel.

Moving to Tribeca from the Lower East Side was like moving to a different city. A block over from where they had lived, on Bleecker Street, and on Astor Place, and on the Bowery and all the surrounding avenues, there was store after store and restaurant after restaurant. The East Village was a scene and a destination. Tribeca was a ghost town. In the daytime, there was some light warehousing and small manufacturing activity. At night, it was spookily deserted. Their building housed a shipping and logistics company on the ground and first floors. During business hours, the tenants were allowed to use the freight elevator, which opened right into the lofts. After business hours, they had to walk up the stairs.

They discovered there was no place to shop for food in the immediate area, not even a bodega, so all their meals had to be planned well in advance. Nor were there any household service stores or convenience stores or laundries close by. On Thursdays, Harold lugged their dirty clothes into SoHo and left them at a laundry on Prince Street to have them washed. On Saturday, he picked them up. The only place to go for a drink at that time was Puffy's. It would still be several years before the Odeon would open its doors.

〜

Both Hardscrabbles advanced steadily in their jobs. Carol received outstanding reviews and well-deserved raises. On her third-year anniversary, she was named as a *woman to watch* in the company's internal newsletter. She was lauded for all her hard work and the exquisite manner in which she handled clients. She shared the article with Harold. It included her picture, in which she appeared seductive in a corporate kind of way. He was very proud of her. One year later, as Carol was being promoted to a director-level job, she was hailed as a take-no-prisoners executive with a strong work ethic and an effortless ability to perform well in a team structure. It was the first time the appellation *executive* had been attributed to her, and she took it as a further sign that her future was bright.

At work, Carol exuded nothing but confidence. At home she voiced all her insecurities. She tortured herself endlessly. She found fault with her decisions. She tried to second-guess what her superiors or clients would think of her work and never stopped speculating about which coworker was plotting to block her advancement. Harold reassured her that everything she was doing had to be right, because, he said, if it weren't, she wouldn't have attained her current position of power and responsibility. She achieved it only because she worried incessantly. Worry was what kept her a step ahead of everyone, she claimed.

Harold surmised it was not worry that drove her performance. Carol was a worker, and he was sure Carol's success was due both to her talent and the fact that she was devoted to her job and worked practically around the clock. She worked while she was at work, and she put in more work when she got home. She was always fatigued. Because home was the only place she vented her emotions and frustrations, it put a strain on their relationship.

Harold had it easy compared to Carol. Because he had been recruited from a competitor's firm, and because he had formerly worked with Charlie, who was one of the owners of the company, his colleagues treated him with a level of respect he hadn't known as a freelancer. Everyone was nice to him. Charlie's partners were affable in varying degrees, and once they came to appreciate his talents they began seeking his opinion on projects that were not his but required an outsider's critical analysis.

While many of Harold's colleagues cringed when they heard a senior partner bark *can you come in here a minute?* over their speaker phone, he enjoyed the opportunity to interact with the partners. He was always able to provide a detailed rationale for everything he had done, on the fly and without his notes, and in the heat of the discussion he often came up with another way to do what he had already done, which might, who knew, be superior to his original effort.

Less than two months after coming on board, one of the partners told Harold, *I always feel smarter after talking with you.* After this observation, he was promoted several times in very short order and given wide latitude in his working conditions, which meant, chiefly, that he was left alone to think and not forced to attend endless *blue-sky* meetings that people called to help *move forward the thinking.* This was great for Harold since he didn't believe in brainstorming. He believed the standard group-thinking exercises produced nothing but doublethink, forcing people to accept the lowest common denominator of an idea while extolling it to be the highest because of the peer and social pressures built into the framework of corporate problem solving. Real innovative ideas were birthed from a lone individual. Harold's gift for producing these ideas stemmed from his intuition, his liberal arts education, and a natural curiosity that sent him off in search of seemingly haphazard associations and relations between seemingly disparate ideas. Ideas had etymologies and taxonomies just as words and species did, and he enjoyed examining them if he sensed there was some value to be extracted. When his curiosity was aroused, he would track down the references listed in the footnotes of the document he was reading, searching out the forebears of the text until he was sure he had come to the urtext itself. Then he would exploit it for all it was worth.

The firm hit its sweet spot not long after Harold arrived. Business boomed. They picked up more clients and hired more people and moved to new, more luxurious quarters. Harold was given a sunny office with windows that provided a view of the Chrysler Building. It included chairs for visitors, a table for intimate in-office meetings, a bookcase, and a couch: all the trappings of power and prestige.

His job couldn't have been going better. He sometimes sat with his feet up on the windowsill and stared up at the Chrysler Building lost in thought, or dreaming, and no one disturbed him. During this time when his thoughts were completely his own, he was often frightened. Because all he could think about was the question that kept nagging at him: *Why am I here?* He felt like an imposter who would be unmasked at any moment. Worse was the gnawing sensation that the so-called career in which he was embroiled was a joke that would have a failed punch line at the end.

It was odd, too, because the more success he experienced at his job, the bigger the joke his job appeared to him. Yet he was incapable of taking any action to relieve his situation.

—Sometimes, I want to laugh because it's funny, he said to Carol. But sometimes I feel like I'm not real, he said, or at least not authentic.

—I don't understand. What's funny? What do you mean by authentic? You know I don't like it when you talk like that. I mean, who talks like that?

Undaunted, Harold pushed on.

—I feel like I'm compromised as a person.

—What's that supposed to mean?

—It means I perform a function that I don't take seriously. It makes my situation either tragic or funny or absurd or all three.

—Don't be so dramatic, she scolded. I don't think it's any of those.

—Well, it's stupid, he said.

—It's not stupid. It takes a lot of brains to do the kind of work you do.

—I put too much of myself in it, and it leaves me with nothing.

—Okay then, but whatever you do, you have to put yourself into it. Work is demanding.

Moreover, she carried on, they had to work to survive, or at least work to survive in the style to which they were fast becoming accustomed, of which, she reminded him, he was fond. So he might as well settle in and stop bothering about the meaning of what he was doing and instead concentrate on doing the best he could.

—That's what everybody does, she said.

There was no question of authenticity to ponder. There was, she claimed, trotting out her sociological training, *the dignity of the function* that work in the postmodern industrial world was supposed to provide. His work, knowledge work, exemplified this. The fulfilling of *the dignity of the function* bestowed a sense of worth in the individual performing the function, especially when it was executed to its highest degree.

—I see, he said. But I'm operating in bad faith. That's what makes what I do a joke.

—You're overthinking it, Carol said.

—What's the difference between thinking and overthinking? I mean, you're either thinking or you're not.

—I'm thinking this conversation is over.

—We haven't settled anything.

—There's nothing to settle. Work is what it is, and you have to get used to it. You're stressing me out by talking about it. And I have enough stress in my life.

—Does that mean we can't talk about it?

Carol had no answer but a piercing, silencing glance.

〰

While Carol's job produced no end of stress, she seemed to thrive on it, and moved from success to success without missing a beat. After four years, she was recruited out of her firm into a larger one and was given greater responsibility and, as she put it proudly, blue-chip clients to tend to. For Carol, work was not only fulfilling *the dignity of the function*. It served as a stage upon which she performed and showed her talents. Carol wanted to be somebody. She wanted to be a star. The harder she had to work—writing draft after draft of a position paper, editing slide after slide of a presentation—the more she affirmed her self-worth and this increased her happiness.

↶↷

Lounging on the couch in his office, staring out the window, Harold's mind often drifted in directions that had nothing to do with his work. One day he found himself pondering the difference between his perception of the clouds floating by and the thought processes he exercised when thinking about the clouds. He didn't know why.

Harold believed the mind didn't differentiate between external and internal sources of stimuli, which made it easy to confuse the two. He was also pretty sure everything mental was nonmaterial. Like most people, he sometimes confused the images and the ideas that popped into his mind for thinking, which involved joining subjects and predicates. It was not hard to do: our consciousness consists of a continuous, largely incoherent flow of phenomena, and many of our waking hours are spent trying to sort through it. Which gave credence to the idea that what we call our *life* is closer to a dream than was supposed. Further consideration of this proposition led Harold to believe that at any particular point in time, most people didn't have a thought in their heads. Which also made sense to him because the inescapable inrush of phenomena overwhelmed our minds and fatigued us, making it difficult to think. The inexorable assault of the material world alienated us from ourselves. He thought: *we live in the society of the spectacle.*[2]

As far as Harold could figure, the only relief was art, for art ordered the whir of phenomena surrounding us, helping

2 Guy Debord, *The Society of the Spectacle* (Detroit: Black & Red Books, [1967] 2002).

us understand the series of events we call our lives. Unfortunately, while most people said they *liked* art, most people didn't have time for it. That was why so many people were incapable of confronting the aching, empty feeling that sometimes took hold of them. Like Carol, they downplayed their malaise, and claimed they led full, productive lives. Yet once in a while they'd slump in a stupor on the couch, or have trouble getting out of bed in the morning without knowing why. They'd write it off as feeling weary or weird or blue. They'd put it down to too much TV or too little exercise. They wouldn't comprehend that their spirit was depleted and they had nothing with which to rejuvenate it. They needed a way to get back to themselves. They needed art. For only art provided the means to break the power trance under which we live and offered the possibility of rescuing us from the dreamscape in which we wander.

Somehow, Harold thought, I have to get back to art.

〰️

Children were inevitable. After the move to Tribeca, discussions about starting a family became more frequent. They were more than a decade into their marriage. They had finished graduate school and found steady employment and enjoyed an advanced standard of living. Carol managed to slip the subject into almost every discussion.

—Do we have to talk about that again? Harold would ask.

—Yes. I'm thirty-three. The clock is ticking.

—Okay. But all we do is talk about it. Why can't we just do it?

Harold knew why. He had ceded the timing of having children to Carol since even in today's world it was still the woman, not the man, whose career was punished for procreating. She had worked hard to achieve her current position of power and status, and she didn't want to jeopardize it by becoming inconveniently pregnant. She wanted to wait for the perfect time before going out on maternity leave. But she didn't want to admit she was the one who was procrastinating.

—There will never be a perfect time, Harold told her. It's like when we plan when to take a vacation. There's no right time. And when you think it's the right time, the minute you book a flight and reserve a hotel an emergency lands on your desk.

—I know, she said sadly. One day we're going to have to bite the bullet and do it. Our idyllic existence will be over.

It was true. Kids would put an end to their dual-income, no-kids lifestyle. Their freedom was on the verge of vanishing, and there was nothing they could do to prevent it. Except enjoy the present. So, they went out to eat, or to a movie, on a moment's notice. They spent long weekends in bed-and-breakfasts in the Berkshires. They had sex in the middle of the afternoon on weekends and afterwards took long, languorous siestas.

Sometimes after sex, Harold would watch Carol as she napped, naked in the tangled, rumpled sheets. She had a profoundly beautiful nakedness. She was the most beautiful naked person he had ever seen. Lying on her side, totally exposed, the curve of her ass, the flatness of her stomach, her muscular thighs and calves still excited him after all these years. Her vulnerability as she lay sleeping made him feel protective and tender and deeply loving toward her. He would sometimes lie down beside her and intertwine his legs in hers and wrap his arms around her and pull her body against his, and he would feel they were one. Half-asleep, she would murmur *I love you*, and he would murmur *I love you, too*. This bliss would end the moment a child arrived, and neither one of them wanted it to end.

They put off having children until the pressure to have them grew so intense they knew it must be time. Their colleagues at work, their parents, friends, strangers at parties all demanded to know their *plans*, hinting that parenthood favored the young, and whether they wanted to admit it or not, they were not getting younger.

〰

The following year Carol gave birth to their first child, Jake. She rebounded rapidly and returned to work with the same élan as if she had only been out with a cold. Sarah came along eighteen months after Jake.

When Carol had been pregnant with Jake, everyone at her firm, including the few female senior managers, told her to take the time she needed, to go on leave and spend as much time as she wanted with her baby since her baby wouldn't be a baby for long. If she didn't, she would regret missing that time for the rest of her life, she was told. Motherhood was one of the joys of life. Work would always be there. Carol couldn't do it. She didn't want her career path to come to a sudden dead end. She didn't want to be relegated to a lesser role, a possibility she had felt as a palpable threat every day of her pregnancy. Despite the feminist movement and the continual call for equality of the sexes in the workplace, she felt that because she was female, taking off too much time for child care would hold her back. She was on a fast track, she told Harold, and she didn't want to be derailed.

—I want to be one of the ones who throws the rock at the glass ceiling, she told him. I don't want to be sidelined.

Carol knew other female colleagues in the industry who had been in her position, and she had watched some of them suffer the consequences of giving in to their so-called maternal instincts to spend time with their babies. Taking time off demonstrated that they were committed to something other than their jobs. No sooner did these women return to work than some of them were laddered down into less demanding roles, which many of them swore they were happy about since it allowed them to devote more time to their families. Carol had also seen the women who threw themselves back into their jobs too soon castigated behind their backs for lacking a maternal instinct. They were considered cold-hearted bitches. Senior management, which was predominantly male, showed its displeasure with this behavioral trait by finding a reason to stall their advancement or by sidetracking them outright.

—What am I supposed to do? Carol asked after Sarah was born. Should I give up my job and be a stay-at-home mom? As much as I love my kids, I'm not sure I want to be with them every hour of the day. Would you?

—That's why we hired a nanny, Harold said, skipping over the question.

—No, really. I'm asking. If I stayed home, what would I do with my spare time? Go to the gym, or shop, or hang around the school with the other overly protective, nonworking mothers who schmooze the teachers in the hope their kids will get preferential treatment?

—You give up the nanny, and then there isn't any spare time.

—I don't want to give up the nanny. Why don't you give up your job and stay home?

—I don't know.

—Why don't you know? What we're talking about has to do with being a parent. Gender doesn't matter. You know that. Everyone, including you, still assumes it's the mother who's in charge of child care. I mean, I want to be able to provide for the children the best I can, the best we can. But I still want to have work outside the house that means something to me. I feel terrible, she admitted. I mean, am I wrong?

—No.

—You work. Why shouldn't I work? We can both work, can't we?

—Of course.

—Okay, then.

The issue was settled. Carol continued her career.

↜↝

Harold didn't know what to make of the children. An only child himself, he had never had to deal with siblings. All the several cousins in his family were the same age as him, so he'd never had the experience of being around infants. Watching his become mobile was both amusing and touching.

When Jake started crawling, he would make his way to the far end of the loft and hide behind the couch or the bookshelves and begin to cry as if he had been abandoned or was lost. Harold would go and pick him up, and Jake would cease his wailing and stare into his eyes with a look Harold took to be pure love.

While Jake was a wanderer, Sarah was mischievous. On any number of occasions, she mushed her snacks into the VCR. She managed to destroy three of them before Harold relocated the fourth one to a shelf she couldn't reach. She regularly unplugged all the lamps and appliances. Too many times, she stuffed the toilet with her toys.

Harold cherished the time before either child learned to use language and had only noises and expressions to make public their needs. Without words, they were unique little creatures with secret lives. He made no attempt to encourage them to speak. Carol cooed and babbled at the children endlessly. Harold remained mute for as long as he could as often as he could. Speech was going to suck them into the social system, and the inscrutable individuals they had been up until that point would be obliterated by the common language that would make them use the same words and say the same things as everyone else. And the clarity and purity, the innocence he read in their eyes, did seem to diminish the moment their minds discovered a channel for their desire in language.

～

When Jake and Sarah reached school age, Harold calculated what it was going to cost to educate them if they stayed in the city. They were agreed that the kids would have to attend private schools, but the number to send them was staggering. The only reasonable thing to do was move to the suburbs where the kids could attend public schools.

—If we stay here, he explained to Carol, practically all our earnings will go toward paying for schools. It'll reduce our standard of living.

—But we'll get to stay in the city. That's the trade-off. I don't want to leave, Carol said.

—We won't be able to save a nickel if we stay here, he said, continuing to build a case for their departure. Whereas, if we move to the suburbs, the kids can attend public schools and we can save the money we would've spent for private schools for the kids' college education and pocket the difference. Which would mean we'd have money for emergencies and be able to make more discretionary purchases.

—I need time to get used to the idea, Carol said.

—We can get the kids a dog, said Harold. Recently this had become a topic of some importance as both Jake and Sarah stopped to pet and coo over every dog they encountered on the street.

—It's not something I want to think about right now.

With the help of a financial planner, Harold convinced Carol they had to move. The rise in real estate prices in Tribeca was such that they netted a significant profit from the sale of their loft, which they had purchased some years earlier. Harold regretted leaving New York, and Carol regretted it even more, but as a conscientious couple concerned for the future of their children, they knew they were doing the right thing.

❧

They bought an elegant older house in an established neighborhood in a riverside town north of the Tappan Zee Bridge. The neighborhood streets were lined with stately, mature shade trees. The yards were immaculately manicured. They had been told there were other young families with children on their block, only television and video games had sucked them indoors, where they played in a cyber-reality devoid of direct human interaction. The adults, too, preferred the indoors, Harold surmised, since he rarely saw anyone outside. Were it not for the occasional car in a driveway and the obvious maintenance of the yards, it could be imagined that the neighborhood was abandoned. It was eerie in its emptiness.

The neighborhood was steeped in the same stultifying suburban silence Harold remembered from his youth growing up on the outskirts of Albany. Which was somewhat similar to the profound silence of the countryside he had experienced while staying with his grandparents in Glens Falls, an hour north of Albany. Every August from the time he was nine up until his early teenage years, his parents had deposited him at his grandparents' house. It's nice for you and Grandma and Grandpa, his mother said.

Harold was eleven or twelve when, during these summer sojourns, his grandfather began taking him to the lakes and ponds he had fished in when he was a young man. He had his own secret places where, he claimed, the fish always bit, and only he knew their whereabouts. He might have been telling the truth, too, for some of the spots were so far off the beaten path his grandfather had a hard time locating them. No sooner did they park the car and set off than his grandfather was at a loss to remember which way to turn when they came to a fork in the trail. Ringed by rocks and trees and bramble, some of the ponds were visible only when you came right up on them.

Harold was not an enthusiastic fisher, and he released all the fish he caught. Sometimes, instead of fishing, he would lie out in the sun on the rocks and read while his grandfather fished.

After he turned thirteen, his grandfather started letting him go to the ponds to fish by himself. It was a break in the tedium of being cooped up in the house all day with his grandparents. In their eighties at the time, they were as oversolicitous of his well-being as they had been when he was five. His grandmother, in particular, fussed over him endlessly, doing anything and everything she could to make sure he was happy. Did he want a snack? Was the house too hot or too cold? What would he like for dinner? Did he want her to wash the shirt he wore yesterday? Only when he'd assured her several times that there was nothing more she could do for him did she return to her household chores. She cleaned incessantly. She washed the windows, vacuumed the rugs, polished the wood, scrubbed the tile and linoleum floors on her knees, dusted the drapes, all the while muttering unintelligible sounds or humming to herself. Harold couldn't remember a time when he saw her sit down, except to eat.

If they weren't going to one of the ponds together, his grandfather would shut himself in his study to work on his history of the Adirondacks. As far as anyone knew, he had never written anything in his life, having earned his living as a traveling salesman. After he retired he began writing about the Adirondacks, which had been his sales territory for forty years. He had been working on the book for a decade. He had a pile of paper over a foot high that he said was the manuscript. Every word typed by me, he told Harold proudly.

His grandfather was a chain smoker. He smoked Raleighs. In those days, each pack of Raleigh came with coupons that were redeemable for merchandise or services. The cartons came with bonus coupons. Upon entering his study, the smoke in the room was so thick that sometimes Harold didn't see his grandfather. There were abandoned cigarettes burning away in almost every ashtray, smoking like incense. The coupons were stacked everywhere, piles and piles of them mixed in among all his journals and photographs and the maps for his book. His doctor told his grandfather his addiction to nicotine was so physiologically intense he would die if he quit. So he couldn't quit. He had to smoke. He would smoke right through his meals, taking puffs of his cigarette between bites of food and swallows of beer or Jack Daniel's. He smoked so many cigarettes he was able to buy a car with the coupons. A Plymouth Valiant, with buttons on the dashboard that you pushed to change gears. He died at age ninety from emphysema and heart failure before the car had five thousand miles on it.

Harold's grandparents had lived alone ever since Harold's mother had gone away to college and his aunt had married her long-time hippie boyfriend and moved to California, more than thirty years ago. The isolation of the small town and their steady withdrawal from social life after his grandfather retired had mummified their responses to the world around them. Most of their friends had moved away or died. As they became feebler, they felt uncomfortable in public places and among strangers. They rarely left the house, and when they did it was only to drive to the local supermarket and then to the gas station and return home. Infrequently they visited the Elks Club, where they would sit at the bar, drink beer, and eat peanuts.

At the ponds, Harold developed a capacity to think outside himself, almost to the point of having out-of-body experiences. On his back with his eyes closed, he sometimes, daringly, took off all his clothes and lay naked in the sun. He saw the light through his eyelids and felt the heat of the sun pressing down on him, and somehow, perhaps because of the weight of the light, he thought he felt the vastness of the universe. He dreamed away, into a future he could not imagine. He was a soul in a body in time, and time was endless and pointless as far as he could tell. For day after day, nothing happened. Day after day there was the blinding white light of summer and the smell of cooking chlorophyll and pine sap and the hot dirt. The sky was empty. The quiet by the lake was unimaginable. No planes flew overhead. There were no wires giving off an electronic buzz and no sound of passing cars or lawn mowers or leaf blowers or any sound from any animate being, except now and then for the whirr of insects or the occasional song of birds calling to one another. Sometimes the leaves scraped against one another in the breeze, when there was any. Sometimes it was so quiet he heard the ants crawling over the rocks.

↔

The commute to work from Westchester proved daunting. When residing in the city, Harold had used the subway to get to his office. He had always thought there was something exotic and romantic about being crammed into a subway car during rush hour, with its hodgepodge of people of all classes and many mental states and indefinable odors. There was something egalitarian about standing shoulder to shoulder with his fellow laborers as the train hurtled down the tracks. From both the Lower East Side and then from Tribeca, it had been a quick ride from the station where he boarded the subway to the station where he exited, followed by a brisk walk to his office.

Riding the train from Westchester to Grand Central Station each morning and back again each evening was different.

He had to drive to and from the train station. In the morning, depending on how long it took him to find a parking spot, and how far away from the station the spot was, another fifteen minutes could be added to his journey. The train was hardly ever on time, and once he was on board, it lumbered along at unpredictable rates of speed, starting and stopping for no discernable reason. While the train cars were cleaner than the subway cars and perhaps more comfortable, Harold felt ill at ease surrounded by all the pale faces, starched shirts, pressed suits and power ties, and the expressions of entitlement shining in the eyes of his fellow commuters.

According to his calculations, because of the commute, on average he was away from home at least twelve hours a day. Unlike many of his colleagues who used the train time to unwind or catch up on reading or finish off a project, Harold thought of the commute as a monster that devoured a significant portion of his life. He didn't complain about it to Carol because the move had been his idea.

Carol complained about the commute, but when she worked late, which she often did, because of her seniority her company afforded her the luxury of a company-paid-for car and driver to bring her home. Three or four times a week she availed herself of this service.

⟨∿⟩

Harold almost never arrived home before seven o'clock. The kids and Buddy, the dog they had rescued shortly after moving, would rush to the front door, vying with one another to be the first to receive a hello and a kiss and a hug. The torrent of activity and togetherness made him feel guilty for having abandoned them for so long because he sensed their intense need for the comfort and love only a parent could provide. They always asked the same questions: *Where were you? What took so long? Why do you have to work? We've been waiting for you forever.* Even Buddy seemed to reproach him with his sad, limpid eyes.

The kids' competition for his attention was so fierce it sometimes led to arguments. Each wanted to be heard, to be coddled and cared for and fed and cleaned, and they would fight for the right to be first. But mainly they were yearning for love. And no matter how tired Harold was, he never ignored them or gave them anything less than what the fullness of his heart could offer. On those occasions when he was delayed at the office or out entertaining clients, and didn't arrive until eight or later, he entered the house to find them weary, glassy eyed from too much television, their welcome subdued, touched, he thought, with sadness from having ceaselessly longed for parental presence over too many hours.

Harold loved his children and tried his best to be a good father. His childhood and its attendant joys and sorrows were so far removed from his consciousness that it was practically impossible for him to recall what had made him happy when he was a child. The very concept of *his early childhood* was fuzzy because almost everything he considered a memory from that time was a memory not because he remembered it, but only because it had been told to him as a story by his parents.

The first memory Harold counted as his own was his father teaching him to play chess. His father was an avid club player, and he had insisted he take up the game. His lessons began at an early age, maybe when he was four or five. The learning process was long, and extended over several years. It had been painful at times. His father made him memorize classic offensive openings for white, including his favorites, the Queen's Gambit, which could be accepted or declined, Giuoco Piano, Ruy Lopez and the Italian. Then his father taught him the logic behind the classic defensive openings for black, such as the Caro-Kann and the French Defense. Never trust an opening that has an animal for a name, his father warned. During his lessons, his father referred to the principles propounded by Lasker in his *Manual*, which he encouraged Harold to read. A classicist at heart, his father did not neglect aggressive, hypermodern approaches such as the Alekhine system, which he urged Harold to study. He had to memorize the main lines of these systems as well as the variations and continuations of lines of play when they deviated from the standard repertoire.

His father was a stickler for theory, but he also instilled in Harold a deep appreciation of the pieces, in particular, the pawns, the simple, undifferentiated soldiers who occupied the second rank of the board. They were pushed around in the service of a grand strategy carried out by the knights, bishops, and rooks under the guidance of the king and queen. If they were lucky enough to reach the opposite side of the board, latent within their undifferentiated bodies was the ability to metamorphose from their humble state into a power as great as any piece on the board in whose service they had performed their duties.

As Harold progressed in his ability, chess games with his father sometimes dragged on for hours and often were more work than fun. However, as he got older, chess ultimately turned out to be an activity that yielded him enormous pleasure.

His other standout memory from his childhood was learning to use firearms and to hunt. The Hardscrabbles had always hunted, his father told him. They had always held firearms. Harold's great-grandfather had served in World War I, and his grandfather had served in World War II, and after they were decommissioned, they kept arms out of an appreciation engendered through their service. Harold's father had served in Korea, where he earned a distinguished marksman badge and a distinguished pistol badge. And he, like his forebears, was fond of guns and hunting. Harold's father had rifles for animals and shotguns for fowl. He kept sidearms, too, as he called them. Semiautomatic pistols and revolvers for home protection. His father taught him how to handle them safely, how to disassemble and clean them and then put them back together. Guns were beautiful machines, especially the revolvers, his father said. The purity of the choreography of the pull of the trigger and the simultaneous turn of the cylinder and the drawback of the hammer was elegantly ingenious. The simplicity was stunning, the mechanics irrefutable.

His father pointed out that in many ways hunting was similar to chess. Both were strategic and tactical exercises except, in hunting, the quarry was not the opposing king but a wild animal. The process was the same: the hunter had to make all the right moves to bring down the prey. The dichotomy between taking pleasure in something as cerebral as chess and something as bloodthirsty as hunting was something Harold never understood about his father. He knew his father thought one was the extension of the other. He didn't see it that way. He hated the hunt.

Harold became a marksman with the rifle, but to his father's dismay, he preferred target practice to the art of the hunt and the slaughter of animals. He could lock an animal in his sights, but he couldn't pull the trigger. He didn't have the heart to transform something alive into something dead.

Nevertheless, once or twice a year, his father would be overcome by the urge to go out and kill animals and insisted Harold join him.

—Hunting is a tribal activity, his father lectured when Harold tried to get out of accompanying him. It's an ancient affair. Part of our humanity.

It was in our genetic code to eat other animals, and therefore we had to kill them. Once in a while men had to assert their dominance over the animals and show they were not afraid to take their rightful place at the top of the food chain.

Harold's mother rolled her eyes at such rhetoric. Yet she dutifully prepared their backpacks with provisions for the day and wished them luck when they set off on their mission. If the hunt was successful, she cooked up delicious dishes of marinated venison, savory stewed rabbit, or stuffed wild turkey.

For his fourteenth birthday, his father bought him a Model 70 Winchester rifle, which was considered the rifleman's rifle. It was a spectacular piece of craftsmanship, light and well balanced. It had a beautiful black walnut stock, a polished blue metal finish on the barrel, and was equipped by his father with an additional gift, a matte-black Leupold scope.

—You can't miss with this equipment, his father said.

During hunting season, they would drive up to the mountains, park the truck and trek through the woods. Dressed in their camouflage outfits, they marched through wide open meadows. They followed creeks or streams in which clear flowing water babbled over gray rounded rocks. Huge trees loomed overhead. There was a chill in the air when they hunted, and sometimes it was so cold their breath materialized into mist.

Picking his way through the brush, Harold would gaze at the streaks of wide open blue sky that appeared through the treetops. He followed the light beams streaming through the matrix of leaves. There was something magical and beautiful about being in the woods. But at some point, his father would say:

—Look! You see that?

All too often it was a deer that he spotted. His father would slip his rifle off his shoulder. Harold would imitate his action.

—Get her in your sights, son.

Harold would get the animal in his sights and watch the creature, and his father would scream softly in his ear: *You got her? You got her?* His father commanded him so intensely and so insistently that his voice took over his consciousness, filling his mind with his words, imploring: *Don't let her get away. Pull the trigger, pull the trigger slowly, son. Pull the trigger, and breathe in as you pull so you don't move the barrel.* He would listen to the excitement in his father's voice and want to please him, but before he pulled the trigger he would lower or raise the barrel a little and miss. Even with his father hovering over him, insisting he bring the beast down, he was incapable of doing it. The deer was too alive. Harold could see the animal perfectly in the crosshairs, twitching with life, bobbing its head, flicking its tail, alert, wary, but—tragically—incapable of detecting the two predators hiding behind the trees.

After witnessing his son fail so many times, his father began lining up the same target and asking his son, *Are you going to do it?* If he did not reply, his father would make the kill.

—Dropped him, he would scream. One shot, he would brag.

His father was jubilant. Harold was despondent, but he dared not show it lest his father would think less of him.

One outing when he was again incapable of pulling the trigger, his father made the shot and dropped a buck.

—Easy, he said, congratulating himself.

As they approached the downed animal, it raised its neck and turned and gazed at them. It made a feeble attempt to rise and run but stumbled and fell, mortally wounded. They drew nearer and the buck moved again, crawling a few feet before collapsing. They moved closer and the poor beast craned its head over its shoulder and stared at them. Its rolling, bulging, pleading eyes spoke of terror and fear of its impending doom, of which, it was clear to Harold, it had foreknowledge. When it collapsed once more, his father in one quick movement pulled out his sidearm and put a bullet through its brain.

—There now, he said.

The animal was dead. The forest was still. The surrounding trees stood in mute witness. His father gave him his rifle to hold and tied the animal's legs and they dragged it to the road. Harold sat with the poor, dead creature while his father went to fetch the truck.

That was the last time Harold went hunting.

↢∿↣

When Jake and Sarah entered middle school, Harold and Carol found the demands to show up at school functions were far greater than when the kids had been in elementary school. They argued about which of them should attend the meetings because they were always scheduled either too late in the morning for them to arrive at work on time, or too early in the afternoon, requiring them to leave the office early. They wanted to do the best for their children, but they were suspicious of the necessity of having to be present for *Picture-Day Parade* or *Show-and-Tell Spectacular*. They boycotted whatever seemed silly to them, always first checking with their children to see how they would feel if one or both of them didn't attend an event. They also determined that there was no reason for both of them to attend so-called official functions, such as parent–teacher conferences, because these colloquies did not require two listeners to hear a report about whether one of their children was having problems paying attention (Jake) or exceeding all expectations (Sarah).

—They're only in middle school, for god's sake. Nothing can be that wrong or that important, Carol claimed.

They settled upon a division of labor. Since Carol's office was north of midtown and required a cab ride or a train ride to get to Grand Central, and Harold could walk to his office in five minutes, he was frequently tasked with attending the morning meetings. One day after a parent–teacher conference for Sarah, he remembered he had left a report he needed on the kitchen counter and returned home to retrieve it. No sooner was he inside than he felt the urgent need to relieve himself. On the way to the bathroom he almost tripped over Buddy, who was blocking the hallway. He wagged his tail, happy to have companionship when none was expected. Emerging from the bathroom much relieved, Harold decided to forego the trip into the city and to work from home.

He made himself a cup of coffee. He set out his papers on the dining room table and sat down, prepared to work. He took a sip of coffee from his cup and, in an instant, slipped into a hypnagogic state. Transfixed in his chair, he became aware of the silence and solitude of the empty house. There was no banging or thumping across the floor upstairs. No screaming from the basement. Carol wasn't calling his name from their bedroom. The intermittent muffled noise from passing cars in the street punctuated the purr of the refrigerator in the kitchen as he sat rapt in quiet contemplation. Light filtered into the room through the lattice work of tree branches and leaves outside. The grime on the windows softened and diffused it so it spread through the room like a fog. He slipped into a daydream that was as elaborate as any of the ones he had at night. It reminded him of his pre-Carol college years when sometimes, in the quiet of his apartment, he would space out, leaning back in his chair, taking long inhalations from a joint, savoring the taste, delighting in the trail of smoke as it left his lungs and wafted in waves through the light, his mind extending outside of him, evaporating into space like the smoke. He wished he had something to smoke right now.

Incapacitated, sitting at the table, Harold experienced the tranquility of being home alone. He enjoyed himself so much that day that he began letting Carol off the hook whenever afternoon meetings came up. He would leave work at lunchtime and wend his way home. He would set out all his papers, pads, and notebooks, and then sit and do nothing. He luxuriated in the late afternoon slanting light that filled the house with a golden glow. There was something indescribably decadent about being home in the afternoon on a work day and not working. The rest of the world was busy performing its assigned tasks. He was out of bounds, outside the norm, indulging in pleasure derived from solitude and nonproductive activity instead of working to increase the wealth of the corporate coffers. The very thought of it gave these interludes a rebellious overtone. The quiet of the surrounding unoccupied rooms further amplified his transgression. The muted sounds of jets roaring overhead, traffic from the valley, and sometimes a siren screaming in the distance, or a train whistle, reached him but couldn't touch him as he sat still as a sphinx and drifted in dream.

On the days he drank too much coffee and was unable to sit still, he wandered through the house, entering each room and inspecting its contents, most of which he swore he had never seen before. There was an overabundance of *stuff*. The house was stuffed with stuff. It was hard to figure how or why he and Carol and the kids had accumulated so many things. It was impossible to link every object with the desire that had preceded its purchase. The very thought of the *wanting* that had led to the purchasing of all these material objects was disturbing. Every room in the house was cluttered with things, most of them, he guessed, worthless.

In his closet, in a box shoved back in the corner, under some old winter clothes, he discovered his old vinyl record collection. He hooked up the turntable knowing it was wrong, all wrong. Listening to music was a weekend or evening activity. But on the weekends and in the evenings, taking this much time for himself would be unheard of. Reliving the sounds of his youth, which were embedded in those vinyl grooves, would be impossible if he was surrounded by Carol and the kids since none of them had been with him when he was a youth. He had to be alone to experience the anodyne effects of nostalgia. He wanted to hear the music in its original format.

He set a record on the turntable platter and lightly lowered the needle on the record. There was a crackle and a pop as the needle fell into a damaged groove, but then he was listening to Jesse Colin Young sing *Darkness, Darkness*, evoking all his adolescent anxiety and pain as fresh and sharp as when he was fourteen. Hearing Eric Burdon sing *When I Was Young* made him feel old. Jefferson Airplane's *Today* was still dumbfoundingly beautiful, with its haunting guitar and confessional, romantic lyrics. Marty Balin's yearning, ethereal tonalities made his heart ache. *All Along the Watchtower* remained as mystifying and metaphorical as ever. Tim Buckley's *Phantasmagoria in Two* almost brought him to tears. He still knew most of the lyrics to these songs by heart. He and his friends used to sit around and get high and spend hours listening to music, often arguing about the meaning of a song's lyrics. Was Paul the walrus? What enigma was embedded in the Moody Blues' song *Tuesday Afternoon?* Did the gentle voices explain it all with a sigh?

The music also stirred up unresolved feelings about what he was doing with his life, of everything he had become since he crossed the threshold of thirty and settled into a career. The specter of *The Port Huron Statement* returned to haunt him. Was he doing the right thing? Was he living a good life? What did *good* mean? He wasn't sure.

Harold was overcome by a fleeting intuition that if he persisted in this line of questioning he would be gripped by a sadness that would not release him. He felt queasy as the suspicion rose into his consciousness that he might have made a wrong turn somewhere along the way. But where? Was it wrong for him to want to be happy, for him to want his family to be happy? He was working toward that end. And how could it be wrong? Wasn't the country founded upon the principle that the pursuit of happiness was an unalienable right? But why did he have to pursue happiness? Why did anybody chase an abstract concept for which there was no tangible correlate in the material world? That made no sense. That was what confused people. That was how things got substituted for ideas. That was why his house was stuffed with material goods. He and Carol had thought purchasing them would yield happiness. Had all these things brought them happiness? Perhaps for a fleeting moment they had been happy. But happiness? Wasn't the freedom to pursue happiness as likely to make you a slave to the pursuit of material goods and services you thought would make you happy? Didn't it transform you into a consumer? Wasn't that what the Rolling Stones were getting at in *Mother's Little Helper* when they concluded the pursuit of happiness was a bore? All in all, wasn't it better to renounce than to pursue? How complicated it all was.

Surprisingly, indulging in these musical interludes left him refreshed. Afterwards, he settled in and focused on his work. The act of grappling with the questions he knew were important somehow assuaged his troubled mind. Of course, he knew he hadn't grappled with the questions. They had come to mind. That they came to mind and that he still recognized them as the fundamental questions of life cheered him some.

✧

Over the years, nannies came and went. Housekeepers were hired and fired. Soccer games were won and lost. Little League practices and karate tournaments and dance classes and summer camps and trips to the orthodontist and family vacations were all, Harold knew, ephemeral arrangements in the kaleidoscope of his life, and that kaleidoscope kept turning and shifting and presenting different images of him and his family as they passed through time.

⟨∿⟩

Harold was hailed a hero at work for spotting the business potential of the Internet. It was still in its commercial infancy when he brought it to the attention of his senior management through a series of white papers that were cogently argued and meticulously referenced. His intuition had told him AOL's massive direct-mail campaign to get people online, where they would become the easy targets of marketing efforts, was going to revolutionize the lifetime value of a customer. Later he insisted, after the dot-com bust, that the Internet was here to stay and the impact of Web 2.0 would have great import for the firm's clients. He wrote profusely on the probable profits the firm would make if it took a leadership role in recommending *new media* strategies to its clients.

⟨∿⟩

Sometimes during his lunch break, Harold rummaged through old issues of the *Harvard Business Review*. Here, he came upon works written by Theodore Levitt and other early business theoreticians about business and marketing strategy. He was able to see how to translate the theoretical and philosophical insights of these authors into practical money-making applications and apply them to clients' problems. While his probity was appreciated by the partners, who liked to introduce him to clients as their resident *big-ideas guy*, his most important practical contributions to the firm revolved around his ability to take complicated concepts and break them down into their individual components and show how they could be used to increase the value of a service or a brand.

Luck also played a role in Harold's success. Having recruited him, the partners at Gingham, Plaid & Taupe remained loyal to him after they sold the firm to a publicly held communications conglomerate. Harold, they said to the new managers as they sidled out the door on the way to the bank with their money, was to be retained at all costs as a key asset. The new owners did retain him, and he was rewarded with stock options and grants, and when the conglomerate that had bought Gingham, Plaid & Taupe was purchased by an even bigger holding company, his holdings vested. Unfortunately, while the sum was not insignificant, it didn't add up to the kind of fuck-you money that would allow him to walk out the door and retire. There was enough money to pay for the kids' college educations, if he invested it wisely, which was a relief, but he and Carol still had to work for a living.

⤳

Carol, too, was having success in her line of work. Unlike Harold, she had changed employers several times. She made no secret that whenever she didn't get what she wanted, or felt she wasn't being treated fairly, she sought new opportunities. She couldn't understand how he had managed to stay in the same company year after year. The American job market was fluid and opportunistic. For educated people such as they were, there were always new possibilities. Harold remarked that he was treated fairly at his place of employ. Why rock the boat? Well, not rocking the boat was one way to fall into a false sense of security and to be thrown off the boat, Carol warned.

—You always have to be looking around for other opportunities, she said.

—Exploring other opportunities is like working a second job, Harold said. One is enough.

Carol disagreed, and whenever one of the many executive recruiters with whom she kept in contact informed her of a job opportunity, she explored it. She used interviews as a way to network and make more contacts even when things were going well at her current job. You learn something every time you go out and talk to people, she said. And she liked to learn. She always wanted to bring her A-game to any endeavor, and she pushed herself to maximize her talent, always working at the edge of her capacity.

Carol was also astute enough to see that another way to network was to join every woman's organization that would have her. The sisterhood, she said, was the only way to overcome the boys' clubs that ruled the corporate world. She joined in the fight for women's workplace rights and was a vocal advocate for equal pay for equal work. Pay inequality was another form of discrimination, she said, of sexism.

⤳

Suddenly they were in their forties. Carol spotted her first gray hair one night while she was taking off her makeup. She pulled it out with tweezers and held it up for Harold to see.

—Look at this! I can't believe this is happening. My mother didn't have a single gray until she was fifty.

—She didn't have the stress you do, Harold said sympathetically.

Carol shook her head sadly. Her ambition to *make it*, which had fueled her workaholic frenzy in her thirties, was still alive but had been tempered by the vagaries of workplace politics and chance. She was frustrated. She had hit a wall and she wasn't sure if it was because she had reached the limit of her competency, or if her superiors were unwilling to recognize her talent because she threatened their competency. In either case, her advancement stalled. Moreover, there were fewer calls for interviews. She was disappointed yet undeterred and continued to work as hard as she could. She rationalized her lack of forward progress by saying that as one approached the corporate apex there were fewer opportunities. She was going to have to be patient and not lose hope. She remained as determined as ever to achieve certain milestones in her professional life and still planned on being a C-suite executive in her fifties.

—That's when you begin to accumulate capital, she said knowingly.

—I've been told that, Harold said.

He marveled at Carol's unshaken belief in the inevitability of her success. Harold admired her spunk.

To help make sure she met her goals, Carol began obsessively reading business books, seeking the recipe for advancement and survival. She started taking classes at the American Management Association and availed herself of every seminar and workshop her company offered to groom senior managers. She warned Harold he was going to fall behind the times if he didn't also start educating himself to improve his performance. She loved quoting Andy Grove:

Success breeds complacency. Complacency breeds failure. Only the paranoid survive.[3]

Harold was unimpressed.

—Corporations all across America brainwash their employees into believing they have to participate in employee performance optimization programs, he said. And why? To increase productivity.

—If we're not productive, we lose out to the competition. Which is global nowadays, Carol noted.

Harold was combative. He wasn't buying into it.

—I think corporate-driven labor productivity is like the food industrial complex stuffing cattle and chickens with antibiotics and vitamins to increase their productive yield at the slaughterhouse. Anyway, everyone approaches self-improvement from a different angle. Reading a novel or a book on history is as legitimate a way to improve yourself as any other, he said, and would potentially help generate new insights every bit as much as taking a course from Steven Covey on how to better manage your time.

Over the next few years Carol collected at least a half dozen certificates of completion for the courses she attended, which she had framed and hung in her office. She proudly listed her accomplishments on her résumé as proof she was a self-motivated, dynamic businesswoman. He was in awe of her drive to continually reinvent herself.

↜↝

---

3 Andy Grove, *Only the Paranoid Survive* (New York: Currency Doubleday, 1996).

Harold began working at home every couple of weeks whether or not there was a school meeting to attend. He needed mental health days, he explained to Carol. She was appalled.

—Nobody needs that many mental health days, she said. It means you're unhappy where you are. You should look for another job.

It wasn't that he was unhappy with his place of work, he explained. It was a bigger issue. He was unhappy doing what he was doing. His belief in *the system* was faltering.

—I don't know what that means.

—Yes, you do. You just don't want to hear it.

—I want to hear whatever you have to say if it will make you feel better.

—Well, I'm aiding and abetting the enemy.

—The enemy? What enemy? The system? What are you talking about?

—It's all part of the same thing. Do you remember Vance Packard's book *The Hidden Persuaders?*

She indicated that she did, although, by her nod, he wasn't sure she recalled any more than the title.

—All I do, one way or another, is help identify and create persuaders.

—I didn't think you created anything. Anything real, I mean.

—Not technically. A lot of what I do revolves around piecing together the foundation of the edifice that creates the persuaders, the marketing concepts. I help uncover so-called unmet needs. I identify trends that lead to *discovering* unmet needs, or worse, suggest ways to invent unmet needs—because an unmet need is only a euphemism for the stimulation of desire through marketing and, ultimately, advertising.

Carol was shaking her head, dismissively, he thought.

—Why are you shaking your head?

—Because....

—No, listen....

He pulled a bottle of water out of her bag.

—How did it happen that we *need* to carry around our own personal and disposable bottle of branded water? he asked.

Carol closed her eyes and shook her head.

—Someone discovered they could make money by touting the health benefits of natural, spring-fed water, that's how. They packaged it with panache and water became sexy. Never mind the old-school water fountains and water coolers. Who wouldn't want their own individual bottle of water from an uncontaminated well in the pristine wilderness? Who doesn't want to stay hydrated? Once you have your own bottle, you don't ever have to go thirsty, for an instant. You never have to suffer because someone discovered that selling branded bottles of water was an unmet need. The idea became a money-making proposition.

—So what? Some smart entrepreneur came up with an idea to make money, and now more people drink water, which is better for them than soda. What's wrong with that?

—That's not the point.

—What is the point, Harold?

—Personal sanitizers.

—Personal sanitizers are the point?

—Ten years ago you never heard of portable personal sanitation dispensers or wipes or sprays. Today, they're as ubiquitous as dirt. Have you been healthier since you started indulging in your desire for cleanliness? Do we need to be that clean? Or have we been manipulated into believing we should want to be that clean, germ-free? That's the whole key to marketing.

—I don't think there's any key. It's an approach to selling stuff. You're a sales guy.

—I don't sell anything. I'm talking about marketing, or customer engagement as it's called today, which is an attack on your emotional vulnerability. Marketing is finding the space in your mind that can accommodate a message that arouses a need, like a secret vice you might not want to acknowledge. There are whole books written about this. It's an art. You, me, all of us are manipulated every minute of every day. Every image you see in a magazine or newspaper or home page or banner ad or on television or your cell phone has been researched and tested and honed to hit home as accurately as a laser-guided drone missile. It has been calculated to pierce your psychographic armor no matter how bulletproof you claim it to be. Everyone who makes anything is in cahoots with everyone who markets anything.

—Harold....

She was clearly irritated. He guessed that at times like this she regretted all the years she had scolded him for keeping everything bottled up inside and had coached him on how to empty his head of all the thoughts that were rattling around inside.

—It's worse than you imagine, he continued. All the social media and advertisers have you under surveillance. They're spies. They're predatory. They share your data. They feed their algorithms with your likes and dislikes. They've got a big target on the inner sanctum of your mind.

—You're beginning to sound like a conspiracy theorist.

—But it's true.

—True?

—I'm not making it up. It's common knowledge. Listen to the founders of the new media companies and their handlers spewing their propaganda about the social good they're creating. Listen to them tell their bullshit stories about the radical change they claim they've brought to communications, the innovation they say they've engineered in human relations by helping you keep in touch and express your likes and dislikes and allowing you to share them. They do that to make you forget what they offer casts a huge net. Anyone who wanders into it is captured and exploited for a value that far exceeds any potential benefit that might be returned to them for surrendering their so-called preferences. It's all a bunch of shit. The so-called social networks are the factories of the new millennium, and every time you use one of their sites you help those corporations make money. Your log-in is labor and signifies your submission to their power over you. You're a slave.

—We're all slaves to something.

—I don't want to be a slave. I'm sick of being a slave. And that's my point. But figuring out how to remain free is hard.

—Everyone has to make compromises. You have to decide what your personal set of them will be, she said.

—I don't want to, he said.

Carol wasn't getting it. She didn't understand that the ideas he came up with were aiding and abetting his corporate masters, who were selling them to other corporate slobs to make millions by promoting rampant consumerism.

—I'm part of the problem, Harold said. I know it. I just don't know what to do about it.

He began pacing around the kitchen, distraught.

Carol sat down at the table and gazed at him. It was hard to tell what she was thinking. She put her elbows on the table and dropped her head into her hands and stared straight ahead of her. She looked tired, or bored, but since she made no effort to interject, he kept talking.

—The cultural war waged in the sixties was won not by the Left or the Right but by consumerism, he said. And the mouthpiece of consumerism today is mass media and advertising, which makes everyone a target for radicalization, although *radical* is not a term one normally associates with a consumer.

Over the years, he went on, corporations mastered their ability to keep consumers receptive to sales pitches for goods and services. They learned that while they want brand loyalty, they also want their customers to remain open to being seduced by new goods and services. Everyone experiences this manipulative scenario. Bought a new iPhone? Don't get attached: a newer version will be available in six months to a year. What are you to do? Corporations claim you are only a click away from improving your life. Everything is available ready-made, mass produced, and can be shipped today and delivered tomorrow if you order online now. At the same time, everything is made to be disposable and ready to be traded in or thrown out so the next disruption in the chain of production doesn't feel traumatic.

Carol yawned, but Harold was riled up, unstoppable.

—In capitalist countries, he said, the idea of social revolution is pointless because no one is attached to anything. From the sixties forward, culture and ideologies have been manufactured and distributed like sitcoms on TV. There's nothing to grasp onto that's worth preserving. All that was solid long ago melted into air.[4] By constantly fueling appetites to feed profits,

---

4 Karl Marx and Friedrich Engels, *The Communist Manifesto* (New York: Russell & Russell, [1848] 1963).

the market economy has undermined traditions, values, and communities. This was the cultural contradiction of capitalism.[5] This circle was voracious and vicious and ineluctable. This was why people went insane.

—Harold? Are you okay? You're scaring me a little.

She appeared genuinely concerned.

—I think I'm suffering from a bad conscience, he confessed.

—Well, you can't have a bad conscience about what you do, she said, sympathetically. I don't think you do anything bad.

—No. I do bad things. I help design the architecture of desire that drives people to want more than they can ever have. That's bad.

—Oh, you're in a foul mood.

—I'm not in a mood at all. A mood is a fleeting set of sensations that comes and goes and doesn't correspond to a mental state. I'm in a state of some sort.

—Well, it's natural to examine things when you reach a certain age. And if it's not a mood you're in, then maybe you're bored, or having a midlife crisis.

He wasn't bored. He wasn't having a midlife crisis.

〜

A few weeks after his conversation with Carol, while sitting in his office after lunch contemplating an assignment with an approaching deadline, Harold had the strange sensation he was floating in and out of his life. Random, bizarre thoughts overwhelmed him. He couldn't concentrate. He couldn't

---

5 Daniel Bell, *The Cultural Contradictions of Capitalism* (New York: Basic Books, 1976).

think. His mind went wild. He snapped out of it and wrote it off as fatigue. But more and more often he fell into this kind of daydream. In the blink of an eye his mental state shifted into a hallucinogenic reverie. Time melted away, leaving him floating like a Brownian point on an infinite vector in space. There was, he concluded, a definitive unreality to his life. While Carol was sure about who she was and what she was, he sometimes no longer recognized himself. I wonder if I'm losing it, he thought. He tried to explain this sensation to her.

—You can deny it, but what you're telling me sounds to me like a midlife crisis, Carol said, assuredly, with all the solemnity of a physician announcing an unfortunate diagnosis. You're not as young as you once were.

—I don't think it's about my age.

—Then what?

—I don't know. I feel empty. I'm working against what my will wants me to do.

—Stop it.

—That's the problem. I can't.

—Harold....

She was exasperated.

—I'm sure whatever you're experiencing is serious. You need to stop torturing yourself. Doubt is debilitating. You're becoming hysterical. Maybe you should see a therapist. You're depressed, she said, changing her diagnosis.

He thought about seeing a therapist. But the most a therapist might do was transform what was becoming his hysterical unhappiness into everyday unhappiness, and he doubted the transformation would afford him any relief.

Harold learned that physical activity distracted him from his mental problems. Soon after they moved to the suburbs, he had become acquainted with Martin, a fellow at his local gym with whom he occasionally worked out. One day while they were spotting one another on the bench press, Martin explained he came to the gym to keep his upper body and core strong, but his principal sport was cycling.

—Do you ride? Martin asked.

—I have a bike.

—A road bike?

—I think it's called a hybrid. My wife and kids each have one.

—That's not a road bike, Martin explained.

After a quick description, Harold understood Martin was talking about the lightweight, thin-tired, multiple-geared bicycles he saw men in tight spandex costumes riding on the local roads.

—If you want to get in shape, you should buy one. We have a group that rides out of the local bike shop every morning.

Not long after his conversation with Martin, Harold visited the local bike shop. He allowed himself to be persuaded to buy a little more bike than he needed, as the salesperson had put it, since he would grow into it as his ability improved. He also purchased all the accoutrements necessary to ride: a helmet, a spandex riding bib, a shirt with pockets in the back, gloves, and clip-in shoes.

On his first foray out on the road he was unable to unclip his foot from the pedal fast enough while coming to a stop and went tumbling over sideways, badly scraping his shoulder and hip, ripping his new shirt, and damaging the front brake mechanism. The salesperson at the shop was not surprised.

—Happens to every beginner, he said.

The bike was fixed in a jiffy. His injuries, his first road rash, took some time to heal. Carol shook her head, disapprovingly. Cycling was a dangerous sport, she warned. It hadn't occurred to him that it was dangerous, but now that she labeled it as such it became even more alluring.

When he thought he had ridden sufficient miles on his own to know what he was doing, he showed up one morning at the bike shop for a ride. Everyone was charming and welcoming. Once they began riding, Harold found the pace was much faster than he was used to, and he had to struggle to keep up. No one else was putting in the slightest effort. He heard the riders talking among themselves and remarked on their relaxed postures as they rose off their saddles and bobbed up and down on their pedals to attack a slight incline. Meanwhile, he was huffing and puffing and grinding away, barely able to hold on to the tail of the peloton. When they came upon a long stretch of flat road, and everyone shifted into their big rings and hunkered down in the drops of their handlebars and got into a rhythm that lifted the speed to the low twenties, they left Harold in the dust like a man chasing after a moving freight train on foot. No one looked back.

When they all met up to ride the next morning, everyone was happy to see him.

—It doesn't come easy, he was told.

The group was comprised of a congenial bunch of local men, and after several months and many hours on the road with them, Harold became friends with them, at least superficially. The men referred to one another by nicknames that were based on each individual's physical traits or personal quirks. No-Talk rarely spoke on rides, but he was a slip-and-fall lawyer. The Landlord owned a real estate and property management company. The Invisible Man joined rides after they started rolling and hung on the back where he thought no one saw him and then disappeared at some point before the ride was over. Single-Speed rode a single-speed bike on race days. The Ring had a penchant for riding only in his big ring, ignoring what the road grade dictated. Einstein appeared to be a slow learner, but he was an excellent athlete. The Abductor drove a beat-up old Ford Econoline van, which everyone said was the type used by kidnappers. The Baker owned the bagel shop in town. Martin, who had introduced Harold to the group, was called The Mope, since he was always sulking about something. They referred to Harold as Skinny.

It took Harold six months of concentrated effort to be able to stay with the group throughout most of their rides, and even then the better riders appeared at the end of an incredibly strenuous thirty-mile outing as if they'd been out for a spin around the block while he would be hyperventilating, still trying to catch his breath.

It took him a year to be able to stay with the peloton on the two fastest weekly rides. The first of these was a rotating double-pace line in which the riders in the fast-moving right line moved up to the front and pulled everyone behind them for several seconds before rotating off to the slower-moving left line, then drifted to the back and rejoined the fast-moving line on the right. Known as the Mambo, this ride took place on Tuesday mornings at six and covered thirty miles of rolling hills at an average speed of twenty to twenty-three miles an hour. How much work each individual rider had to perform depended upon how many riders showed up. On days when riders from the surrounding communities joined and there were as many as twenty men, Harold made it through the course like a champ. On days only ten men participated, he still might fall off the back of the pack.

The Friday Special was a longer and no less intense ride. It was more of a race than the Mambo, and it attracted more riders. It covered approximately fifty miles and included one big climb and several sprints. They rode the course at about the same average speed as the Mambo, sometimes hitting speeds of up to thirty miles per hour on the flats. Here, the best strategy for Harold was to pick someone's wheel and follow it, hiding in the peloton, drafting to save energy for the accelerations. When he was situated perfectly in the center of the bubble, it felt like he wasn't even pedaling. If he played it smart and followed a strong rider and mimicked his gear shifts and anticipated the power surges and didn't drift to the front where he might be expected to pull, he finished this ride. If he miscalculated as they approached the big climb, the peloton would speed away from him as they began the ascent, and while he would be pumping his legs as hard and as fast as he could, they would slowly break away from him, and although he would continue to move forward, it felt like he was moving backward as he watched them ride away.

〰

The endorphins his body released while riding were powerful enough to suppress Harold's rising anxiety about his life. But like any drug the effect wore off, and then the questions that were demanding answers hounded him.

A few months after he told Carol about his daydreaming, he announced he was afraid he wasn't leading a morally purposeful life. His life had gotten away from him, he told her. He needed to take it back. He needed to find some meaning in what he was doing that was positive.

—If you would stop being negative, that would be a positive, Carol counseled.

She said it wasn't healthy to keep questioning and analyzing everything, looking for some sort of meaning. You had to give meaning to things since they didn't come with it as an ingredient.

—I understand that, he said.

Finding meaning in what he was doing, and doing the right thing, was only part of Harold's predicament. He also worried about whether or not he was free, or as in chess, whether he was nothing more than a pawn in the service of forces over which he had no control. And if he was a pawn—the evidence of which was becoming clearer to him every day—then what, as *The Port Huron Statement* had asked, could he do to attain a determining influence over his circumstances of life? How could he, at this stage in his life, effect a transformation that would allow his full potential to be known? How could he find freedom?

Carol's forbearance with these college-boy discussions, as she referred to them, was waning. She would give abrupt and indifferent answers to his rhetorical questions. She pooh-poohed his increasing unease about his life, insisting he was going through a midlife crisis and he was going to have to outgrow it. She didn't want to hear about it.

—You're not twenty-one anymore. Demonstrate a little maturity, she said.

She spoke rather peevishly, he thought.

꧁꧂

Harold tried to comply with Carol's command. But his concern about how he was living became overwhelming and manifested itself at work. Assigned a project to sort through the debate between old and new media and the role of advertising in each, he focused primarily on television and television commercials. He approached the assignment from a hypercritical point of view, borrowing from David Foster Wallace[6] and Noam Chomsky.[7] He intended to send a shot across the desks of the bureaucrats. Just to see what would happen.

In his paper, he accused television and advertising of being responsible for all the evils in the world. There were several well-accepted truisms about television, he wrote. It had reduced our attention span, suppressed our appetite for complexity, and altered our perception of reality. Over time, this triumvirate had softened our brains. It tricked us into believing that what was presented on television was reality, when it was the furthest thing from it. What we watched on television was nothing but stylized rituals. The spectacle in full regalia. Television, and here he indicated he was using the word synecdochically, was nothing but a masquerade for the power structure behind it. The news, the talk shows, the reality shows, the sitcoms, everything on the screen was nothing more than the projection of power by the commercial interests that underwrote it with the aim of making a profit.

---

6 David Foster Wallace, "E Unibus Pluram: Television and U.S. Fiction," *Review of Contemporary Fiction* 13, no. 2 (1993): 151.
7 Edward S. Herman and Noam Chomsky: *Manufacturing Consent: The Political Economy of the Mass Media* (New York: Pantheon Books, 1988).

Commercials, he wrote, were the lifeblood of television, and they had led the way in destroying the mind's ability to think and to find solutions to problems. Because so many people dreamed of transcending their ordinary lives by any means they could, when they were confronted by a pitch to purchase a product that promised it would change their life, they were easily persuaded that, yes, I should buy that, yes, I have to order that, yes, I have my credit card right here and will purchase that right now in order to receive two for the price of one. Who wouldn't? Who could resist?

Senior management fired back at Harold. They were very unhappy with the direction his paper had taken. There was no strategic value in it, they said. It was more of a screed than a balanced piece of writing. One of the managing directors was quick to point out that Harold hadn't included an assessment of network television's actual declining power due to the impact of the Internet and the growing use of mobile devices. Subversive thinking, another commented.

During dinner, he proudly distributed the paper for all to read.

Sarah, now in high school, shrugged her shoulders.

—So? she said. This is the same stuff you always talk about.

Jake claimed he found substantial evidence on the Internet that his father was right about the pernicious effects of television and advertising, none of which was new.

Carol was aghast and critical.

—It reads like something you cobbled together from some left-wing socialist blogs. Have you lost your mind? She wanted to know.

—I felt great writing it. I had to do something.

—I'm sure you did. But look, you're successful. You're re-spected. You're paid well. You do what you want most of the time. Do you want to throw it all away because you feel the need to act out? Because if you keep this up, you'll get fired. Then what? What about me? What about the kids?

Harold had nothing to say.

—You're biting the hand that feeds you. Please stop.

Harold knew he was in trouble the minute Shirley, the head of human resources, or HR, showed up in his office. He knew it wasn't a chance visit since he never had unplanned inter-actions with HR. One of the managing partners must have suggested someone talk to him about his paper and that someone should be Shirley.

She must have checked his calendar and knew his sched-ule was clear before walking through his door and half closing it behind her.

—Do you have a minute? she wanted to know.

The inquisition began with niceties and chitter-chatter.

—How's the family?

Shirley had never met any of them. She only knew they existed from the health insurance forms he had filled out.

—Your kids must be big now. Getting ready for college, right?

—Yes, Harold said.

—How is Carol?

—She's fine.

—Happy at her job?

—Very happy.

—Everything at home is good?

—Very good.

—And how are you doing?

Well, right now he was cornered in his office by the head of HR, who was undoubtedly trying to coax out of him the reason for his seditious paper. So he wasn't doing great. He thought it despicable that she was subjecting him to a line of inquiry designed to assess his mental health or, worse, his morale. While Shirley wasn't taking any notes, signifying this was an unofficial, informal chat, she would be sure to write something up after she returned to her office. The partner who suggested the visit would want a report. *How'd it go? What do you think? What's the risk?* For the first time in his working history, something negative would be entered into his file. And I don't care, Harold thought.

Shirley smiled as she extolled his virtues and told him he was considered to be one of the preeminent thinkers in the firm. She crossed her short, stubby legs, making herself more comfortable in her chair, and folded her hands over her notebooks and slouched down a little, so she appeared smaller, trying, no doubt, to show she had come in peace, not to intimidate. But as he was reticent and she was finding it difficult to articulate lines of questioning that would reveal useful information, she began spewing out the mission of the firm, harping on its commitment to its clients, telling him how everyone had to work as a team and each team member had to fulfill his or her duties within the parameters laid out by the team leader. If he didn't sense she was nervous, he would have thought she was talking down to him as she went on to make a point about the necessity of fulfilling expectations and how behavioral differences were signals of mental states and emotional shifts.

Then she tapped out some words about how it was necessary for everyone to be marching to the same drum or the rhythm of work would suffer.

Yes, he thought, that made sense. For it was Shirley who, shortly after the last takeover, had spearheaded the effort to bring the new corporate mission to life and to disseminate it to the employees. He remembered going into the executive conference room for a meeting one afternoon and noticing two beautifully framed photographs hanging on opposite walls. One was of two shirtless mountaineers on the face of a sheer precipice, both dangling over an abyss, one man pulling the other man up by one arm. Underneath this dramatic, doubtlessly staged, photo was copy that read: *Teamwork*. The other photograph showed a track race: the winner, his eyes focused, his face contorted in pain, had crossed the finish line a fraction ahead of the racer next to him. Underneath this stop-motion, full-color photo was copy that read: *Achievement*. Harold had wondered how he, or anyone else, was supposed to work with these visual and verbal platitudes shouting down at them from the walls. They were royalty-free stock photos available all over the Internet, and yet here they were hanging on the walls of a conference room in one of the most prestigious consulting organizations in New York. It was embarrassing. Additionally, the messages appeared to be contradictory since, in one photo, working together would appear to be the message, and in the other photo the message appeared to be that a single individual would triumph over others who were striving equally as hard to achieve the same goal.

Upon leaving the conference room that day he had also noticed, behind the half-closed door, in the same spot where hotels posted their room rates and all appropriate taxes, a plaque. On it was inscribed the company mission. The mission statement summed up the two inspirational photographs hanging on the walls. Beneath the corporate logo, it read: *Through teamwork we achieve our goal: client appreciation.* And then Harold knew: this idiotic phrase, as well as the hackneyed photographs, had the stench of HR written all over it.

Shirley smiled at him, trying, he thought, to be conciliatory. She didn't fool him. She and her cadre of spies were always looking for troublemakers, ready to pounce on anyone who was denounced by a fellow worker for even an insignificant infraction. In reality, HR was no more than an internal police force.

After the second takeover, Harold had become convinced that the more entrenched HR was in management, the less well run was the company. The more power HR wielded, the less innovative the company was because HR was a parasite and contributed no intellectual property to the enterprise, built no assets, only sucked income away from the people who produced it. They undertook idiotic initiatives and put up intellectually embarrassing photographs, like the ones Shirley had installed in all the conference rooms, the kitchen, and the open shared-space areas. As far as Harold was concerned, the only thing HR was qualified to do was fill out the paperwork for his tax withholdings and enroll him in the health and benefits plan. Sometimes they even fucked that up.

Yet here sat Shirley, a nincompoop, trying, it appeared to him, to counsel him on how to behave in an appropriate manner.

—You know, she said, if you are disgruntled there are various pathways you can follow to make your feelings known rather than sabotaging work.

Harold was surprised at her word choice. She couldn't possibly have come up with *sabotage* herself. One of the partners must have fed her that word, and she was parroting it since she was not that bright. Moreover, it was an odd interpretation of his paper. He had wanted to provoke a reaction from his superiors, but he hadn't intended what he had written to undermine or subvert the company. It was where his mind had taken him while he was working on the assignment. Back in the old days, when the firm had been privately held, and he was personally known to the partners, after perusing his paper they would have chortled and sent it back to him with a one-word note: *rewrite.* And that would have been the end of it.

But corporations had no sense of humor. That was the point Shirley was here to make. He worked for a corporation. He had to share the goals and aspirations of the world in which he functioned. And that was a problem for Harold. For the longer he worked for a corporation, the stronger his belief became that no other modern institution was more destructive to the American way of life than the corporation. It was something his father had repeated to him many times. Corporations undermined the very idea of individuality and American exceptionalism. They instilled the need to conform in their employees. They made people fat and lazy. They encouraged the multiplication of timid little men and women and forced them to live timid little lives because corporations needed timid little people to sit in their tiny little cubicles and work for the good of the corporation. Which corporations claimed was good for America because the business of America was business.

And here was Shirley, trying to understand why he had strayed outside the straight and narrow lines of solid corporate citizenship. She was trying to make him aware of his place within the organization and put him back in it. All for his own good. For nothing good would come from his supposed dereliction of duty, as the senior partner had warned. Carol had predicted exactly this outcome.

Harold didn't have his mental resources sufficiently organized to defend himself. He couldn't recall exactly why he had written the paper the way he had. Or why he had decided to provoke senior management. Or what sort of response he had expected, or wanted. His mind began to wander. He couldn't focus. He felt dizzy.

Shirley was staring at him expectantly.

—Are you disgruntled?

He took a moment to think about her word choice and tried to imagine what its implications were.

—No, he said.

Then he had an epiphany.

—No, I'm not disgruntled, he said.

—Then what?

—Disenchanted.

〰

Harold shared the details of his discussion with Carol. He recounted at length the stupidity of their talk. He verbalized his deep hatred of HR but said he had remained mute on that subject, practicing total and complete self-control, never showing his true feelings.

—You would have been proud of me, he told her.

Carol saw the exchange in a different light, particularly the conclusion.

—You told her you were disenchanted? She was incredulous.

—Yes.

—Are you mad? Why would you ever tell someone from HR you were disenchanted? Who even uses that word, *disenchanted*?

—Well, she was trying to imply I was disgruntled.

Carol shook her head.

—You gave them ammunition to use against you.

While Harold had been through a merger and acquisition, and then a buyout, and had spent time with HR people during transitional interviews and departmental reshufflings—the very interactions that had formed his opinion that the HR department represented an internal threat to an organization—he was uncertain how to interact with them, or how to protect himself from them. As intelligent as he was, he did not understand the difference between sharing a fact external to himself and sharing a state of mind, or what the implications of sharing one versus the other might be. Until these last few years, his job had always been protected: first by the founders and then by the senior partners. But as the company had grown in size and added layers of management, he was pushed further and further away from his protectors. The addition of directors and team leaders and managers that resulted from the mergers had diminished his standing. So much so that in one of the corporate reshufflings he had been relieved of his windowed office and given a small windowless one that faced an internal atrium. Whenever his name came up in conversation or during talent reviews, it was still tagged with *smart guy* or *sharp*, but he was now considered merely one of the members of the general class of knowledge workers that management referred to when they spoke of putting their *intellectual capital* to work for clients.

—I don't understand why you would tell her you were disenchanted. That's worse than saying you're disgruntled, Carol proclaimed.

—I thought it was a better choice, he explained. More accurate. What was I supposed to do? I needed to give her a word.

—You didn't need to give her that word. It is one thing to tell me. It's another to tell her. Well, now you're going to have to deal with it, she concluded.

⟨∿⟩

Carol thought he had made a mistake by sharing his feelings with Shirley. But for Harold, the moment he had blurted out *disenchanted* was the moment he recognized how radically unhappy he was with his work. Rather than be traumatized by a failed encounter with reality, his unconscious had spoken, albeit impulsively. His unconscious censors had failed, allowing the truth to slip out. He now knew for certain that the only so-called good he was doing was helping the corporate masters he served make money.

Recognizing the truth placed him in a paralyzing situation. He had to weigh his obligation to his wife and kids against his conscience, which now told him that what he was doing was wrong. What should he do? An alarm was going off in his head, but he was standing still instead of running for an exit.

—I should quit my job, he proposed to Carol.

—Quit?

She was incredulous.

—You mean I shouldn't quit?

—That's not what I mean. Harold, honey, she said, lapsing into her soothing admonitory voice she often used with the children when trying to get them to do something they didn't want to do. You're a smart man and held in high esteem at your company, and compensated accordingly, I might add, for the intellectual contributions you make. The minute you quit and find yourself on the street you'll be worth less. And then you'll be sorry.

—Worthless?

—Worth *less*, she clarified.

—Less than what?

—Less than you're worth now, she said. Trust me. I know what I'm talking about. My friends have been through it. And you should understand it. While you're employed, your value is the link in the chain of the system you support. The second your link breaks and you're outside the chain and want to be added on to a new chain, all your accomplishments and core competencies and education sit on a piece of paper, which, like any commodity, is traded and purchased for the lowest price obtainable. You're at the mercy of forces over which you have no control.

—Yes, that's the problem, he said. I have no control. I'm not in control of my life. That's what I've been telling you. But what can I do about it? How do I take control? By continuing to do what I'm doing? I don't think I can keep on doing what I'm doing.

—Of course you can. We all do it every day. You think I like getting up every morning and going to work?

—You love your job. You've said so a million times.

—Look, on a good day it's good, and on bad days it sucks.

—That's not what I'm talking about. I'm philosophically opposed to what I do.

—I don't like every assignment that comes my way either.

—I think you're being purposefully obtuse, he said.

—I'm not. You're unhappy, and you want to take some drastic action to relieve your distress. Quitting is not going to help. Quitting never proves anything. Even if you are totally miserable, you can't walk away, or you'll walk away with nothing.

Carol paused. She stared at him, sympathetically, he thought.

She began again.

—If you want to quit, at least be smart about it. Start interviewing. Find something else first. Keep taking their money for as long as you can. Or slack off. Let them fire you. Let them tell you they have gone in a different direction, that the team is being restructured, that your functional responsibility has been eliminated. Let them tell you anything that will make them negotiate your exit package. Based on your age and how many years you've been there, at least you'll walk away with something.

—Then what would I do? he asked.

Now that he was on the defensive, Carol changed her stance and began offering advice on how to quit correctly.

—Find another job first. You can't sit around here. Our lifestyle is not supportable on a single salary.

—I'm afraid I'd end up doing the same thing for someone else. I'd still be supporting the status quo.

—Honey, I hate to break it to you, but we are the status quo, she said.

—I don't understand that either. How did we become the status quo? We hated the status quo. How did we end up here? Remember when we were in school, and we used to have dialogues about how we were going to live our lives. What happened? Now when we talk, it's like we're only exchanging words, passing them back and forth. Like there's nothing deeper. I mean, how the fuck did this happen?

—Harold....

—We used to talk about what we were going to do, of who we were going to become. Remember? And what have we become? I don't know ... what became of becoming? How did we stop becoming and end up as the status quo? That's the question I want answered. That's the overwhelming question, if you ask me. That's what's killing me.

Carol was calm.

—Life happens around you: you make it.

—Those are two separate thoughts.

—Okay. You're responsible.

—Well, then, I don't like what I've made of it.

—There's nothing wrong with the status quo, Harold.

〜

Cycling saved him. On his bike, the intense focus required to ride in the peloton and to stay alert to the cars and potholes and the technical challenges of the road calmed him. Traveling fast, with another rider's wheel not more than six inches in front of him, and another rider's wheel six inches behind him, and sometimes riders on each side of him, required a degree of concentration that banished all other concerns. Going downhill at thirty or forty miles an hour required as much commitment to the moment as a mountain climber scaling a sheer face without a belay. And while the sport was inherently dangerous, it was, he thought, as much fun as one could have without being under the influence of a drug.

The pure sensual satisfaction of experiencing the changes in velocity and the scenery flying by were only part of the pleasure. The real thrill came from being one with the machine. Watching his speed, power output, and cadence on the Garmin, he listened only to what his body told him: the overwhelming physical demands pushed every other thought out of his head. With his feet clipped into the pedals and his legs providing the mechanical source of power that made the bike move, he was motion itself.

He rode almost every day. Once Jake got his driver's license, and Harold no longer had to worry about chauffeuring him or Sarah to school, he would go out early in the morning with his cycling buddies and get in twenty to twenty-five miles. Then he would go to work, his endorphins still riding high. His skills and conditioning had arrived at a point where he was able to compete in local races at the master's level.

On weekends his cycling group would carpool and take road trips, sometimes traveling to Ulster County to ride the roads around Peekamoose Mountain or to Harriman State Park, where they would climb Perkins Memorial Drive to the top of Bear Mountain and afterward ride the roads through Seven Lakes. They cruised through the park, surrounded on all sides by forest. The light fell through the leaves, dappling the road. When Harold was riding exceptionally well, his movements were as smooth and precise as a clock's. He hunkered down in the drops and pedaled through the technical turns, rising out of the saddle to attack the next grade without losing momentum, and then coast down the following descent, pedaling again as the grade picked up, keeping a perfect tempo. At moments like these he felt weightless and abstract. It was as if he were experiencing the space-time continuum itself.

〰

Riding was therapeutic. It was not a cure for his problems. At work, Harold thought some of his colleagues began exhibiting a slightly different attitude toward him. Up until the time of *the debacle*, as Carol referred to his confession to Shirley, all the assignments he'd turned in had been accepted more or less in their entirety, with very few edits requested. In the meetings where he'd presented his ideas, questions were raised, points challenged, conclusions debated, in an open, collegial manner, and he'd dismissed the irrelevant or tangential comments while accepting the legitimate criticisms, and had reworded and rewrote where necessary.

Recently, after presenting his ideas, he noticed a subtle antagonistic response. He had to defend his ideas more aggressively than previously. His ability to memorize data and cite the references backing up his points was useful, but it did not silence the more pugnacious detractors from criticizing his thinking. They thought it was acceptable to attack his propositions using such banalities as *I don't want to seem negative, but ...* or, *I'm just playing devil's advocate, so ...* trying to negate the value of his insights and elevate the value of their analytical powers.

Fortunately, after listening to his response, his direct supervisors were smart enough to conclude his theses were well founded and his arguments and creative solutions sound. Once they got it, they put a stop to the critics. Harold came to believe that the working sessions in which everything had once gone so smoothly were now forums where his ideas were vetted and subjected to a rigorous internal quality control procedure so the executive directors could be reasonably certain that what ended up on their desks was a legitimate piece of work and not a philosophical treatise. They didn't want the responsibility of having to distinguish between the two.

The trial-like atmosphere made these meetings uncomfortable for Harold. They also forced him to work harder than he had been working. For to make sure everything he did was buttoned up and beyond reproach, he found himself becoming even more meticulous than he usually was. That he succumbed to what was no more and no less than peer pressure galled him to no end and made him feel incredibly guilty. He hated his work, but he was still seduced by the intellectual challenge. And while he was toying with the idea of quitting, he was simultaneously exhibiting behaviors consistent with maintaining the dignity of the function. He was stuck in an absurd position. It was mentally exhausting.

⟨∿⟩

His epiphany had exposed the reality of his situation and now he couldn't stop thinking about it. His abhorrence of his job stayed front and center in his consciousness and refused to recede into the shadows. Reeducating himself for another career at his age, just as his kids were on the verge of going to college, was out of the question. Very few jobs would pay the money he was making. His family would have to downgrade their lifestyle to accommodate his bad conscience, and that wouldn't be fair.

Harold was flummoxed.

Carol either didn't understand the acuteness of his dilemma or didn't want to acknowledge it, and in either case, she had no patience with him. She was tired of talking about his *plight*, as she now called it. She did her part to pay for their lifestyle. No matter what issues he was having, she expected him to continue to help maintain the family's overall standard of living.

—We're both adults, and we have obligations. We have to think about the kids, she said, indicating her position was not a self-interested one.

—You live in a bubble, Harold said.

—Maybe.

—Not maybe. You do.

—Okay, so what? I blew it, and I like it.

—What if it bursts?

—Can you stop, please?

He had to stop, or an argument would start, and he didn't want to engage her any more than he already had. These days she rarely conceded any of his points, and in his effort to get her to see what he was seeing he would become more aggressive and she more defensive, and the impasse that ensued would lead them to utter inanities, if not, sometimes, insults, leaving them both frustrated and fatigued.

〜

Harold suspected Carol's lack of sympathy toward his predicament was partly caused by the fact that she had never quite forgiven him for moving the family to the suburbs. Carol was a city girl. She had grown up in Boston and gone to college in Ithaca, which she had enjoyed, especially after meeting Harold. But the town was insufferably small, and she had looked forward to nothing so much after graduation as moving back to a real city, even if it was to live in the hole in the wall they had first occupied when they moved to New York. While she hadn't been able to fight the facts he adduced in making his argument for moving, she had let him know she was emotionally opposed to it. At one point she had accused him of not being sufficiently sensitive to her feelings. She had never gone as far as to say that she would hold it against him or resent him, yet shortly after they became suburbanites, he had sensed a subtle shift in her attitude toward him that fell somewhere between a grudge and indifference. Over the years these sentiments had grown more pronounced.

After the move, Harold often had a hard time eliciting any more than a wan, half smile from her. She would sit nicely with him on the couch while watching television and permit him to enfold her in his arms. A gentle kiss on the cheek or a pat on the hand was about all he got in return when he said something affectionate to her. Not that he expected a lot more. Already, after they were married and had settled down, as it were, she had become less generous with her hugs and kisses, and her emotions in general. After the move she became down-right stingy, and the times she chose to show some warmth, its expression was tepid at best. Their lovemaking, which had never been the same since the arrival of the kids, was now intermittent and devoid of passion.

Carol's chief objection to having sex when they had lived in the city was the proximity of the children's room to theirs. Now their master bedroom suite was far from the children's rooms, but this did nothing to make her more receptive to his advances. Before she could think about responding to his amorous initiatives, she needed to be well lubricated with copious amounts of alcohol. It helped her unwind, she explained, and enjoy *it*.

He tried to assuage her smoldering hostility. The distance growing between them depressed him. But according to her, nothing was wrong with their relationship.

—I'm fine, she claimed. We're fine.

—You don't seem fine. I want you to be happy, he said.

—I can't be happy here. I wasn't meant to live here. After the kids are gone, and we move back to the city, I'll be happy. Until then I have to cope.

—There's a difference between coping and living.

—While I'm living here, I'm coping. You have to tolerate your job, and I have to tolerate being here. We each have our cross to bear.

Carol didn't consider herself a suburbanite. Her commute to and from the city, and the weekend routine she created for herself, insulated her from contamination by the community. She had made no attempt to reach out and make friends. She interacted with other parents only if she was forced to do so and thwarted all attempts at socializing.

From time to time Carol was obliged to attend events organized by Harold's cycling friends—drinks or dinner in the winter, barbeques in the summer. Despite his insistence that his buddies were all nice, friendly, down-to-earth people, she saw nothing appealing in any of them, or their wives, who were, she said, the same, but slightly older, vicious hausfraus who had bullied her for years when the children had been attending elementary and middle school. It was during those years that she had been subjected to no end of snarky, bitchy comments about the fact that she worked and wasn't a stay-at-home mom.

—Most of them don't have half the education I do, and yet these are the same women who tried to educate me on the benefits of a mother's presence in the home when the children are young. I'm sorry, I didn't go to school for all that time to have kids and then stay home with them. I'm there for them if they need me.

He tried to preach tolerance.

—Why should I be tolerant? They weren't, and they still aren't. They still talk down to me because I work. I have nothing in common with them. They fill their days with yoga, shopping, manicures and pedicures, and making dinner and theater plans for the weekend when they'll change out of their workout clothes and get pimped out to go into the city to reap their reward for the insufferable boredom of being a suburban stay-at-home mom.

—They're not all like that, Harold said.

—Oh, you don't think so?

—They can't all be that bad, he said.

—Oh, they're that bad, she said. They get dumber as they get older. As their kids move forward in the educational system, their brains atrophy from years of lack of intellectual stimulation, and from reading *Mademoiselle* and *Cosmo* and *People*. They can't hold a conversation about anything more complicated than which nail salon has the best manicurists. Or the merits of going to Cancun or Aspen during spring break, and which hotels have fluffier bathrobes and better-looking cabana boys. There's not a working woman anywhere who would disagree with me.

—Why do you let it bother you?

—I don't know, she said, her anger subsiding some. Maybe I would have been better off if I was like them. Maybe I made a mistake.

—No, he said firmly.

—I mean, am I wrong to want to make money and have some control over my life and have some choice over how I labor and some power over my circumstances? Isn't that what you're always ranting about?

—Yes.

—Well....

She had worn herself out. When she became vexed, her mode of presentation came close to veering into hysteria. In their college days he had always been impressed by the passion with which she argued or expressed an opinion. Age had attenuated some of her fervor, but in cases like this, where she perceived she was being personally attacked, she worked herself up to a screaming pitch impossible to ignore.

—I don't mean to be negative, she relented. If I didn't live here, I'd be the happiest person ever.

Harold knew what he had to say.

—As soon as the children graduate, we'll move back to the city. We're not married to this place, but to each other. It's only a little longer.

—I hope I make it, Carol said.

—It's just like you said. If I can be disenchanted with my job and keep working, you can hate our social environment and still tough it out. The worst is over. It's only another year or two. And then we're done here.

Neither of the Hardscrabbles was happy. Harold was disenchanted with his job. Carol was discontented with living in the suburbs. Thankfully, having received all the benefits that accrue to children growing up in a dual-income bourgeois household, their kids were doing well.

From the time they were little, Harold had tried to provide his kids a solid cultural and moral education. He had spent many nights reading to them, not the usual bedtime stories by Dr. Seuss and P. D. Eastman, but *The Iliad* and *The Odyssey*, Greek myths, *Aesop's Fables* and *Grimm's Fairytales* and stories from the *One Thousand and One Nights*, and the Bible's Old and New Testaments. He wanted them to be familiar with the classic mythical archetypes and the literary foundations of the canon. He thought this knowledge would whet their appetite for books. He was sure early exposure to the classics would reap rewards later. He was wrong. His library contained all the books, great and otherwise, he had read in college and graduate school and had carted around with him all these years. They rested untouched on the shelves despite him urging his children to delve into them. Both Jake and Sarah were more wrapped up in the seductions of television and the Internet. No matter how hard he tried, he couldn't convince them reading was a joyous intellectual activity. Even when they had nothing to do and pronounced they were bored, they wouldn't read a book.

—I can find a summary or overview of any book you name in milliseconds, Jake boasted whenever Harold suggested he pick one up.

—It's not the same thing as reading the book, Harold tried to explain.

—Exactly. Reading is too time consuming, and there are plenty of other things that are fun and don't take as long.

It was a losing battle. Nobody read books anymore, both children averred. Books were a twentieth-century phenomenon. Now, when they *read* anything, what they read was online. They lived their lives online. They had no passionate interests in anything except what came to them over the Internet, a trait they shared with their entire generation. We are the future, they said, and the future is online.

Jake spent hours and hours locked in his room playing games on the Internet. The gaming had started with *Pokémon*, which everyone considered a harmless video game. All his friends were playing at the time. Harold and Carol had never sought to curb his habit as long as he finished his homework. Then came *Tiberian Sun*, which, Jake said, despite the mild violence, presented serious strategic challenges that had to be solved to survive in a hostile environment. The game would improve his ability to reason, he said. After this, he moved on to *World of Warcraft*, which required a paid subscription, and with its opportunities for social interaction, it became its own little world from which it was hard for his parents to pull him away. Jake claimed *StarCraft* was an advance over *WoW*, and he would sit in front of his computer screen with his headset on for hours, lost to the world around him. When he grew bored with these so-called intellectually challenging games, instead of picking up a book, he turned to *Grand Theft Auto*, *Halo*, or *Call of Duty* for relaxation.

Sarah also played video games, but she spent more time on social sites with her friends or watching music videos or visiting news and gossip outlets, the feeds of which alerted her to all the latest dirt on the people she followed.

Harold had tried to get both children interested in chess, which, he informed them, was a strategic game and could also be played online, but they told him chess was old school for old farts like him.

The high hopes he and Carol had had for their offspring when they were babies had long faded. Like the concerned parents they were, they had anxiously scanned every developmental stage of babyhood and childhood seeking evidence of genius or exceptional talent in one area or another. There had been glimmers of hope. Jake had demonstrated some musical talent on the violin, but lessons revealed that while he had nearly perfect pitch, he was no more than a mechanical learner and had no notable ability for either composition or interpretation.

Their hopes had been raised again by Sarah. Early on, she appeared to have a gift for languages. She didn't. Her facility was due to rote learning and her fearless ability to adopt the tonalities of her teachers on tape. Later, she became interested in theater and was given the leading role in her class play, which received positive reviews. Subsequently, she had some acting lessons, but by this time boys and parties and teenage angst were her chief occupations.

One of those harsh moments in life occurred when Harold realized his children, despite all the advantages they had been given, might not be smarter than he was, that there was always the regression to the mean, and that given the state of the economy and increasing global competition, it was conceivable his children might not realize the same success he and Carol had achieved.

Even though they didn't excel academically in high school, Harold had not given up believing Jake and Sarah were capable of accomplishing big things. Jake had an affinity for numbers. He was proficient in mathematics and able to memorize formulas and solve complicated problems in his head. He had voiced his desire not to work in an office like his father and mother. When Harold asked him what kind of work he wanted to do, he was unsure. The only thing he was certain about was that he wanted to be an entrepreneur of some sort, like Grandpa Hardscrabble, only much more successful.

—I want to be a billionaire, he proclaimed.

Sarah's ambitions and interests were more amorphous than Jake's, and she was adamantly unapologetic for not having a clue. She and her mother were at war over the fact that, according to Carol, it was never too soon to start developing a clue.

—The world won't wait for you, Carol told her.

—I'm not asking it to.

—You have to start thinking about schools.

—I have time, Mom.

—You apply in six months.

—Then find some schools you like because I don't care, Sarah challenged her.

Carol was beside herself after these discussions. She had done nothing, she explained to Harold, but lead her daughter by example, showing her through her own hard work that power and economic rewards were achievable for women. She had spoken to her about glass ceilings and how she and women everywhere had to continue to fight for a seat at the table of the established power structure, which was still chiefly dominated by men. And yet her daughter had no goals. It didn't make sense to her that Sarah couldn't define a future for herself other than hanging out with her friends. Carol feared Sarah could become the very type of woman that she despised.

—She's still young, Harold reminded her.

—I set an example every day.

—It's never that simple, he counseled. Remember, her friends have mothers too.

Carol appeared stunned and frightened at this self-evident observation.

—Do you think they got to her? I mean, maybe that's it. I try to set an example, but I'm not here every day like those other mothers. Do you think Sarah could accept a stay-at-home mom as a role model? That the mani-pedi culture corrupted her?

—Of course not, he said.

—I hope you're right. But what was I supposed to do? Stay home and have more contact with her, hoping to have greater influence over her decisions? Then how would I tell her she should grow up and do something with her life while I was stuck at home doing nothing but telling her what she should be doing? Those are the stupid kinds of contradictions women get sucked into. How do you win that battle?

Harold, like his daughter, had no clue. He was happy the children had avoided serious drugs and excessive alcohol abuse.

Jake, on a dare, had gotten a tattoo, his initials, inked on his left buttock.

—This way, if something ever happens to me you'll be able to positively identify me, he said reassuringly.

Sarah had her bellybutton pierced, and if snippets of some overheard conversations with her friends were to be believed, one of her nipples.

〜

Harold looked at himself in the mirror. Standing stock still staring straight at his reflection was not a smart thing to do at his age, or maybe at any age, but certainly not at his age when mirrors began to turn against you and magnified your imperfections rather than show your reflection. And shit, it was incredible: over the years he had purchased and applied cleansers, moisturizers, balms, salves, lotions, notions, and potions and he still hadn't managed to prevent the wear and tear that he saw under his eyes. Rough, dry, imbricated layers of skin. How depressing. Switching on the light built into the mirror for a closer inspection, he saw the skin was thin and almost translucent, like late autumn leaves.

He had never had a line on his face until he was thirty-five. His skin had always been perfectly clear and smooth and soft, without a blemish of any sort. He looked much younger than his age, people said. Sure, after thirty-five one or two small creases appeared at the edges of his eyes, and he was able to live with those. At fifty, this was something different.

He went to his dermatologist for a consultation.

No moisturizing agent in the world was going to bring his epidermal mask back to its former turgid state, she told him. She could correct some of the damage, but it would involve a little nip and tuck and some filler. He said he would think about it.

He thought about it every time he gazed at himself in the mirror. He couldn't decide if he was more afraid of the knife or more afraid of admitting to Carol that he was vain enough to be considering professional cosmetic help. He decided he was more afraid of his wife.

Carol, however, had her own idea about aesthetic self-improvement. She shared it with him one evening as they were finishing dinner.

—I think I need a boob job, she announced.

She took a sip of her Cabernet and stared right at him, smiling. Denial of her assertion would, he feared, wipe away her smile and expose him to an expression that would be much less pleasant. But if he agreed, there would be a protracted examination as to what was wrong with her breasts. She would want to know why he was dissatisfied with them, and how long he had been unhappy with them, and why he hadn't previously said anything about them. And, if he had been neglecting to tell her about her breasts, what else was wrong with her that he was afraid to mention? Of course, if he didn't agree she needed a boob job, he would be stuck singing their praises and arguing against the surgical enhancement of one's body, an option he was considering for himself. In any case, it would involve a long and torturous discussion, and there wasn't enough wine left in the bottle to dull the pain it would produce. Since she had hidden her desire to have her boobs done behind the qualifier *I think*, he took the easy way out and didn't offer an opinion.

—Why?

—Oh, come on, you know why.

The combative nature of this assertion, as well as the insinuation that she had access to his mental state, and knew what he knew, was frightening and signaled that resistance of any sort would be futile. The opening moves in a conversation such as this one were as important as the opening moves in chess, and they would determine the entire course of the discussion and whether it would end well or badly for him.

—I don't know why, he protested.

—You don't look at me anymore.

—That's not true.

—You don't touch me.

—I try to touch you. You don't want to be touched.

—Only because you seem to pick the most inconvenient times. Or when I'm not in the mood. I think you do it on purpose so you don't have to touch me. Anyway, you don't look at me. And I don't blame you. I don't like looking at myself either.

This was patently not true. She spent an inordinate amount of time in front of the mirror, vamping with one outfit or another, fixing her makeup, adjusting her hair. Sure, she sometimes expressed displeasure with what she saw, but over the last few years she had indulged her vanity several times, having minor facial work performed, chemical peels, some resurfacing, a pinch of Botox here and there, some dermal fillers, nothing major. Just what a girl needed to keep in the game.

Harold thought Carol had aged well. She was still, indisputably, a beautiful woman. He was still attracted to her. Even after her pregnancies, her figure had remained trim and athletic. She was preternaturally fit. Minimal workouts produced maximum effect in her. When she had the time, she ran on their treadmill in the basement on weekdays, and on weekends she went to the gym to work out with weights. During the summer, she swam laps at the local community pool. She took yoga classes at lunch with some of her colleagues when she could fit them in. These far from intense or lengthy workouts somehow kept her in top condition. Good genes, she explained. It was that, but it was also her diet, about which she was fanatically conscientious.

Only in the past several years had she filled out a little, becoming a little softer around the edges, as it were. Her curves gave her a wholesome, yet sensual look that she knew how to exploit with her wardrobe.

Harold didn't believe the boob job, like her tactical forays into superficial facial improvements, was intended to keep her in the game. This was something different. For while Carol was a striking woman, she had average-sized breasts, and these, after the children were through with them and the predations of time had their way with them, were, he had to admit, lacking their former youthful perkiness. They were weepy. Her nipples no longer looked up, but down. Somehow, they had flattened and stretched. He did have to admit that now and again when he caught glimpses of them he longed to have them back in pristine condition. As it turned out, Carol shared his longing. She wanted back the breasts of her youth. As a gift to herself.

—It will make me feel young again, she said.

—I see, Harold said.

—I don't know if you do. Your tone is very condescending.

—I'm not trying to be. I guess I don't understand. You go along all these years apparently without even hinting at it, and now all of a sudden you decide you need new boobs.

He didn't know why he was arguing. Why wouldn't he want his wife to have the best-looking breasts the medical profession could provide? Didn't he just acknowledge to himself that he missed their youthful perkiness? What was wrong with him?

—It's one of the most common cosmetic operations performed today. And it will correct the deformity the doctor says I have.

—What deformity?

—All the fat has been depleted from breastfeeding, and there is too much connective tissue, which gives them an odd shape. Sometimes they hurt me.

This was the first he had heard of this. Now that she had shifted the rationale for the operation, making it a medical instead of a cosmetic issue, he knew he was going to be subjected to a public relations campaign she had mapped out well in advance of announcing her intention. The shift from an aesthetic rationale to one involving her health was the tip-off. She must have spent a lot of time coming up with a plausible explanation as to why she needed to improve her breasts. Perhaps she had engaged one of her work confidants to help her explore a variety of story angles so that no matter which perspective it was told from her desire would appear rational. Over time this process had eliminated weak storylines and yielded one that could be defended without making her feel guilty or embarrassed or selfish. Understanding it was pointless to fight this sophisticated presentation of her desire, he shifted gears and brought up his cosmetic issue.

—What if I wanted to get my eyes done?

—Go ahead.

—You mean you're unhappy with how they look?

—No.

—You're okay if I indulge myself in an aesthetic desire?

—If it makes you feel better about yourself and makes you happy, then why deny yourself?

—So, we should both go out and have work done so we feel better about ourselves?

—Why not?

—Will it change the way we feel about each other? I mean, do you think I'll love you more if you get new and improved boobs?

He knew every word exiting his mouth was idiotic. The conversation was swinging wildly out of control. Yet he couldn't help himself from questioning her motives. Nor could he suppress his suspicion that her desire to improve her appearance was a harbinger of something more sinister.

—Maybe you'll love me more. Maybe you'll look at me more. Anyway, I'll feel more attractive. And if I feel that way about myself, then maybe you'll want me more.

—I love you the way you are.

—It's my body, and if I want to change it, I should be able to.

He was going to point out that she was giving in to societal standards created through advertising images, and that she would therefore be tacitly ceding control of her body to the image factory, but it was disingenuous of him to continue to fight her since some of what she said was true, and because of his own aesthetic concerns.

At any rate, she had dragged out the feminist verbiage *my body*, and this, coupled with the previously posited medical rationale, let him know that his wife was going to get a boob job whether he liked it or not.

❧

A month later, while he was working at home, Harold noticed a pile of mail in the front hall. Below the mail slot, scattered on the floor, were any number of envelopes and magazines and catalogs. On the bench next to the coat tree there was more mail. At various points during the week, Carol sifted through it and pulled out the junk, giving him only what was important, which wasn't much, and sometime after that she threw out the rest.

Harold was surprised at the quantity of mail that arrived daily. The number of pieces pushed through the mail slot was staggering considering almost all of it was unsolicited. So, on the days he stayed home, when Buddy barked, which he did each time the mailman began shoving the mail through the slot, Harold inspected the paper that littered the floor. There were postcards, magazines, envelopes of every size, flyers, plastic bags chock-full of coupons, brochures, catalogs, newspapers, bills. Every piece bore headlines and pictures and teaser lines screaming *open me, open me now.*

—Doesn't it bother you that we get all this crap in the mail? Harold asked Carol.

—What difference does it make? I throw most of it out. But I like the catalogs, she said.

—You don't buy anything through catalogs.

—No, but when I see something I like in a catalog, I check it out online. It saves time.

—Nevertheless, it's scary how much junk finds its way to us. She was indifferent.

—It's crazy, he said.

—I think most people accept it and figure out how to take what they want and ignore the rest. It all gets recycled, so who cares?

—I find it frightening that even though we've switched over to electronic delivery of our banking and most of our bills, the onslaught doesn't stop.

—There's no stopping it, she said.

—It should stop, he said. I want it to stop.

—Harold, are you okay?

He dropped the subject, but the more he thought about it, the more perturbed he became. It was unsettling that he couldn't stop the delivery of junk mail. There was something absurd in the fact that mail came in the front door and was thrown out the back door. The spam that polluted his in-box on his computer was also hateful, but he received less of it than physical mail due to the spam filters his company had installed on his computer. Moreover, the mail that made it through the filters was quickly disposed of with a mouse click. That the mail delivered to his house was physical matter with dimension and mass, and gained entry to his house without his permission, made him angry. The mail was like an intruder against whom he couldn't defend himself.

He didn't want to admit it, but his fascination with the mail was partly instigated by his knowledge that he had, in many ways, contributed to the very phenomena he deplored. After all, his job involved developing the psychological under-pinnings of concepts and ideas that would drive desire. Over the years, through a series of papers and PowerPoint presenta-tions, hadn't he resurrected and updated John Caples's *Tested Advertising Methods*, borrowing from him ideas about how to find the right appeal and how to reach broad audiences? He had given a half-day workshop to several of the firm's major clients on the chapter *How to Appeal to the Masses*, updated for the digital age, which resulted in significant new business for the firm's direct marketing division. He had also managed to subsume the principles of Claude C. Hopkins's scientific ap-proach to advertising and increase the response rates to offers and coupons, whether in print or on the web. Doubtless, some of what was showing up on his foyer floor was the direct result of his work. He was being hoisted by his own petard.

Delivering messages to people. Communicating. Putting a brand in front of eyeballs. He knew all about that. He knew that was why Weichert and ReMax and Century 21 kept sending him postcards, the lowest form of mass mailing, showing photographs of houses their agents had sold, often with a picture of the agent who was responsible for the sale. He had no intention of selling their house until the kids left for college. But the real estate companies were following accepted marketing principles. They knew from their transaction records when he and Carol had purchased the house, how much they paid, how much it was worth today, how much it would be worth tomorrow, and what the turnover rate of the housing stock was in their neighborhood. The real estate companies knew that if they had young kids at the time of purchase, those kids would be approaching college age, and soon there would be an empty-nest discussion about if one needed all this space. And each of these realty companies that kept bombarding him with mail wanted the opportunity to sell his house when the time came. They knew that to obtain the contract, they had to keep a constant presence in his mind.

Insurance companies also attacked him relentlessly. They too had done their homework and knew he was getting older and, presumably, feebler. One wrote:

Now here's something else to think about. Nearly one-third of all adult Americans will become disabled for at least 90 days between ages 50–65, and the average disability lasts 2½ years. Quite frankly, your chances of becoming disabled are far greater than your chances of dying prior to age 65. The truth is that if you're under 65, disability protection is as important as, and sometimes even more important than, life, health, auto or even homeowner's protection. You need to protect one of your most important assets—your earning power— your paycheck!

The letter went on for three pages, and each and every paragraph on every one of the pages had embedded within it a frightening statistic related to the consequences of becoming disabled. Some poor copywriter stuck in a cube somewhere was scribbling away, crafting these threatening scenarios about what would happen to him without insurance, or since he had insurance, not enough insurance. It was obscene. Still, he was intrigued by the dire consequences that could befall him, and he read the entire letter agape with terror but unmotivated to take action. The sensation was similar to how he felt when he got sucked into an infomercial that exposed him to the world of slicers or dicers or car floormats or sealants on a Sunday afternoon after he returned from a long ride and didn't have the physical energy to change the channel, or the mental energy to tune out the insistent repetitious offers available only on TV. He listened in awe but was paralyzed and incapable of taking any action.

He started keeping track of how much mail arrived. He gave instructions that no one was allowed to throw anything away unless he gave his permission. He collected all the deliveries. After a few weeks, he decided it would be interesting to count the number of pieces that arrived on any given day and classify them. He bought a notebook for keeping track. He also began weighing the day's delivery. Sarah came into the bathroom while he had a pile of mail on the scale.

—Daddy, what are you doing?

He offered an explanation, but his daughter sensed the absurdity of his enterprise and ran to tell her mother.

—Harold, are you serious?

—The mail is like ordnance being set off in this house every day, he explained. They measure ordnance by weight. I'm curious to see how much is being thrown our way. You said yourself it can't be stopped. I'm curious to see how much of it there is.

—I think you're losing your mind, Harold.

At work, several months went by, and aside from his discussion with Shirley, there was no other response from management about his wayward paper. Carol said that was a good sign, but she was convinced his comment to Shirley had been noted in his record and at some point would come back to haunt him when decisions about his future had to be made.

—I know how these things work, she said.

Moreover, the paper would be kept as evidence of nonperformance of his duties. She was of the opinion that he should start to look for another job before anything bad occurred because from this point forward if someone had it in for him, they had the ammunition to take him out.

—I don't want to look for another job.

—Well, then you're at their mercy, she said. Just stay there and see what happens.

It wasn't clear if this was advice or a threat.

—Okay.

Harold's business tolerated some outside-the-box think-ing, which was what clients always claimed they needed to make headway in crowded, mature markets, but his little show-stopping extravaganza had stirred up trouble. His long tenure and known abilities were, more than likely, what had saved him from immediate termination. That didn't mean he was safe. In the ecosystem in which he functioned, once you were marked for having exhibited deviant behavior of any kind, you were doomed. Rehabilitation was not considered an option. He knew of many examples where one wrong move had tainted a person's reputation, and no matter how well that person per-formed thereafter, his or her work was seen in an unflattering light. This occurred more among junior people and midlevel managers, and sooner or later the poor souls would tire of the constant cloud of suspicion under which they functioned and leave on their own accord. Or they would be forcibly replaced, all of which was done with no fuss and bother since junior people and managers were interchangeable.

At Harold's level, there was no internal candidate who could replace him. Conducting a search to find someone of the same caliber would be a long, painstaking endeavor. Which didn't mean the firm wouldn't pursue that option. That was why Carol was concerned. He believed he had time on his side, and to show his errant behavior was only a one-off, he forced himself to have an attitude adjustment, as Carol called it, and redoubled his efforts to stay out of trouble. Soon, he was os-tensibly back in everyone's good graces, with one exception.

Prior to his foray into self-expression, Harold had always had easy access to the executive managers. Now that his ac-tions and motives were no longer fully transparent to them, and his dedication to the team was suspect, they put some distance between him and them. He wasn't exactly shunned. He was still greeted and brought into debates and invited to meetings and included on high-level conference calls as he always had been. But, while continuing to smile and slap him on the back when they met, these executives had politically and psychologically distanced themselves from him. He understood. He had betrayed their trust. The place where he worked, which had functioned for almost three decades under one name or another and where he knew all the people from the receptionist to the janitor to the CEO, was not only a place where people came to work for a living, but a social construct with its own rituals and complex rules and codes and shared values. Management had interpreted his action as a violation of the social contract, an abnegation of faith, an act of sabotage, as Shirley had put it. So, although senior management had declined to move against him, to show their displeasure and disappointment, they kept their distance.

❧

Harold continued to work as hard as he could. He put so much effort into redeeming himself that his colleagues noticed. Some of his recent work was outstanding, they said. He also helped win new assignments and solidify existing pieces of business. While these successes did not put him back in favor with his superiors, they did bring him closer to his colleagues who handled the day-to-day business, many of whom had formerly been only hallway acquaintances. For up until the time of his disgrace, he had spent a majority of his time in the offices of one senior partner or the other. Now that his access to that level of social intercourse had been cut off, he discovered new socializing possibilities in a different milieu.

The day-to-day tactical teams welcomed him with alacrity. Through gossip, more and more of his coworkers had learned of his daring attempt to stand up to management. Many were jealous. Some of his colleagues considered him a gutsy hero who had followed his ideas to their logical conclusion. Others thought the assignment given to him had been flawed, and that it was a stupid idea from the beginning. They were of the opinion that Harold had done his best under the circumstances. His action gave them hope that at some point in their careers if something was wrong with an assignment, they would have the courage to put their convictions down on paper and not be influenced by career or political considerations. His perceived lack of concern over the self-destructive nature of his act was the type of event that was slowly woven into the mythic fabric of company life. Soon it became legend. It was recounted as a cautionary tale to the new hires and junior wannabes who were always threatening to act out and strut their stuff.

Of course, for many of the junior people, putting anything down on paper appeared to be an issue in and of itself, Harold discovered. Some of them could barely string together two sentences, and those were often marred by mistakes. A few of them couldn't even write in PowerPointese, the official language of the marketing services business. They were incapable of combining a headline and subhead, let alone arranging the bullet points beneath them on a slide in a logical manner. Sometimes it took a working session with the team, with the document up on a screen, to pound out a presentation.

Writing in prose was torture for these people. They failed at anything that took more than a paragraph to describe.

Which was a demonstration of a substandard education or a habituation to texting or tweeting, or both. It was embarrassing. Fortunately, the firm employed a staff of experienced editors, many of them from Harold's generation, whose job it was to make sure everything made sense before it was presented to a client.

One day a team member on a project to which Harold was contributing strategic insight sent him the rough draft of the paper he had just completed and asked for his input. Harold was flabbergasted at the writing, at the shallowness and lack of cohesiveness, aside from the simple rudimentary grammatical goofs. He diligently went through the paper, marking all his comments and edits using the track changes function. By the time he e-mailed the document back, along with an encouraging note, he had written more text than was in the paper itself. Soon thereafter, Clayton, the fellow who had sent him the paper, turned up at his office with a hard copy.

—This is why we need you, he said. This is great! Thank you so much.

—No problem, said Harold.

—You saw what I was getting at but was unable to communicate, and now it's all there, clear as day, Clayton said.

—Happy to have helped.

The young man wasn't embarrassed at all about the substandard quality of his work. He said he hadn't understood some of Harold's comments and questions, which was why he had wanted to go over the paper with him. Of course, Harold helped him.

Suddenly, thanks to Clayton, Harold was a mentor. He developed a following that championed him. He made friends among the midlevel tactical staff to whom he gave ideas when they had none of their own, or only a germ of one, which they didn't have a clue how to cultivate and bring to fruition.

Harold offset his loss of support at the higher levels by replacing it with support at the lower levels. The senior executives were suspicious of him, but they needed new thinking. The firm was fundamentally an idea factory and the constant throughput of intellectual property was what kept the revenue stream flowing. Because the senior executives couldn't churn out enough ideas on their own, they turned to the lower level tactical teams. These latter were too inexperienced to come up with the quantity and quality demanded of them, and therefore they turned to Harold for help. And when he helped them, they duly credited him for his contribution. Thus, a symbiotic relationship developed, and nobody could say anything negative about Harold.

〰

Carol had her breasts done six months after announcing her intention to Harold. In the months prior to the operation, the two of them had spent hours reviewing photographs of other women's breasts. Her plastic surgeon had a library of hundreds of before-and-after images of his work. The faces in these photographs were either pixilated or had white or black boxes over them to assure patient anonymity. As the breadth of her doctor's portfolio of breast types didn't satisfy Carol, she consulted the online libraries of other surgeons who also had images of breasts before and after surgery. She was determined to find as many pairs as she could that closely matched her own so she could imagine what her hoped-for results would look like. She compared degree of sagging, nipple location, malformation, size, skin tone and texture. Any number of times during these working sessions, she would lift up her shirt and ask Harold to confirm that hers did indeed match the pair in the photographs.

Some of the photographs didn't show the head of the woman at all. It didn't take long for Harold to become exhausted from staring at one headless torso after another with fully exposed mammary glands. Few, if any, looked pretty, either before or after surgery. None of them stirred in him the slightest desire to put his hands on them. In fact, often, if the breasts in the photographs exhibited an abnormality before the surgery, the operation itself further enhanced what was wrong instead of correcting it. If the nipples were tilted one way or another or appeared as dried and desiccated teats, then after the surgery they appeared much the same. They were still misshapen, only, due to the increased volume produced by the bags of saline or silicone, they appeared to be under tremendous pressure and ready to explode. The skin was stretched so thin over some of the implants the blood vessels showed through, giving the breasts the appearance of a marbled piece of steak. Some of them reminded him of Francis Bacon paintings.

Carol also needed to consider which implant technique she wanted used when she went under the knife. Particularly important, it turned out, was deciding where to place the implants, under or above the chest muscle. Some doctors believed putting the implants behind the chest muscle reduced the potential for capsular contracture. This might also interfere less with a mammogram than if the implants were placed behind the breast tissue. However, placement behind the muscle might be more painful for a few days after surgery than placement under the breast tissue. It was a personal decision more than anything, the doctor said, barring, of course, any technical or anatomical issues.

There was also the question of where to make the insertion, either in the crease where the breast met the chest, around the areola, or in the armpit. Carol was leaning toward having it made in the armpit as she had small, light-colored areolas, but her surgeon told her it might be harder to achieve a perfect placement that way.

The operation took only a few hours. Harold took Carol home from the clinic and helped her into bed. She fell asleep immediately. Upon awakening, she was in pain. Her nipples felt like they were on fire. At the last minute, under her doctor's advice, due to her particular anatomy, she had opted to have the insertion done through the areolas. She took her pain medication and fell back asleep.

To Harold's great disappointment, her breasts were wrapped in bandages, and there was nothing to see.

〜

While Carol had said she was only interested in correcting the damage done to her breasts by time and children, what burst out of the gauze bandages on the evening of their unveiling was a startling full C-cup.

Harold was bedazzled.

—Are those the ones we chose?

They were clearly not. They were much larger.

—I changed my mind at the last minute. Remember, we were always considering two options, these and the other ones, which were a little more modest. I went with silicone. Do you like them?

—I do.

No other answer was possible.

—Most men would be ecstatic, she said, gazing at them in the vanity mirror.

—I am ecstatic, he said.

He went to stand beside her as she turned sideways to look at them in profile, and then forward, pulling her shoulders back.

—I'm going to have to buy all new bras.

He tentatively extended his hands in their direction.

—See, you can't wait to get your hands on them. You'll have to wait, she said, turning away coyly. They're still very sore and sensitive. I go back to the doctor next week, and he'll take out the stitches. And then, right after that, they'll be ready for prime time.

He stared at her breasts as she vamped in front of the mirror. She obviously adored her enhancement. Yet, as magnificent as they were, somehow, Harold thought, her breasts no longer seemed part of her. Yes, they were impressive, imposing, even a little intimidating. But like the women's breasts in the strip clubs he sometimes visited with clients, they looked, for lack of a better word, professional.

⟨∿⟩

Jake went off to school that fall. And Sarah the following fall. Jake went far away, to the University of Southern California, and Sarah stayed close to home, choosing to attend Colgate after visiting at least half a dozen schools with Harold and Carol in tow. They heard from Jake infrequently. He texted or called only when he needed more money than his allowance permitted. Sarah and Carol were on the phone talking or texting every day for the first month after Sarah's departure, after which time she made a sufficient number of friends to keep her occupied.

Now that the kids were gone, there were no televisions blaring, no music playing, no one walking from room to room while talking on the phone, no friends coming and going at all hours. All the activities that one time or another he had complained about, Harold now regretted making a fuss over. He missed his kids. Without them, the house was eerily empty, devoid of joy. He and Buddy occasionally visited their rooms for consolation. Buddy sniffed at the closet or the bed, seeking signs of life. Jake's room was exactly as it had been while he was still at home. It was as if he had left behind a shrine to his existence, taking with him no more than an oversized backpack stuffed with his favorite clothes, wanting nothing from his childhood or adolescence to accompany him. All the posters and pictures and awards and miscellaneous keepsakes, magazines, and worthless bric-a-brac that he had accumulated over the years, he abandoned.

Sarah had vacuumed up every piece of her life and emptied it into her half of her dorm room, re-creating the same nest in which she had lived for the last fourteen years. Her bedroom was a stark, empty shell, the walls covered with tape marks where her posters and pictures had hung. The floor too looked strangely empty without the usual clutter of shoes and underwear and makeup and scrapbooks and her collection of plush animals covering almost every square foot.

The Hardscrabbles made dates with each other in the city after work to avoid having to face the empty house alone. On weekends, they performed chores that had long been written on their to-do list hanging inside the pantry door. Little by little, they came to grips with their loss and began to enjoy, if only tentatively at first, their newfound freedom.

↜

Harold began spending more time on his bike. He had mastered all the requisite cycling skills and could now keep his cadence constant by shifting his gears without thinking about it. During the winter he trained with his power cranks, which allowed each leg to work independently of the other and enforced the idea of spinning perfect circles so that each leg continually delivered maximum power on both the upstroke and the downstroke. The summer after Jake left for school he began entering competitions.

His first race was the Tour of Battenkill, billed as America's toughest race, a sixty-four-mile loop through rolling countryside of both paved and unpaved roads with over five thousand feet of climbing, and grades attaining 18 percent. After hanging with the peloton that comprised his age group for the opening half of the race, he went with a breakaway of five riders. They all worked together nicely over the next twenty miles, but as the finish approached, the tension mounted. The chitchat stopped. They still took turns at the front pulling, but the struggle between the riders had become palpable. Someone was going to have to make a break, and Harold knew it wasn't going to be him since he didn't have the experience to know when to jump. If he took off too early, everyone would grab his wheel and draft and let him burn his legs out. Then, at the last moment, they would charge out from behind him in a big acceleration and leave him in the dust. He waited for the group to make a decision and settled into an easy gear he could stomp on if he had to make a quick move. The break came in the last mile. Two of the riders took off together in a nasty acceleration, hoping to leave everyone behind. Harold went with them. He closed the gap without losing too much energy. Should I pass the leader? Harold wondered. No. It wouldn't be prudent. The guy evidently had plenty of power to spare, judging from the way he was pedaling and looking behind him for challengers. As the finish line loomed up in front of them, with about fifty yards to go, the leader acceler-ated again and Harold charged after him, coming around from behind the man in front of him. Out of the saddle, he sprinted for the line. He finished second.

↜↝

As the months passed, Harold and Carol saw each other less often.

On weekdays, Harold departed early for his bike rides, and by the time he returned home, Carol had left for the city. Since she frequently worked late, or had drinks or dinner with clients or colleagues after work, he was often home alone. To keep himself busy, after dinner he sorted and weighed the mail, Buddy his only company.

He began writing letters to the corporations that most frequently bombarded him with catalogs and coupons and in-surance offers, asking to be removed from their mailing lists. He also sent cease-and-desist letters to the more egregious purveyors of schlock housing goods and home improve-ment companies and gutter cleaning companies and window replacement companies. Virtually no one responded to his demands. The few companies that stated they would remove his name from their list did remove his name, yet they continued to send letters and catalogs to his house, only now it was no longer addressed to him but to *resident*. The piles of mail grew taller and taller.

On the weekends, Harold rode his bike, played chess, and cataloged the mail. Carol spent hours on her computer working, surfing the Internet, and updating her social media sites. There was a vacancy in the air. It wasn't long before their date nights fell into abeyance.

⟨∿⟩

Having made it through his semi-annual performance review, which, he was sure, had served as some kind of check on his capacity to stay in the game, Harold was once again handed interesting assignments. He completed the first few without raising any red flags among management, although he had identified issues he could have legitimately brought forward for deeper discussion. Then he was handed a more open-ended assignment. A client was looking for the firm's ideas on a *data-driven world*, and how big data sets interconnected, and their relation to advertising in content-driven multimedia platforms, and if it was feasible to super-infuse branding into data.

—You're the one best equipped to handle this, let alone understand what it means, a senior partner told Harold at the input meeting.

Upon review of the scope of the work, Harold wasn't sure what it meant either. He began reflecting on data. He researched related issues and compiled notes from numerous sources. He developed what he thought was an interesting thesis and wrote a rough draft of a paper, which he shared with a colleague. His approach was too radical, he was told. You're looking for trouble, his friend warned. Tone it down, he was advised. But Harold couldn't help himself. He was overcome by a compulsion to write what was on his mind, heedless of the consequences.

In the paper, he postulated that data was problematic. And if you were going to depend upon data to support a marketing thesis about a brand, you were going to fail. Because, paradoxically, increasingly, in the postmodern world, for those who believed in a thesis, or a proposition, or an accusation, no back-up data were necessary, and for those who doubted a thesis or a proposition, all data put forward as support was suspect.

He invoked Heisenberg's uncertainty principle and the observer effect to argue that all data was tainted by the observer. Raw data could be understood only when given a voice, and in giving the data a voice, one encountered the problem of metaphor because the voice that spoke corrupted what it spoke about. No one should forget, he wrote, *data cannot speak for itself*. Just giving people data in an attempt to influence them was a waste of time. Data was neutral until someone added meaning to it. People made decisions based on what the data meant to them, not on the data. This was why, for example, there were climate-change deniers and people who doubted whether the proposition $r > g^8$ was responsible for the ever-increasing inequities in the distribution of wealth. For any given issue, conspiracy theories abounded, propounding the view that one side or the other was misrepresenting the data. Today,

---

8 Thomas Picketty, *Capital in the Twenty-First Century* (Cambridge, MA: Harvard University Press, 2013).

there could be no certainty based on data. Paranoia pervaded the population.

He went on to argue for a new vision for advertising. He claimed data sets had become so devalued they were superfluous. He posited a new humanism in marketing, one in which data was ignored and stories recounted. He argued that if a marketer was going to succeed, he had to ignore data and instead tell a story. He provided a detailed logic tree demonstrating how to construct a selling story for a brand in such a manner that no one would notice there were no features or benefits associated with it, that there was nothing to substantiate any product claims at all. Everything was smoke and mirrors. He titled this paper *The Barker's Cry*. He couldn't decide if any of it made sense.

〰

Harold had his annual physical on his birthday. He dreaded this event since every additional year he lived, the likelihood that one or another of his bodily systems would malfunction increased. But each year he was given a clean bill of health, and that made the fourteenth of September worth celebrating. The physical part of the exam was very minimal. His doctor listened to his breathing, took his blood pressure, and performed an EKG. He also provided him with the results of his blood work, which Harold had done at a clinic several days before going to the office. Generally, his cholesterol was within the normal range, his hemoglobin great, and all his chemistries perfect.

The only worrisome issue started when he had turned forty-nine. His PSA number was elevated, which raised the specter of prostate cancer.

—The number's not conclusive of anything, his doctor told him. It's a little unusual in a man your age. It may be an artifact of your changing body chemistry. Many men experience a rise in their PSA as they age. Sometimes it's benign prostatic hypertrophy. Sometimes it's nothing. We'll keep our eye on it. There's no cause for concern yet, his doctor said.

Nevertheless, Harold had altered his diet to try to reduce his risk of cancer. He drastically cut back his intake of red meat and fat. He ate as many tomatoes as he could stand, for the purported anticancer properties of the lycopene. He bolted down broccoli. Anything coniferous, everything with a superabundance of antioxidants, he ate, regardless of the taste. He cut back on his alcohol consumption as well.

Nothing helped. Little by little, his PSA number kept going up. It increased incrementally, not a lot, just a little, every year creeping up, and this year, it went over the threshold.

—You should see a specialist, his doctor advised.

—Why?

—He may want to do a biopsy. That's the only way we'll be able to determine if something is wrong.

—Is something wrong?

—I don't know. That's why you need to see a specialist. You're still on the young side, but I would have it checked out.

The doctor gave him the name of a well-known specialist.

—He's one of the best. Call him.

Harold left the office in a state of shock. He and Carol had plans to go out for his birthday celebration. On the drive home, his mind was muzzy. He couldn't concentrate on anything except the fact that his doctor was transferring his care to a specialist, indicating he no longer considered himself qualified to manage the situation. His *number*, the doctor had insinuated, was far enough outside the normal range that it could no longer be ignored.

When he got home, Carol was sitting in front of her vanity, applying her makeup, preparing for his birthday dinner. She was naked from the waist up. Since having her breasts *adjusted*, as she referred to her enhancement, she liked having them out where she could see them whenever possible.

—How did it go? she asked.

—My PSA is very high.

—*Unhuh*, she purred, preoccupied with her preparation.

—He said I should go see a specialist.

—Is that right?

—Yes.

—Do you think they're even? she asked, throwing her shoulders back and thrusting her breasts forward. I mean, is the left one a little lower than the right one?

She wiggled, and they shook, tantalizingly. They weren't real, but they were spectacular.

—I might have cancer.

—You don't have cancer. You have a high PSA. You've had it for years.

—But now the doctor thinks I should see a specialist.

—You probably have BPH. From riding that bike. It drives up the PSA number.

—Really?

—I don't know. But look: do you think they're even? Look, she commanded.

—They're going to do a biopsy, he said.

—It's a precaution to protect themselves, a liability issue. Now, are they even? Tell me what you think.

He couldn't think.

〜

When Harold started to think, he remembered what had happened to his mother. Five years earlier a seemingly innocuous lump in her breast had turned out upon biopsy to be malignant. She had the breast removed. The next year in a follow-up exam, her doctors discovered a lump in her other breast, which was also malignant. It too was removed.

—They're chopping me up, his mother complained from her hospital bed.

Her mental state deteriorated after these operations. She was often confused and never again herself. One night she wandered out of her bed, fell down the stairs, and broke her hip. In the hospital, she developed pneumonia and died. It had been barely over thirty-six months from diagnosis to death. And now he was going to see a specialist to receive a diagnosis. Was he going to die, too?

Seeking comfort through knowledge, he began reading as many books and pamphlets about prostate cancer as he could find. He studied all the treatments and their effects. None of what he read was encouraging. There was no cure. There were very few treatment options for a man his age aside from surgery. After scrutinizing secondary sources and review articles, he located the bible of prostate cancer treatment itself: *The National Comprehensive Cancer Network*, the NCCN, which published guidelines on the standard of care and best practices for oncology. Absolutely none of the words in this document were optimistic words. There was not a sentence of solace in any of the literature. *Radical prostatectomy, histopathologic grade, radiation, risk, salvage, staging, recurrence, chemotherapy, nomogram,* *life expectancy,* *death* were not the types of words to comfort someone with an elevated PSA number. There was nothing in the documents that said he would die, necessarily, but it was all very bleak.

〜

Harold went to see the specialist recommended by his doctor. He was part of a progressive practice associated with New York University, one in which the practitioners, as advised by the NCCN guidelines, were involved in clinical trials.

After he signed in, a nurse took him from the general waiting room to a smaller reception area where only patients in his doctor's group sat while waiting for their examinations. He spent some time with an administrator who took all his personal information. Then he met with the specialist, Doctor Pavani, who reviewed the records his primary care doctor had sent, as well as his recent lab test results. The doctor didn't look happy. He asked Harold what he wanted to do. Harold wanted to go home. He wanted to go home and have a Scotch and forget the whole thing. That wasn't in the cards. The doctor suggested he have another blood test and, as long as he was there, submit to a digital rectal exam.

Harold thought his primary care doctor was always a little timid about inserting his finger in his ass. This young man had no qualms about jamming his finger in and feeling around with such exploratory gusto Harold swore he was going to pull his prostate out right then and there. No such luck.

—Everything feels fine, Doctor Pavani said. Of course, this is a nondiagnostic procedure, and it doesn't mean you don't have a malignancy. Something is driving those numbers.

The admission that the rectal inspection was basically a useless procedure raised a host of questions in Harold's mind. He didn't bother to pursue them. A phlebotomist came in and took his blood, and then, instead of going back to work, he went home. He poured himself a glass of Scotch and stared out the window.

At his next visit, Doctor Pavani informed Harold his PSA was indeed well over the limit of what was considered normal, and because he had a history of cancer in his family, he advised him to have a biopsy.

—When you reach this stage in the diagnostic process, aside from waiting and watching, there aren't any other options to discover what's going on inside, the doctor explained.

Harold knew he was going to do it. He didn't want to say it.

—Is it going to hurt?

—Of course not, Doctor Pavani assured him.

All he was going to do was numb the area and take tissue samples with some needles. He would do it right here in this office, and Harold would be able to go home the same day. He might experience mild discomfort for a few days after the procedure, and there would be some blood in his semen, but that would be about it.

The following week Harold arrived at the appointed hour. He was escorted into a changing room, where he took off his clothes, donned a disposable hospital gown, and was led to the operating room. It was an unsettling sensation knowing someone was going to do something to him that would determine how he would live the rest of his life, however long that might be. It was unlike going to the dentist with pain in a tooth, knowing that if the X-ray showed a cavity the dentist would drill a hole, fill it and that would be that. The results from this test would determine his fate. Like his mother, he might never be the same. Or, despite whatever subsequent treatments he received, survive.

Lying in wait on the long Naugahyde table covered with white disposable paper, he began meditating about the various results of this exploratory investigation. Somehow, he knew none of them were going to be positive.

The Xanax he had taken was not having any effect. The room was either too hot or too cold. He couldn't tell which. He stared at all the equipment and the sterile packages of bandages and gauze. He listened to the hum of the ventilation system, contemplating how it was going to feel to have the doctor stick a long, proboscis-like instrument up his ass to numb *the area* before plunging in with the needles to perform the procedure.

It didn't feel great, he soon discovered.

After the anesthetic had been administered, Doctor Pavani informed him he was going to stick another instrument up his ass, one that held the needles. He would then extract the core samples. At first, Harold didn't feel anything. But he didn't feel anything because the doctor hadn't begun the procedure. When the doctor asked if Harold was ready, he knew to expect the worst.

THUNK.

It was the sound of a nail gun. The reverberation hammered through him, and something pierced him, deep within. He shivered from the inside out. He gripped the table more tightly.

THUNK.

—I thought this wasn't going to hurt, Harold said.

THUNK.

His nails were digging into the Naugahyde. It wasn't going to hurt, he distinctly remembered the doctor telling him.

—Does that hurt? Doctor Pavani asked. He offered to withdraw the mechanism and apply more anesthetic if it was too painful.

What could Harold say? He was lying on the table, on his side, with cables dripping out of his ass and the doctor's gloved hand on one of his naked butt cheeks. He tried to gauge what the doctor would think about disrupting the procedure to administer more anesthetic. It wasn't worth it. The whole thing was absurd. Harold told him to continue.

THUNK ... THUNK, THUNK, THUNK.

↜↝

Through the glass panel that made up one of the walls of his office, Harold watched the parade of senior managers, the CEO Marc, and Shirley, enter the large conference room off the rotunda. Like his office, the conference room had glass panels, some clear, some frosted. From his vantage point, he saw Ed, the COO, look in his direction and notice Harold staring at him, and he seemed nonplussed by this. Shirley was walking around the room, handing out folders to each of the meeting attendees. Something was afoot. A shiver of paranoia shook him. He was sure he was going to be the topic under discussion. He became keenly alert. His ears pricked up, and so hard did he concentrate that he swore he heard their discussion.

Marc asked the attendees, but no one in particular:

—Okay, who wants to start?

There was silence. No one wanted to throw the first stone. Harold knew that no matter how they felt about him, no one would say anything inflammatory about him or utter a statement that would reveal their personal feelings toward him. There would be no breech of corporate protocol. The truth would never be spoken.

—Frank, you called the meeting. What's the story?

—There's no story. We're a little worried about Harold.

—I gathered that. Why?

—He might be going off a little, losing it, you know.

—No, I don't know.

The rise in Marc's voice was sufficiently sharp to indicate he was aware of the meaning of the idiom but wouldn't accept it was true of Harold. Marc had been told by the former partners that Harold was an asset and was to be protected.

—Yes, well. Some of his work has been peculiar, Peter pointed out.

—As I understand it, his work has always been known for its idiosyncrasy.

—We know.

—He's an original, Marc said.

—Yes, but....

—His recent work seems out there.

—Out where?

—Farther away from normal than usual.

—He always provides a different perspective. Sometimes it's helpful. Sometimes it's not. When he hits, it can be a home run. We have enough people here who can hit singles and doubles without too much trouble, but sometimes you need someone who can hit a grand slam. Marc looked at each member of his team individually, then stared into space.

—There have been fewer and fewer of those recently, said Frank.

There was silence.

—Not to say he hasn't been contributing. He's been doing wonderful work with the midlevel staff. But he has been hitting quite a few singles.

—Sometimes striking out.

—These last few jobs have been complete misses. Have you read them? asked Charles.

—They're included in your folder, Shirley said. Including the latest one.

Marc opened the folder.

—*The Barker's Cry*, he read out loud. The title is worthy of the man. It's a nice double entendre. Melancholy, don't you think?

—Yes, but....

—So what are you saying?

—We're a little worried.

—I got that.

—It's not that what he's doing is necessarily wrong. He gives everyone a lot to think about. But it's not productive.

—And at his billing rate, said Ed.

—What do you think it is?

—We don't know, Ed said, looking around the room for general consensus.

—Disenchantment, divulged Shirley.

They all turned their attention to her.

—Disenchantment or disgruntlement, Marc wanted to know.

—Disenchantment, Shirley said. I wrote it down.

—Hmm....

Marc was the one person in the agency who came closest to being wise rather than smart. Marc was a man of high culture and appreciative of the finer things in life. In an age where hoodies were fashionable among entrepreneurs, and senior executives prided themselves on their countercultural all-black, tie-less ensembles, he wore impeccably tailored suits and sported shirts with collars, French cuffs, and monograms. He liked silk ties with intricate, interesting patterns. His untroubled and unhurried demeanor was offset by his decisive, almost dictatorial pronouncements that were spoken with a hint of an accent picked up at prep school.

—He's not angry. He's simply out from under the spell, said Marc.

—What spell?

—The spell we're all under as we spin our webs of illusion for our clients. At a certain age people like him begin to see through the bullshit. They start to see themselves as an oracle.

—An oracle?

—Look it up, Marc snapped.

—What do we do?

—What do you want to do?

—That's what we wanted to discuss, said Frank.

—You wouldn't have called this meeting if you didn't have an idea.

—We lose billings every time he goes off strategy.

—I mean, I love the guy, but....

—I have nothing but the greatest respect for him, Marc said. Can you move him out of the line of fire?

—Yes, yes, we could do that ... but then we lose all his utility, and at his billing rate, we can't acquire someone else without negatively affecting the margin.

—I see.

—There aren't a lot of options.

—He isn't happy, Shirley said.

—So you want to help him out?

—We don't know what to do. That's why we came to you.

—Ultimately, you people have to make the decision, Marc said.

—We wanted to make you aware.

—I am now aware.

—What do we do?

—Protect the business.

Everyone nodded their heads. Marc stood up. The meeting was concluded.

When Harold saw the glum faces file out of the conference room, he imagined his fate had been sealed.

↞∿↠

After the biopsy, Harold hardly thought about sex. When he began to think about it, and tried to interest Carol in it, she was reluctant. She claimed she didn't want to cause him any unnecessary harm.

—It's too soon, she said.

Harold's hormones said otherwise. One night after they had shared a bottle of wine over dinner, he convinced her it would be all right. As they were undressing, he recalled what Doctor Pavani had said about the potential for some blood in his semen. He warned Carol he didn't know what to expect.

She was a bit squeamish about the possibility of having blood ejected in her so instead of fucking they kissed and cuddled and caressed and touched, only using their hands, slowly working their way to climax.

Everything was going great until the orgasm, Harold's orgasm, that is. At which point he saw red everywhere. It was blood. His dick had spewed red blood all over both of them. Not a filigree of bright red in the usual milky white fluid, which is what he had been led to believe. No, his semen was infused with blood: a deep, dark-purple red, the color of an old scab. It was disgusting. Carol was repulsed. He had sullied her new breasts with blood. She was aghast, insulted, infuriated. He began screaming as if he were wounded, but chiefly to keep her from screaming, which would mean he'd have to calm her down. This strategy succeeded. In the shower, cleaning off, she kept telling him everything would be okay, promising him everything would be all right. He wanted to believe her, but he knew it wasn't true.

❧

The only hope Harold had that his biopsy would come back negative was that Doctor Pavani had appeared fairly sanguine about his chances of having an elevated PSA for reasons other than cancer. His prostate felt healthy, he had said, and he had no reason to doubt this after the thorough exam he performed, even if it was nondiagnostic. It might also be an infection, the doctor had postulated, in which case he would treat it with antibiotics. Or it might be BPH, which was also a possibility since he did have some of the symptoms, including urinary hesitancy, and if that were the case, he would treat him with finasteride.

Of course, three weeks later when he returned to the doctor's office, he was told it was none of those things. It was cancer.

—Malignant.

Doctor Pavani pronounced the word Harold had most dreaded. Harold nodded his head back and forth as if he understood, but he had gone into a daze.

—It's unfortunate in a man your age, the doctor said. He shook his head sympathetically.

Harold nodded again. He felt lightheaded and a little woozy. He was no longer listening to what the doctor was saying. He was staring at a five-by-seven picture of the doctor and his family that was perched on his overstuffed bookshelves. They were at a beach somewhere. The doctor had his arm over his wife's shoulder and was holding her protectively. Their two children, both girls, were kneeling in the sand at their feet. Everyone looked happy. The kids had zinc oxide on their noses. They were tan and energetic looking. The doctor appeared to be in excellent physical condition. With more hair on his chest than Harold would have imagined. His wife had a fantastic figure and a wonderful, engaging smile. Harold wondered who had taken the picture.

—Six of the core samples were cancerous, the doctor reported. The malignancy is in both lobes of the prostate. It's not news you wanted to hear.

Harold took in and exhaled a deep breath. Having read the guidelines, he knew what his options were. Removal was the preferred treatment for someone like him.

—You should have a radical prostatectomy, the doctor said, but the decision is up to you.

Radical, the word reeked of violence.

—Is it going to hurt?

The doctor appeared perplexed.

—Hurt? Of course not, the doctor said. You'll be completely knocked out. You have to be under general anesthesia for an operation of this kind.

—Totally out?

—Totally.

—So I won't feel a thing?

—No.

—The techniques for removing this particular organ have advanced tremendously in recent years, Doctor Pavani said.

He would remove it robotically. He wouldn't lay a hand on him, he bragged. Using the robot would help spare the nerves around his urethra, which would minimize the possibility of incontinence and leakage. Robotic removal in skilled hands had also been proven to help preserve erectile function.

Harold fell back into reverie. His eyes wandered back to the photograph of the doctor and his family. He wondered if the doctor's wife had had a boob job. He wanted to ask at what beach the photograph had been taken, but he thought the doctor might think that too personal a question.

—Do you have any questions? Doctor Pavani asked. Is there anything else you'd like to discuss? the doctor asked, in a tone of voice that Harold judged to be both solicitous and sincere.

—No.

—People get through this, the doctor said. My success rates are very high. Cancer is never good news. However, we've caught it early, and there is every chance the post-operative prognosis will be good.

↜↝

Harold would have had to have been closely monitoring every minute of Carol's ever changing mental states in order to have sensed her increasing inattention, her growing introversion, her emotional indifference to him. The subtle shifts in her psychological life that he missed occurred gradually, over time, but had accelerated in recent years. Perhaps if he had not been so caught up in his own personal emergencies he might have intimated them, although even then his ego would have forced him to deny that after all the decades they had been together anything of great import was occurring, which made it more difficult for him the day she announced she was moving back to the city.

—What do you mean? Harold wanted to know.

—I've been saying how much I hated it here for years. Now the kids are gone. There's no reason for me to be here.

—And you've made the unilateral decision to move.

—Yes.

—What if I don't want to move?

—I'm not sure how to put this nicely.... I'm moving without you.

—What does that mean?

—It means I'm leaving. The timing's not the best. And I feel bad. But there's nothing I can do.

—You're leaving me, he said, not sure if he intended to utter a statement or ask a question. Is there someone else? he managed to stammer.

—I don't want to hurt you, Harold.

This wasn't an answer to his question but provided all the information he needed.

—You're leaving me for someone else, and what am I supposed to do?

—I'm sorry.

—You're sorry?

—I don't know what else to say. I'm sorry. Things happened, and I couldn't stop them, and because I couldn't stop them, I have to go. I know it seems cruel with everything that's going on with your job and your health, but I can't do anything else. You're going to be okay.

—I'm going to be okay, he echoed her.

—I'm sorry, she said again. I really am. She began to cry.

Caught off guard, he didn't know what to say. His world was collapsing in on him, and the enormous weight of it was suffocating him. His emotions were in such turmoil he couldn't find the words to express them. He kept fumbling for some response, but he was muted by shock.

Harold felt the sky had fallen. His job was in jeopardy. He had been diagnosed with cancer. Now his wife had left him. His life was swinging wildly out of control. He was numb. His body tingled like a foot or finger that had fallen asleep.

However, he could hardly bring himself to think about the heartbreak Carol's abandonment caused him because there was something malignant growing inside him. His cancer preoccupied him. Carol was gone, and the void she left was filled by his disease.

Harold's father called and tried to cheer him up. But he was beginning to exhibit signs of memory loss or dementia and he rambled on during their conversations, often wandering off on long tangents that made no sense.

His kids texted him continually. *Are you okay? Is everything all right? How do you feel?* They were in constant communication with their mother. They, too, wanted to know what had gone wrong. Her departure had shocked them as much as it shocked him.

Eventually, Carol confessed to Sarah that she was living with another man.

—It's someone she met at work, Sarah informed her father.

The *someone* had left his wife just as she had left Harold, and the two of them moved in together. The only explanation she would give Sarah as to why she left was that one day she would understand.

Harold appreciated everyone's concern. They were all worried about his physical and emotional well-being, about his cancer and his cuckolding and how well he was coping.

—I'm going to be okay, he told them.

Every night he sat on the couch, nursing one Scotch after another with the only family member left home, Buddy, his canine companion, who curled up next to him. Sometimes he couldn't keep Carol from entering his thoughts. When this occurred, he didn't know which produced more pain, the fact that she had moved on to a new life and was no longer part of his, or that she had been in a relationship with another man before she left him and had thereby subjected him to the lowest form of human behavior: betrayal. Either way, he felt horrible.

༄

In their own inimitable way, his cycling buddies became his support group. They provided practical but heartless advice. Before and after rides they would mill about, chatting. On rides of forty miles or longer they would stop at delis or cafés to purchase food or replenish their water bottles, or sometimes to drink a coffee and relax a little. During these breaks, they shared stories and gossiped about their lives. Harold had informed them he had cancer and would soon face the knife, after which he would be off the road for some time. He had also, from time to time, obliquely hinted at his troubles at work. Now he shared the news about Carol.

—Wow, dude, you just hit a triple play, said The Ring.

—What do you mean?

—Work, wife, health ... when all three go south in a short time span, your risk of dying goes up exponentially.

—Be careful, said The Landlord.

—You should seek counseling, The Mope advised.

Everyone concurred.

What was incredible to them was that from what Harold had told them there had been no warning of Carol's intended desertion. She hadn't issued an ultimatum he might have agreed to live under. She had said nothing. She announced she was leaving, packed up all her belongings, and bolted. While most of the group thought this story chilling, some claimed he should have seen it coming the minute she got the boob job.

—You should have realized right away those weren't for you, fella, Einstein said.

—I was suspicious, Harold claimed.

—Yeah, when they go for the boobs they're on their way out the door, The Abductor said, backing up Einstein.

—She claimed they were a medical and psychological necessity, Harold offered in his defense.

—Right. And there was no way to say no.

—I didn't have much choice.

—Of course not.

—Well, we've all seen it before, The Landlord said. It's part of the cycle of life in the burbs. As soon as the kids are old enough to drive, the wife wants to feel young again and starts with the plastic surgery. Then the kids go away to college. Then the wife leaves to love again. Then the family pet dies. Then you move back to the city. Then you either meet someone else or end up sitting on a park bench, muttering obscenities at passersby.

When Harold got home he cuddled on the couch with Buddy and poured himself a Scotch.

〰

Doctor Pavani's office staff sent him photocopies of pages from a patient-education brochure explaining what he should expect after the operation. They would be considered dry. Approximately 75 percent of patients would be dry by three months after the operation. With any luck, 85 to 90 percent would be dry six to twelve months later. This was cheery news compared to the information about the accompanying erectile dysfunction, which, it was stated, took longer to overcome than the control of urine. Most men would require at least six months of healing and perhaps as long as eighteen to twenty-four months to have an erection. Twenty-four months, that was two years. That was depressing. Thankfully, counseling services were available for those who required them.

On the Internet, Harold found information about the robot the doctor was going to use to perform the operation. The manufacturer had posted a picture of it with a doctor sitting in an enormous lounge chair with arms coming out of it. The doctor was staring at a screen. The accompanying copy went to great lengths to make sure patients understood the robot was not in charge, the doctor was in charge. The doctor controlled every aspect of every movement of the robot, directing it as he stared at the surgical field through the hypermagnified screen. The machine was designed, the copy said, to repair your insides while leaving your outside as intact as possible. It would allow the doctor to perform complex and delicate procedures with precision. The minimally invasive approach would reduce the physical and emotional impact of the surgery. Only six ports would be carved open in his belly rather than cutting an unsightly six-inch slit. This advance in surgical capabilities would yield less post-operative pain, require less anesthesia, cause less blood loss, and ensure a shorter hospital stay and a quicker return to his life.

This was smart advertising copy. It touted all the benefits succinctly. It was disappointing that due to the patient- and procedure-specific nature of the surgery, none of the benefits were guaranteed. All the benefits mentioned in the copy were potential benefits. He might not receive them. He might be incontinent forever. He might never have another hard-on. He might die on the operating table. Why did he have cancer? How the hell did this happen? How did he end up in this situation? It was beyond his comprehension.

Harold's diagnosis was his introduction to mortality. An introduction that had nothing to do with anything he had ever talked about or heard about or read about. It didn't matter that he had always known he was going to die someday. It didn't matter that he might have died in an accident on his bike or from a different disease. It didn't matter that his mother and any number of other people he knew had died. That's what other people did—they died. Death was for other people. Up until the moment he was told he had cancer, he had been immortal. He was never going to die. Nothing was ever going to interrupt his existence on this earth. Nothing was ever going to interpose itself between him and his future. The more science advanced, the longer he would live. That's what everybody said. But everybody was wrong. And now, suddenly he understood that one day he would die. That his dream of immortality was nothing but a dream, and it was over and lost forever.

On the appointed day, very early in the morning, No Talk drove Harold to the hospital. The highways and streets were empty, and they arrived there all too fast. Harold got out and leaned into the open car window to give thanks for the ride. No Talk nodded and sped away.

Harold walked down a long, half-lit, deserted corridor in the basement of the hospital. The hum and buzz of electricity filled the air. Through some double doors, in a small, not particularly clean room, an orderly provided him with a bag for his belongings. He also provided him with socks and a surgical gown to wear during the procedure. He then attached a plastic band with a number and a barcode to Harold's wrist.

—There's a changing room down the hall, he said. Bring the bag out with you. One of the nurses will put it under the operating table and it'll go with you to the recovery room.

This was the final moment. Alone in the changing room, Harold removed his clothes, donned the surgical gown, and was transformed into a patient identifiable only by the tag fastened on his wrist. He was so depressed he would have cried had he not taken a Xanax before leaving the house.

Doctor Pavani came into the waiting area. He, too, had relinquished his clothes. He was wearing green nondescript surgical scrubs. They were both dressed in the costumes they would wear in the drama that was going to play itself out in very short order.

Harold asked to see the robot. The doctor obliged. The operating room was down the hall. They stared at it through a window. It was motionless, its arms extended in space at odd angles. Machinery at rest fascinated Harold, particularly cranes and overhead loaders and bulldozers and such. He swore he felt the potential energy stored in the steel, ready to roar into action like a predator after prey at the turn of a key. They both stared at the motionless beast shining in the sterile light. A nurse came and announced they wanted Harold in the prep room where they would begin readying him for the anesthesia. He shook hands with the doctor and wished him luck. As Harold walked away, he called over his shoulder.

—Do me one favor.

—Yes? the doctor said.

—Don't fuck it up.

∽

After the operation, it took Harold a while to come back to his senses and realize he was in a bed, and the bed was in a hospital. The last thing he remembered was the anesthesiologist telling him to count backward from ten. He recalled saying *ten*. He was sure his mind had been ransacked while he was anesthetized because he was unable to think. An aide noticed he was awake and came to ask how he was doing. Harold shook his head, okay. The aide patted him solicitously on the hand and volunteered to get him some water.

He had no idea how long he'd been unconscious. He did know someone had been mucking about inside him because there were tubes coming out of his nose and his dick. And there were holes in his sides with tubes coming out of them. The tubes in his nose were delivering oxygen, the tube in his dick taking out urine, and the tubes in his sides were draining fluids and blood into little plastic bags so he didn't swell as his body reacted to the trauma of the robotic invasion by sending white blood cells to the site of the incisions. He felt horrible. He wanted to go home. Sarah, who had come to stay with him, told him he had to spend the night in the hospital.

Doctor Pavani came by and said he thought the operation had been a success. He wouldn't give Harold a definitive answer until the pathology reports came back. Some of his cycling buddies who worked in the city came to wish him a speedy recovery. He slept fitfully and intermittently, and every time he fell asleep someone woke him up to either administer another drug, take a sample of blood, empty a bag, or ask how he was doing.

〰

Sarah took him home from the hospital and stayed for a few days to help him around the house. He had to wear a Foley catheter for two weeks. Before he left the hospital, a nurse had explained how to use it, demonstrating how to empty the urine from the bag and then reattach it, but he was too sedated to comprehend everything she told him.

On his second day home the bag stopped filling with urine. He couldn't figure out what was wrong. Sometime after lunch, he began to feel vaguely uncomfortable. Soon his bladder felt full, then alarmingly bloated. The pressure inside him was building. He was swelling up like a water balloon. Checking the bag, curious as to why there was no urine in it, he noticed the arrow with the word *up* embossed on it was pointing down. In the haze brought on by his pain killers, he must have reattached the bag upside down after the last time he emptied it. Upon disconnecting the tube to rectify this error, urine began squirting out of the tube like a fire hose gone mad. It soaked him and everything in the bathroom. Sarah helped him clean it up.

It was wonderful having Sarah around to help him, but at the end of the week, she had to return to school.

—Are you going to be all right, Daddy? she asked as she got in the taxi that was to take her to the bus station.

He promised her he would be fine. Now that he had mastered emptying the bag, what else did he have to do? He had Buddy to keep him company.

—Well, stop taking all those pain pills when you drink, she yelled out the window as the cab drove off.

He promised her he would, but he didn't.

↜↝

Harold's pathology report came back positive.

—You're good to go, Doctor Pavani proudly told him over the phone.

He didn't feel good to go.

To see if he could improve his state of mind, Harold began visiting prostate cancer blogs. He read the testimonials of the happy, smiling people who had undergone the same operation. He didn't understand why he didn't feel as wonderful as the people in the photographs said they did. He couldn't explain why he wasn't active. He was at a loss to comprehend why he wasn't smiling and optimistic about getting back to his life.

Or why he kept taking the oxycodone when he wasn't in physical pain.

Well, he had some idea. He would never be the same again. And this knowledge, coupled with the loneliness of living alone that was lurking in the corners of every room in the house, ready to pounce, was incapacitating. His friends and his children advised him to see a psychological counselor to help him over the trauma. He was too depressed to make an appointment.

↜↝

His depression fueled his need for self-medication. He couldn't sleep without being knocked out by the one-two punch of Scotch and oxycodone. Between the time he took the pill and the time he began to nod off, there was an interlude where the combination of the alcohol and the narcotic made him feel heavenly, as if he were floating outside himself and didn't have a care in the world. The worries about his job, his health, and his soon-to-be ex-wife all vanished. It was such a seductive, lovely sensation. It was the moment that in his tortured mind Ixion's wheel stood still and his heart didn't ache and he felt all was well with his life.

Of course, then there was the morning.

He woke up dead, put a pillow over his head and lamented his condition. He couldn't move. His limbs felt leaden. Sometimes he heard music playing in a distant room. Usually, it was a piano in a minor key. It was ominous-sounding, like a soundtrack from some old film noir. The dissonance was depressing beyond description. He kept his eyes closed until it stopped. Even after his limbs lightened and his head cleared a little and he forced himself to get up and out of bed and turn on the television or look at the flashing messages on his computer screen, he said to himself—who gives a fuck.

Everything filled him with disgust. Since the operation and Carol's departure, the meaning had drained out of everything. The thought of returning to his job nauseated him: the constant idiotic e-mails, the banality of voice mail, the stupidity of the search for *big* ideas, the drudgery of resetting his password, the documents littered with inanities circulating from one in-box to another in-box, meeting after meeting. There was no reason for any of it. None of it made any difference. He wanted to scream.

He tried to pull himself out of this funk by seeking solace in something Carol had said to him, something about *the dignity of the function* that work in the postmodern industrial world was supposed to be, the fulfilling of *the dignity of the function.* It was a lie. Everyone was lying. There was no dignity in performing a function. How could there be? Functions had no value. They expressed relationships. And relationships were tenuous and fragile, abstract and evanescent.

〰

The oxycodone also made him dream odd dreams, some of which recurred. Death appeared in these dreams. In one, he saw himself walking on a quiet country path of bright brown soft dirt that cut through thick brush and tall trees. The brilliant light of the sun illuminated everything in a glow that felt like eternity. The day was calm and tranquil, and as he walked along he had not a care in the world, and he was happy. Then in the stillness, some leaves quivered as he passed, and out of curiosity he parted the curtain of green shrubbery and saw, hidden deep within, underneath the lightened leaves, deep in the shadows, a bird thrashing in its death throes as its head was being ripped off by a cat. Horrified, he released the branches. The leaves stirred again for a moment, perhaps as the bird's final flutter fanned them to a rustle. This time, he ignored the sign. He didn't look again. He had seen *it*. He walked on in the heat and the light, abandoning the prey to its predator, perturbed but not guilty. Intercession would have been futile. Death was certain.

〰

Two weeks and two days after leaving the hospital, Harold went back to Doctor Pavani's clinic to have the catheter removed. A nurse and an assistant informed him they would perform the procedure. They had him lie down on an examining table. They opened his gown, exposing his nakedness. The nurse explained that first they were going to test his bladder. They were going to connect a bag of fluid to the tube and fill his bladder to capacity.

—Is it going to hurt? Harold inquired.

—Of course not, the nurse said.

They proceeded to drain a bag of saline into him until he felt his bladder was going to pop. It was far worse than when he had attached the bag upside down.

—There, that wasn't so bad, was it? Harold was informed as they drained out the fluid. It was clear the nurse didn't mean it as a question.

He had passed the test, the nurse informed him, which meant it was okay to remove the catheter. Harold asked if an anesthetic would be necessary.

—No.

—It's not going to hurt? he asked.

—Of course not.

—Really?

—Nope.

—How do you take it out? Harold asked.

—I'm going to pull it out.

—Just like that?

—Just like that, big guy, the nurse said. I do it all the time.

Harold cringed. Lying naked on the table, he reminded himself that everybody lies about pain they don't have to experience. Whenever he had asked anybody if something was going to hurt, he was always, invariably, emphatically assured it wouldn't hurt, and it always, invariably, emphatically did.

—Now hold on, the nurse said. He placed one gloved hand over Harold's testicles, wrapping his thumb around the base of his dick, and with the other hand he yanked out the tube like a carpenter pulling a ten-penny nail out of a two-by-four with a claw hammer.

Harold yelled.

—Did that hurt? the nurse inquired.

Harold was too busy hyperventilating to answer. This did not dissuade the nurse from offering his own judgment of the procedure, which was that it couldn't have hurt and most people didn't complain at all and were relieved to be rid of the tube. The assistant gave him a diaper to put on and a big pack of adult Depends for the road.

—It's a gift, he said. You're going to need them.

The nurse and the assistant both wished him luck and told him he was free to go.

He went home a wounded animal and curled up in bed. He had an ache deep inside him. It was part physical and part mental. The physical part of the pain he numbed with oxycodone and Scotch, but the emotional assaults would not be assuaged.

⌇

Harold met with the sex therapist some weeks after the catheter had been removed. This jolly fellow told him in no uncertain terms that he had to use his dick or it would atrophy and become useless. To prevent this, he prescribed every erectile dysfunction drug available, and gave him some free sample packs as well, and instructed him to take one every night before bed since, he said, the blood rushed into the penis during the nocturnal hours and the drug would help expand the blood vessels. In addition, he insisted Harold buy a pump.

—A pump?

—A pump, my friend. It's a suction device that draws blood into the erectile cavities near the base of your penis and then up through the shaft.

He drew a crude, almost obscene illustration on the disposable sheet of paper covering the examining table.

—It will make your dick stand up straight once again. Like this, he said, pointing to his artwork.

—A pump? Harold said again. Just like the ones they advertise in all that spam that finds its way through my security filters?

—Perhaps, the therapist said. You have to buy it online. They send it in a discreet brown paper package.

—So it has come to this, Harold lamented. There's no other way?

—Well, try the pills first, the doctor advised. If they don't work and you don't want to pump, we can move on to injections.

—Injections?

—Yes, he said, injections into the base of the penis. He pointed, once again, to his drawing. It hurts much less than you might think.

There was no way Harold was ever going to ever stick a needle into his dick, so he bought a pump and religiously and rigorously pumped his penis. Over the next several months, this did bring about the desired result. Little by little his dick regained its strength and stood up, at first wobbly and without commitment, and then straighter and straighter. It wasn't anywhere close to being as hard as it formerly was, and it wouldn't stand up by itself, but it did get up. It took several months more for him to coax it into an orgasm, which brought more mental anguish than physical pleasure because despite the fact he was once again able to achieve the pinnacle of somatic pleasure, his achievement was ruined by the discovery that it yielded nothing. His dick shook. There were spasms. There was shuddering. A heat wave washed over him. Nothing launched out of his loins. There was no money shot. He was bankrupt.

He returned to Doctor Pavani.

—You don't ejaculate because all the seminal vesicles, as well as the prostate, were removed, he said.

Harold didn't remember being told he was also going to lose those glands. The doctor said he wasn't surprised. He said Harold hadn't been paying attention when he explained the sequelae of the operation. He had been staring into space. But, yes, they were gone, and thus so was his ability to ejaculate.

—Will it come back? Harold asked.

—No. I'm afraid not.

—Will it ever get as hard as it used to be? Harold asked abruptly.

—It's too early to tell.

—It's not the same, Harold complained. It's … different.

—I've been told that, the doctor demurred.

Different didn't do justice to describing the change in sensation. His orgasm was now like hitting a flag pole with an aluminum bat. The vibrations he experienced in his limbs were powerful, but felt hollow and empty and unsatisfying.

—It'll never be the same again?

—Most men get used to it, Doctor Pavani offered by way of consolation.

∽

No longer the man he used to be, Harold wondered who, as he began his life over again, would want to deal with him in his diminished state? The ability of a man to give pleasure with his penis was an inalienable right in which every man took great pride, he thought. How could his debilitated member be counted on to do the kind of job it formerly excelled at performing? How would he be able to satisfy the demands of a partner who was in his embrace screaming *fuck me, fuck me, harder, harder* when he could hardly get hard? It was a crushing blow to his ego. For every man experienced the yearning to fulfill the fundamental pleasure need of the Other. And the drive to provide pleasure was every bit as basic as the drive to supply food and shelter and protection for our loved ones so our seed could grow and multiply. His lack of faith in his capacity to meet the physical demands of a partner was nothing short of cataclysmic. Irrespective of whether it was a one-night stand or a long-standing relationship, the ability to carry through with the promise of penetration and its attendant pleasures were paramount to a man's mental self-image. His image of himself was now shattered.

⌇

The systematic derangement of his senses by drugs and alcohol achieved its intended effect. It kept Harold in an altered state of consciousness and prevented him from wallowing in self-pity. No matter that his mind was becoming addled from the abuse.

Fortunately, he ran out of oxycodone. This meant he didn't have to stop drinking since technically he was effectively

cutting his drug consumption in half and on his way to reha-
bilitating himself.

〜〜〜

Just as damaging and in many ways more painful than the
betrayal of his body was Carol's abandonment. No matter
how hard he tried, he couldn't understand what he had done
that was so wrong, why after all those years she had decided
to leave him. He had long ago realized that while he loved
Carol, she was not, as Swann[9] had characterized Odette, *his
style*, but he had never thought of leaving her because of that.
Why had she left him?

At every meeting throughout the divorce, whenever he
talked to her, he had inquired about his inadequacies, begging
her to help him understand how he had failed as a husband.
Her stock answer was that there was nothing in particular, they
had outgrown each other, that was all. He knew that wasn't
all. He sensed she mouthed this platitude to protect him from
a truth she didn't want to reveal. Nevertheless, he was com-
pelled to seek it out in order to bring closure to the drama that
was causing him misery.

After the divorce was finalized, he continued to call her,
seeking enlightenment. Finally, in a fit of pique, she threw
this out:

—I don't know what to tell you, Harold, I really don't, except that living with you was like being nibbled to death by
ducks.

—What do you mean by nibbled?

—There you go, she said.

---

9 Marcel Proust, *A la Recherche du Temps Perdu* [In Search of Lost Time] (Paris: Gallimard, 1913–1927).

—There I go?

—Harold, honey, I have to go, she said, and she hung up the phone.

Her answer left him dumbfounded. Apparently his failure as a husband had been ongoing and systemic. If he understood her correctly, nothing he had done had been horrendous. There was no one precipitating event, no one isolated incident or blunder that had turned her heart against him. His deficiencies had consisted of subjecting her to small but persistent and petty annoyances year in and year out. It was clear she considered herself the victim and him the villain who had tortured her for years on end.

He didn't understand. He thought he had been a good husband and provider. His kids said he was a good father. He was respected and well liked at his job. His cycling buddies thought he was a terrific guy. He was thoughtful and polite. He helped people whenever he could. He confronted rudeness with grace and patience. He rarely passed a beggar or homeless person on the street without donating something. He contributed money to numerous charities and nonprofits, supporting everything from women's rights to animal rights. He supported the environment by not littering and fastidiously separating his trash. How could Carol not see that?

He was perplexed. He continued to analyze his failure but it was like examining a lost game in chess: if there was no obvious blunder, it was extremely difficult to identify the one move that led to defeat. You might find a lot of moves that were less than ideal, but you couldn't pinpoint the one that caused the downfall of the king and his empire.

☙

After the management team's meeting, which at this point was months ago, Harold thought he was a goner for sure. Following his operation, every day throughout his two-week recuperation period at home he had awaited his dismissal letter. Upon his return to work, from one hour to the next, he expected to be called into a conference room where Shirley would be sitting with *the folder*. One of the management team members would be sitting next to her as a witness. Shirley would explain his benefits, tell him what would happen to his 401(k), go over his long-term incentive plan options and grants, and provide information about how his health-care coverage would be handled, how much it would cost and how long it would last. It would be fruitless to protest. By the time he sat down with Shirley, the IT department would have locked him out of his computer, if not removed it from his office. He would be asked to sign some papers that acknowledged he was accepting his package and in return would not sue the company. Accompanied by Shirley or some other HR factotum, he would be walked to his office to collect any personal items, and then he would be escorted to the elevator and shown out of the building. Rarely was security called in.

Harold expected that meeting to take place at any moment, and he had prepared for it by removing all his personal belongings and as many files from his computer as he thought would be useful to him in the future. But his day of reckoning didn't arrive. The only explanation for the delay he could think of was that the signal Marc sent during the meeting had been too ambiguous to be interpreted, and this had stymied any further forward progress in firing him.

The executive management team's job was no more and no less than to interpret and execute the CEO's vision and pronouncements. If they hadn't come away from the meeting with a clear understanding of what they were supposed to do, they would be too cowardly to take any action. Seeking additional elucidation about what Marc meant when he said *protect the business* would be anathema as it would demonstrate a lack of contextual listening skills, and an inability to read the nuances of his directives, when these were the very prerequisites required to serve on the management committee. So if among them the team agreed to fire Harold without being positive they had been given the go-ahead, one of them would be obliged to sit in the room with Shirley while she informed him he was being terminated, and that person would be fingered as the hit man. Very soon thereafter this person would be called to task when Marc asked the question: *Who fired Harold?* No one wanted to be held accountable if they weren't absolutely certain they had understood what those cryptic words *protect the business* had meant. No one wanted to have to answer the follow-up questions Marc would be sure to ask: *Weren't we all in the same room? Did you not understand what I meant? Didn't I see you all nodding your heads?*

Cowards all, Harold held on to his job.

From a certain vantage point, his job couldn't have been going better. The junior people loved him. The senior people now ignored him altogether. He had more free time on his hands than ever before. Left undisturbed, he sat behind his desk and worried about his future.

Yet all the worry in the world wouldn't save him from what was to come. The reason a decision on his case was not made immediately, and then fell to the bottom of the to-do list, had nothing to do with the management team's inability to interpret Marc's words. Between the time of the meeting and the first follow-up debriefing, one of the largest communications holding companies in the world had made an offer to buy the firm. This caused considerable consternation among the management team members. Their focus became figuring out how to increase their odds of survival in the coming melee.

A deal was finally struck, and for the third time, Harold's place of employ changed ownership. Marc ceded power to the acquirer, took his buyout, and went his merry way. The new CEO arrived and called for a review of every function. When this was completed, due to the structural redundancies that were uncovered, it was announced that a rationalization of the staff was necessary.

The reorganization did not include a place for Harold. He received an exit package. They were fairly generous with him, Shirley snidely informed him. Certainly, she said, after explaining how many months he would continue to be paid, he wouldn't have any immediate financial worries. His close colleagues threw him a wonderful going-away party at a local restaurant. The following morning, he had nothing to do except ride his bike.

❧

Harold told his cycling group he had been fired.

—Wow. You'll have to switch gears completely, No Name said.

—What do you mean? Harold wanted to know.

—You were in marketing or consulting or something like that, right?

—Yes.

—Well, that's a young man's game, isn't it? And you're fiftyish. And you think you're at the top with all your years of experience and know-how. But it's not the same game anymore. A generation is approximately twenty-five years. You're a generation out of touch. You're obsolete, dude.

—He's not obsolete, The Landlord said. He needs to find the right place. A smaller shop or a startup that's looking for senior-level help.

—I don't want to go back, Harold said.

—You're angry now. You'll get over it.

—Come on. You're a fierce guy. You can fight your way into something.

—I don't think I want to. I was over it.

—What'll you do?

—I don't know.

—You'll find something.

—Yeah, said Single-Speed. And if you can't get a job, why don't you teach?

—Teach?

—Sure.

Single-Speed informed Harold that his son, who had been thrown out of Syracuse University for drugs, was attending the local community college. They used part-time instructors, he told Harold. With his advanced degree, he might be able to land a teaching gig. Probably nothing permanent. But if he didn't need a lot of money to live on, teaching could be interesting for someone with his intellectual abilities. It could at least keep him busy until he resolved what to do next.

❧

While Harold had been having philosophical and moral issues with his job, it was strange to have been released from all his responsibilities and have nothing to do. For the first time in a very long time, he found himself outside the world of work.

He would continue to receive his salary along with his health benefits for an extended period of months. Thus, as Shirley had remarked, for the moment his financial situation wasn't dire, but since the divorce had depleted just about all of his savings, he was going to have to go back to work.

Sitting at the kitchen counter in the morning, drinking his coffee and reading the *Times*, he was at a loss as to what to do with himself. When he was employed, he would read the headlines and a paragraph or two of each article and then rush off for the train. Now he read entire articles to forestall facing a looming void. How was he going to fill all those empty hours?

Everyone said he should use the time to think about what to do next, and he tried to think about it. He had a hard time focusing. His imagination, upon which he had depended to make a living for the last thirty years, failed to inform him what his next steps should be. Which terrified him.

For the first few weeks, after awakening he stayed in his bed. He rolled around and stretched and rearranged his limbs until he perfectly distributed his weight across the mattress so that he felt weightless, as if he were floating in space. Then he stared at the ceiling for as long as he could.

He had received all the obligatory how-are-you-doing phone calls and had spoken to his kids and his father numerous times. He had explained everything again and again because they all wanted assurances he was okay. They reiterated how sorry they were for him and how they were sure he would show those bastards they had made a terrible mistake by achieving wild success at his next job. They also wanted to hear what his next job was going to be and how he was preparing to find it. The children's curiosity was somewhat self-interested as they had their lifestyle to consider, which Harold helped them maintain. His father's concern was more spiritual since a man's job was to work, and no one could be idle for very long without ill effects. It wasn't good for the soul. Buddy, too, stared at him and seemed to be asking, *What next?*

Whatever was next, the first thing Harold had to do was hold himself together. His Yankee work ethic dictated he should rush back into the marketplace and assert himself before he lost his edge, but he wasn't up to organizing the mental energy necessary to charge back into the world of work and fight for his fair share of the rewards. That's what he would have done when he was younger and unenlightened. Now that he was fully aware of the contradictions inherent in his profession and recognized the harm he had been causing, he couldn't do that. Any urge he had to reenter the morally ambivalent fog of his career was attenuated by his knowledge that he would be doing it only to satisfy some atavistic machismo instinct, to show the world he was unbowed, to prove to everyone he still had it, that he could hack it. And he didn't want to hack it.

In the morning, as he lay in his bed, questions about his identity began to plague him. Who was he? He wasn't sure. On some level, he knew he was nothing more than an aggregate of facts, and these facts were, metaphorically, woven together by his memory over time. Of course, facts were subject to continual reinterpretation and degradation, while new facts were always added. The new ones that had been added to his life were nothing less than catastrophic: His wife had left him. Cancer had ravaged him. His firm had fired him. What was the significance of it all, he wondered? How did that impact who he was? If he was nothing more than a set of facts, the aggregate of the constant conjunction of events he experienced, what did that say about his life? Was he no more than the last fact added on to the chain of facts that comprised his life up until this point? In which case he was an unemployed, middle-aged man. Did that constitute his being? Was that who he *was*? Or was he an unemployed former executive? Or a divorced, unemployed, former executive in his fifties? He had to be more than that, didn't he? But what did *more* mean? How could he become more than the narrative sum total of the events that he had experienced? How could he overcome himself? Who would he be?

In the end, he hypothesized, it was quite likely we were nothing more than the constant conjunction of descriptive events that befell us, and anything *more* we layered on top of that was the work of our imagination. As he lay in his bed, he wondered if it might be true that we had no essence, that our personality, our core being, was nothing more than an ongoing conceptual exercise, something we ourselves create to fit our needs, something we construct and then deconstruct as the situation demands. We might be nothing more than the hollow men[10] Eliot had written about.

✺

On most days Harold woke up with good intentions of accomplishing something productive. Although he was

---

10 T. S. Eliot, "The Hollow Men," in *Poems: 1909–1925* (London: Faber & Faber, 1937).

ambivalent about seeking employment in his field, since it gave him something to do, he reached out to people he knew to inquire about opportunities. He sent his old, out-of-date résumé to some friends who promised to pass it along. But his good intentions weren't enough to impel him to move out of his own way to accomplish anything.

Some days he did nothing. It was all too easy to stay in bed until either his bladder forced him to get up to go to the bathroom or Buddy's bladder forced him to let Buddy outside to go to the bathroom. He would then check his e-mail, make a cup of coffee, climb back in bed and, with Buddy stretched out beside him, watch the morning news shows. He stayed in bed as late as nine or ten if his phone didn't ring. At some point during the day he rode his bike for twenty or thirty miles. Or he went to the gym. If he had no calls or e-mails to answer upon his return, he walked Buddy. Then he would sort through the latest mail delivery. The piles had become quite impressive, lining both sides of the front hallway and one wall of the living room.

He caught up on his topical reading while eating lunch. He read the *New Yorker*, yes, the *New Yorker*, or the *New York Review of Books*. There was a stack of each on the island in the kitchen. Often one of the articles started his imagination, and with no pressing task at hand, he soon found himself wandering into a daydream.

In the late afternoon, he snacked. He settled for any scrap of food left in the refrigerator. A peanut butter sandwich and an energy bar sufficed if there was nothing else. And if the cupboards were bare, he sometimes sucked down a pack of GU, which he normally used for quick energy on long bike rides.

Since he couldn't seem to organize himself to pursue any purposeful activity, Harold thought he might be suffering from problems in everyday living. He located his copy of Thomas Szasz's *The Myth of Mental Illness* in his library. None of what he had underlined was helpful. One underlined sentence reminded him of Freud, and in an old copy of *Civilization and Its Discontents*, he read a marginal note, mixed with some fragments of highlighted text, that expressed the thought: *our responsible, ordinary selves working under the taskmaster of the reality principle can be sustained only by the constant expenditure of psychic energy devoted to the maintenance of the repression of our fundamental desires.* This was enlightening. It might explain why he had no ambition to do anything anymore. It made him think: I don't have any ambition. This must be why I lounge around in bed so long, an activity that was, until recently, unnatural for him.

By six o'clock he began to think about dinner, but first he had a protracted cocktail hour during which time he read fiction. He had to watch himself, however, since it was easy for him to keep reading and drinking instead of eating. Somehow, food wasn't important to him anymore. Material objects were less meaningful as well. It was mental states he cherished most. That was why he wasn't working very hard at finding another job. If he landed another job, he would have hours and hours of his day confined in some corporation's mental map with all the routes marked out for him. He couldn't bring himself to submit to that now. For years he had labored to provide for his family and had no time for anything else. Now, for the first time, he had time, and he wanted to use it for his own devices.

❧

Harold couldn't figure out how to crawl out from under the weight of the wasted decades of his life he had spent working for companies whose goals he had come to loathe. All those years wasted working. He drank to forget them. And though he knew the alcohol was affecting his ability to think, he didn't give a shit: it dulled the ache in his heart. His depression dictated it was better to numb the pain than try to forge forward in search of a new direction.

One night as he was sinking into a stupor, he stared at the walls around him. The colors depressed him. They were horrid colors. They were wretched colors. They were Carol's colors. He had always hated them. He now grasped the import of Oscar Wilde's complaint as he lay on his deathbed and looked at the wallpaper in his room and said, *Either that wallpaper goes or I do.*

He hired painters. They stripped, sanded, primed and painted every room. He replaced all the dark, serious, saturated blues and reds with white and tan and earth tones. At once, the house felt fresher, lighter, brighter.

There were still too many vestiges of Carol echoing through the rooms. A further purge was required.

He got rid of all the furniture and window treatments, which, like the old paint, were heavy and ponderous and incredibly bourgeois. Then he decided he wanted to decrease his inventory of possessions altogether. He needed to relieve himself of all the stuff he and Carol and the kids had accumulated over the years. He cleaned house. He donated most of his clothes, anything that Carol had left behind, and any object he had not touched in the preceding six months to any charity that would take it. He sold off what remained in online auctions. There was virtually nothing left in the house except a few oriental rugs, his bed, and the kids' beds.

He ate standing at the kitchen counter. He worked at his computer on the floor with Buddy beside him. The house-keeper was aghast. Since there was less for her to clean, he had her subdivide the voluminous piles of mail by category.

When his kids came home from school for the holidays, they were distraught. They pleaded with him to purchase some furniture. He gave in. But he bought very little, only that which took up a minimum of space and provided a modicum of com-fort. Jake and Sarah were upset by his newfound asceticism.

—You can't live like a monk, Sarah claimed.

—Why not?

—Because it's unnatural. And besides, monks do it so their minds won't be distracted by earthly, material things so they can concentrate on eternal things.

—Well, I'm changing my life, he said.

—Going back to work would be a big change, Jake said, somewhat flippantly.

—I'm still updating my résumé, Harold replied, realizing the inclusion of *still* made it seem he were either incompetent or procrastinating.

—I can help, Sarah offered.

—I'll be fine. Don't worry.

—We do worry about you, Daddy.

Sarah looked at Jake, who nodded his head in agreement.

—I love you both so much, he said.

—And we love you, Sarah said. We want you to be okay.

He almost asked what she meant by *okay* but held himself back because it occurred to him that asking a question like that might have been what Carol had meant by *nibbling*. Instead he smiled and gave each of them a kiss.

⟨∿⟩

Little by little Harold started to develop new habits. On the mornings he got out of bed early enough to ride with his group, after they headed home, he stayed out on the road, putting in anywhere from thirty to thirty-five miles on weekdays. Going to the gym in the afternoon picked up his spirits and kept him from succumbing to a midafternoon lassitude during which he would idly and aimlessly surf the Internet. In the evenings he studied famous chess games and then played in online tournaments until his concentration failed from too much Scotch.

Despite his newfound penchant for drinking, he was in peak physical condition. His maximum heart rate had increased, his body weight was down, his body fat had all but disappeared, and his aerobic capacity had increased. His upper body was lean and muscular from working out in the gym. He felt fine when he wasn't thinking about his life.

Riding kept him at the greatest distance from himself. It required so much concentration that his mind couldn't wander. Clipped into his pedals, his hands down in the drops of the handlebars, he was one with the machine. His mind and body worked together in perfect harmony, propelling him forward through the air that rushed around him, encapsulating him in a bubble of bliss. Climbing uphill, out of the saddle, the rhythmic swinging of his body from side to side as he shifted his weight from pedal to pedal was like dancing. Descending downhill, hunched low on the handlebars, at speeds of up to thirty or forty miles an hour, he imagined he was flying through the gates of heaven. And he was happy.

〰

Against his better judgment, Harold began seeking employment. He completed updating his résumé and began making phone calls and setting up appointments for interviews. He met with any number of former colleagues or friends of colleagues who expressed an interest in talking to him. In follow-up e-mails, both he and his interviewers acknowledged their satisfaction with how the interview had gone. They mutually agreed Harold would be a perfect fit in their organization. He would bring a wealth of knowledge and experience to any team he was assigned to. Unfortunately, there was never an immediate opening. And while many of the people with whom he talked said they were willing to take on the task of creating a position for him, since it would be a shame to pass up an opportunity to acquire an asset like him, over the next several months nothing materialized except vague promises to stay in touch.

He was forced to contact an executive recruiter to keep the search going. One of his former colleagues recommended the person who had placed him in his current job. The recruiter's name was Sandy. Over the phone her vibe was very upbeat. She was impressed with his credentials.

—This should be a no-brainer, she said. I have several places that would see you immediately.

Sandy asked him to make some minor changes to the format of *his paper*, as she called his résumé, before she sent it out. Once this was accomplished, Sandy began setting up meetings.

The meetings Sandy set up were not the same as the meetings Harold had arranged for himself or that had been arranged through colleagues. Most of the time, to see an actual prospective employer, he now had to go through an intermediary, the hateful HR department, since it turned out the majority of Sandy's business was contractual work with large holding companies. Once again, he was forced to interact with people like Shirley, officious know-nothings who entered his name into a computer and told him with whom he would be meeting. The process was painful and degrading. While Sandy arranged for him to meet with senior people on some interviews, for the most part he met with people at his functional level or lower. Sandy said this was necessary because they were part of the screening process to check for cultural fit and general overall competency. He had to pass muster before being allowed to move on to meet with senior managers whose time was too precious to waste unless everyone on the team agreed they had identified a viable candidate. Sometimes he was interviewed by two people at once, a higher- and a lower-level employee, the purpose of which, it was explained to him, was to give the team a chance to see how he interacted with people of different functional levels simultaneously. The two compared notes after the meeting and turned them over to HR, where a decision was made about whether he would be allowed to proceed upward in the chain of command.

The questions he was asked in these meetings were all taken from HR handbooks and career-building websites and employment consultants' blogs. They were stupid beyond the words used to articulate them: How do you handle criticism? Describe a decision you made that was a failure. What happened and why? Why do you think you will be successful at this job? What did you do during this six-month gap in employment? What is your preferred way to communicate: instant message, phone, or e-mail? Do you check voice mail and e-mail when on vacation? If I gave you one minute, how would you convince me to hire you?

It was all he could do to remain civil during these interviews.

Eventually, he made it past all the screens at one corporation and was scheduled to meet the chief strategic officer, who was also one of the managing directors of the company.

—He's very persnickety, Sandy warned. Show up on time and dress sharp.

Harold followed her advice. He arrived fifteen minutes early wearing his best suit and was kept waiting thirty minutes for his trouble. He cooled his heels in the reception area, watched over by a smiling and aloof receptionist who whispered into her headset. The reception area was elegant, with marble floors, Mies Barcelona chairs, Oriental rugs, flat-screen TVs flashing world news, house phones for visitors' use, and the company's annual report splashed out over a low mahogany coffee table. It was all a sham. The minute you passed into the workspace proper, it would be like stepping behind the curtain in Oz, where instead of finding the all-powerful wizard, you encountered the frightened little old man with a megaphone. Behind the spacious, elegantly appointed reception area were the workspaces that resembled nothing so much as a rabbit warren, with workers tucked into tiny offices or cubes no bigger than coffins to perform their daily duties. Or they were arrayed at open tables in open spaces where there wasn't a shred of privacy. Or they were organized into collaborative workgroups and sat in open meeting rooms. It was all an abomination.

At last, the chief was ready to receive him. He followed the assistant who came to fetch him. He was led beyond the door into the bowels of the office. And sure enough, just as at his old firm, people were crammed into every inch of space. He was unable to recall why he had ever thought of returning to the corporate world. He was becoming nauseated following the woman through the maze of hallways and corridors and workspaces and row after row of cubicles. The towers of Manhattan and every other world-class city were filled with companies like this one, whose workers performed useless, idiotic tasks senior management duped them into believing were important. And here, as at his former job, everyone was clattering over their keyboards or talking into their headsets, trying desperately to come up with something of value, something that would at least earn them a positive evaluation. The hive was alive. Harold heard the hum. Now he was ready to throw up. From Intel to Microsoft, Apple to Google, Facebook to Twitter, Instagram to Snapchat, by the time a company had employees and went public, the innovation had been sucked out of it. Once the founder's vision was exhausted, which happened rapidly, the inanity of groupthink took over. One person after another was hired. All with vetted pedigrees and impeccable credentials. What difference did it make? None. Everyone on payroll was there only to keep the ship afloat. No one had anything to do except make sure the goods and services rolled off the assembly line. Everyone was happy to collect their paychecks every ten days and hope that ten days later another one would be deposited in their accounts. Once we hunted, then we gathered, then we seeded the soil and created surplus. Excess freed us from the earth. Yet that connection to the earth had been the fundamental defining factor of life. When that was dissolved, there came religion. And when religion got old and God died, what emerged was modern man, who became lost in the solitude of his own heart. Lost! Just like everyone here, Harold thought. Just like me.

And here they all sat. Working away. Secure in their belief they were protected from the vicissitudes of the economy by their brand-name company and their long tenures, wearing their fancy clothes, sporting their fancy titles. Right now they were complacent because things were going well. That was for today. Today they could afford to be smug and self-important. Today they were one of the team. Tomorrow, the team might have to be reshuffled. Tomorrow, their names might be moved to the other side of the ledger, and the smallest global hiccup that reduced corporate profitability could result in their being called down to HR to receive a pink slip. Sorry. Tomorrow they could be out on the street calling all their friends. Desperately reaching out to all their connections on LinkedIn. They were just like him: isolated economic units, part of the exchange system in which labor was traded for money.

And here he was, on a mission to rejoin the corporate world, to once again enlist in the ranks of the labor force, to be accepted and appreciated and valued. He wanted to puke.

—A client call, the chief said by way of excuse for his tardiness as Harold was shown into his office.

They shook hands, warmly, Harold thought.

The chief motioned for him to take a seat. No sooner did he make himself comfortable than the phone rang. The chief took the call and then, covering the mouthpiece, asked Harold if he would mind if his shoeshine guy sat in during their meeting. Harold assented and a muscular old black man with the air of a broken-down ex-boxer, toting a wooden box, shambled into the room.

—Hey, boss, the man said.

—Hi, Willie. I've got an interview so mum's the word, right?

—Yes, boss. Willie winked at Harold.

—Willie can maintain confidentiality, right, Willie?

—That's right, boss.

Willie pulled up a chair and began to work on the chief's shoes.

—Here's what I don't understand, said the chief. You've talked to many other companies, I'm sure, who, like us, are in the service business and deal chiefly in intellectual property and ideas and creativity.

Harold agreed to this with a nod.

—And you were in a senior position at your firm, so I'm sure you're aware that when an organization comes under profit stress or suffers through an M&A and has to rationalize the staff, typically the bottom ten percent of performers are lopped off. He paused.

Harold had nothing to say.

—You have an impressive résumé, and from what I've heard you have all the requisite talents … and you present well.

—Thank you, said Harold.

—But given the way reductions work, why are you sitting here?

Watching Willie work, Harold became distracted. Willie's assiduous attention to his task was admirable. From the way he was making the chief's shoes shine like black mirrors, it was clear he took pride in his job and would probably agree to the proposition that there was dignity in fulfilling one's function to the best of one's ability. Harold stared at the chief's cuff links and his monogrammed shirt while deliberating about how to frame his response to the question. The man was curt, supercilious, but his question had cut right to the point. How should he explain why he was sitting here? How could he best describe the issue of his so-called *sabotage* that had gotten him fired at his last job? Should he bring up the fact he had become disenchanted? What about mentioning his cancer to elicit some sympathy?

Then, as Willie worked and he listened to the snap and crack of his rag over the toe cap of the chief's shoes, he thought he must be crazy to want to reenter the system and once again harness his mental capacity for the betterment of corporations like this one. He was on the verge of saying something humorous to break the tension, when he sensed the nausea rise up within him. And instead of trying to convince this pompous ass that he should hire him, Harold said:

—Shit happens.

—I see, said the chief, nonplussed.

Harold shrugged his shoulders.

The chief cracked a smile.

—Willie would agree with you. Right, Willie?

—Sir?

Willie demonstrated his ability to maintain confidentiality.

—Shit happens, right?

—Yes, boss. Shit happens. But you're young. You can handle it. Yes, sir.

✧

Harold told Sandy he was no longer interested in finding a *position* and stopped interviewing. There was no point. He was never going back to the corporate world. He didn't want to go back to work at all. He started to come to terms with the fact he despised what had been *his career*. As he had suspected years ago, it was nothing but a joke with a failed punch line. Moreover, despite his lofty title and the esteem in which he once had been held, he had never been anything more than a corporate drone. *Drone* hadn't been in his job description, yet that's all he had ever been. He had to laugh. There was nothing else to do.

⟵∧⟶

A few weeks later, Harold thought over what Single-Speed had said about teaching. He had long ago foregone his dream of becoming a writer or a critic or working in the arts, but now the idea of becoming at least tangentially connected to the creative world as an educator buoyed his spirits. The possibility of getting back to texts and ideas for the sake of ideas, and not to sell something, seemed like a means through which redemption of his wasted years of life was possible.

Single-Speed put him in touch with the appropriate authorities at Westchester Community College. Harold filled out the paperwork, secured recommendations from colleagues, interviewed, and, two-months later, was hired to teach a literature course.

He put together a syllabus. The theme was *The Searchers*, the same name as the John Ford movie. The texts included *Kim*, *The Asiatics*, *Siddhartha*, *The Razor's Edge*, *The Stranger*, and *On the Road*. The course was intended to be a study of the search for self and authenticity. Possibly transcendence. Issues that were weighing heavily on his mind.

❧

Fifteen students signed up for Harold's class. For the most part they were young. Some right out of high school. A few had failed out of, or dropped out of, a four-year university and wanted another chance at higher education. Some of the older students were from the workforce and wanted to earn a college degree of some sort to increase their earning potential.

On the first day of class, they arrived more or less on time. They greeted Harold as they entered. They clutched their coffee cups and bottles of water and phones and notebooks, looking tousled and dazed and confused and bored. Settled into their seats, they focused their attention on their electronic devices. A couple of them looked like they had wakened from a nap they had taken in some other class.

They were edgy in an urban-suburban sort of way. Several of the women were attractive, including one who had introduced herself as K. She smelled vaguely of peppermint and wholesome natural spices, although her black clothes and the small tattoo on the inside of her wrist made him think she was a bit on the rough side. She wore a short skirt revealing long legs he couldn't stop himself from admiring. While polite enough to introduce herself, as soon as she sat down she turned her undivided attention to her phone and kept it there throughout the entire class.

Harold was surprised at the degree to which his hormones kicked in when he found himself in the presence of the young, attractive women who made up half the student body. It was disheartening to discover he was invisible to them.

Discussing his new job with his cycling group, he brought up the issue of his invisibility.

—That happens, The Landlord said. As you get older your testosterone levels begin to fall, and women sense it, which is why they ignore you. Which means your chances of getting fucked are dismal ... unless you're married. And even then....

—Yeah, even your smell changes as you get older. It goes from being a virile, salty, sweaty mix to one of dirty socks and stained underwear, said The Ring.

—Yep, The Mope concurred.

—I'm not old, he protested.

—It's not that, Einstein said. It's that after a certain age, no matter how good-looking you are, your animal magnetism, your manliness, which is related to your testosterone levels *and* the potency of your pheromones, diminishes. Sometimes it simply disappears. And those are the things that throw out your aura, so when they're gone, younger people—women in particular—have a hard time seeing you. Sometimes, just like you're saying, it's as if they don't see you at all.

—What do I do? Harold wanted to know.

—Don't chase younger women. Older people always recognize one another, so they're a better bet, said The Baker.

—And keep away from your students. That will get you fired in a heartbeat, predicted The Landlord.

—I think if you have money, it's different, The Ring said.

—Yeah. Money is the only antidote for invisibility, said The Mope.

—I lost most of it in the divorce, Harold said.

—Then you are shit out of luck, my friend, said The Landlord.

—There's nothing you can do, Einstein said. You could try to force yourself into their consciousness. But the kind of obnoxious flirting that it would take to get you noticed will be seen as weird and creepy and would classify you as a dirty old man. You don't strike me as that type.

—I'm not.

—Then, as the man said, you're shit out of luck, dude.

Sometime toward the middle of the fall semester, as Harold walked through the parking lot on his way to his car, he caught the scent of marijuana. No sooner did he identify the car from which it was emanating than he spotted one of his students, K, in the car smoking a joint. He nodded to her in a friendly, professorial sort of way as he passed by. He was continuing on toward his car when he heard her call out.

—Hey, hi, you wanna hit?

She held the joint out the window for him to see.

He approached her car.

—You look like a stoner, she said, by way of explanation for her invitation.

He hadn't smoked marijuana since college, and the only reason he spontaneously accepted her offer to take a hit from the joint was because there was something incredibly provocative and exciting about the fact that, for this young woman, he existed. She saw him.

—I knew it, she said with great satisfaction as he passed the joint back to her.

—Knew what? Harold asked.

—That you were a stoner.

He was wearing his usual school-teaching attire, a classic blue blazer, a tie, and khaki slacks, so it wasn't clear to him how he looked like a stoner. He was going to ask her but instead he accepted the joint back from her and took another hit.

—I like your class, she offered.

—But you don't participate.

—I know, she conceded. I wish I had time to read all those books.

—Are you prepared for the midterm?

—I will be. Hey, we should hang out sometime, she suggested.

—Hang out?

—Chill....

Harold was skeptical. He didn't want to risk a disciplinary action or get fired for dating a student.

—I'm not sure that's a good idea.

—Neither is smoking a J in the parking lot. But hey.... Anyway, just 'cause I'm a student shouldn't be a problem because I'm only a part-time student, so who's going to care? Give me your number, she demanded. I'll text you.

—Okay, he said, suddenly swayed.

—My name is K.

—I know, he said. That's what's on the roster.

—I know you know it's K, but do you know it's just K?

—I thought K was an initial.

—Well, it's a letter. My name is K.

—No last name?

He was confused now and thought he might be trapped in one of those ineffable stoner dialogues. He had only had a few puffs but had rapidly succumbed to that wonderful, ethereal, peaceful state in which everything was blissful and beautiful.

—Yes, I have a last name, silly. Castle.

—I know, said Harold.

—But my first name is K. There are no vowels in my name.

—So it's not an initial?

—No, it's a letter.

—Your first name is a letter? Just like K in *The Castle*.

—My last name is Castle.

—I understand that. Just like the novel.

—Yes.

—Oh, K, he said. I get it.

She looked at him quizzically.

—I like you, she said.

↜↝

K texted him the following day suggesting they meet that evening at a local restaurant near the campus. He accepted her invitation.

The restaurant was a low-key place, one step up from a diner, one step down from a tablecloth restaurant, with an unhurried pace and sympathetic but inefficient wait staff. They took a booth at the back. K ordered a vodka and tonic, and Harold followed suit.

—Wednesday is the only night I can get out without having to pay, she said.

While K didn't speak in class, she was loquacious at the table, the alcohol, and the marijuana she had smoked before arriving, having loosened her tongue. In short order, he learned she was from Connecticut but was staying with her grandmother in White Plains, who had agreed to watch her son, Cody, one night a week for free. Any more than that and she wanted to be paid. This arrangement was designed to keep her from abusing her grandmother's good graces. K's husband had been indicted and convicted of mail fraud, or a securities violation, or maybe both, and was doing time. She had divorced him right after they sent him away. She had been dealing marijuana to make ends meet, small quantities, exclusively to friends, and then to friends of friends, and then to students at Wesleyan, where she had studied art for a year or so before dropping out to try to become an artist, which she was, at heart. Someone had ratted her out and she got busted, and the police and social services threatened to put her son in protective custody so she split and came to New York. She didn't have any money since the government took it all, as well as the marital home, to pay the fines her husband incurred from his conviction. Now she had little time for her art and was working freelance as an art director and designer at various local companies. Some of her employers had been quite frank with her, telling her outright that she needed more training and some kind of degree to secure better-paying jobs.

—You know, I don't have any friends, she said out of nowhere.

—No, I didn't know. I'm sorry.

—Don't be. I don't give a damn. I don't like most people. Most people are fake. I hate fake. I hate almost everybody and everything actually. I don't really want to be in school, even though I think I need to be.

Harold wasn't sure what to say. Mesmerized by her rambling tale, he kept staring at her. The luster in her hair, the turgidity of her skin, her posture, the tone in her muscled arms, the clarity and fire in her eyes, everything about her spoke of youthfulness. Her body bristled with passion. He wondered how old she was.

—Are you listening to me or trying to guess how old I am?

Harold was taken aback by her perceptiveness. The only response possible was the truth.

—Both.

—You don't know my age?

—How would I know?

—But you want to know?

—Yes.

—Thirty-four. And I'm guessing here, you're fifty-something.

Harold admitted it.

—What did you do to get here?

Rather than explain his failed marriage and talk about his children, he began to recount his working history. K stopped him.

—Wait a minute. You were, like, a corporate guy or something...?

—Depending on what you mean by *corporate*, I suppose so.

He was about to go into detail when she interjected:

—You? You were one of those motherfuckers? Just like my ex. She rolled her eyes, unable to hide her disgust.

—Aren't you ashamed of yourself?

—I got sucked in, he said in his defense.

Hearing her classify him as a *motherfucker*, he understood he wouldn't be able to justify himself to her by claiming he had always thought of his job as nothing more than an intellectual game. That was the story he told himself. A convenient lie. She wasn't going to buy it. The stark reality of the situation, when you got right down to it, was that his job had been to exploit people's dreams for a better life. She was right: he was no better than a con man, like her husband. Ashamed, he thought he felt himself blush.

—Well, I guess I can forgive you, she said. But it's weird, very weird. Because you seem intellectual or artistic, not like a business guy. Anyone can see that. And businesspeople *are* scumbags. My ex tricked me into believing he was different, but he was nothing but a thief. How could you have been like that? Why would you ever want to work for a marketing company? Or any company? That's what I don't get. That's what I never got. When I was in college all I wanted to do was art, and all these other kids were trying so hard, striving to get good grades and to secure a job in some stupid corporation because their parents wanted them to. Fuck that. Why would I want to do that? Realize myself through the work given to me by my employer. How does that happen? How do I realize myself in the service of an employer? You tell me.

Harold sat mute.

—My father worked for GE for years. For that bald motherfucker with the squeaky voice who preached all that Six Sigma shit. It was all a trick to get you to compete against yourself or someone else. Some bureaucrats set some objectives that don't mean crap. They don't want to get the best out of employees. They just want to make themselves rich. The system is a succubus. It's out to fuck everyone. I don't want to give it anything. I don't want to help. I don't want to grow the economy. I'd rather rob a bank. I only do what I want with who I want. I don't want anything, really. Just basic survival shit. I'm off the wheel of desire. The only thing that is real is the inner self, but reaching it is a struggle. It's work. And I work every day. I'm trying to make art, and that's all I care about.

Suddenly she stopped.

—I hate talking about myself, and that's all I'm talking about. I'm such a long story, and I hate stories.

—We're reading stories in class, Harold said.

—I know. I like reading non-fiction. I don't like most stories, only weird ones. I thought the books you picked were weird. Besides, I needed the credits.

They drank and talked of everything from cabbages and kings to Scylla and Charybdis.

A little inebriated, Harold blurted out:

—Why do you want to hang out with me? I'm a not-so-young, bourgeois baby boomer.

—Maybe. But I think you're real, not fake. And, while I'm younger than you, according to some people I'm an over-the-hill single mom with a bad attitude facing years of downward mobility. Not that many people are banging down my door to go out with me. And those who knock politely don't stick around long once they find out my ex is in the slammer and that I have a touch of bipolar.

—I can't tell if that means we have anything in common.

—I can. What's your favorite band from the nineties?

—I don't know.

—Come on.

Harold struggled.

—Morphine.

—That's crazy. Mine's Nirvana.

—So?

—Don't you see? You need morphine to get to nirvana.

—I guess, but....

—No, no, look, she said. From her bag K pulled out a copy of Breton's *Nadja*,[11] of all things, opened it to a page marked by a piece of yarn and handed it to him. She had underlined: *it is by an extreme capacity for defiance that certain unusual people who have everything to hope and everything to fear from one another will always recognize one another.*

—Isn't that us? she asked.

—I don't know.

She reached across the table and took his hand.

—Trust me. It's us. We're both unusual. We're different.

⌇

Harold and K began to see each other regularly. They met in bars and bistros and cafés near the campus. Talking to her made him realize how lonely he'd been. How much he'd craved company. And how much he missed having someone to talk to about all the things he cared about. K was an autodidact. She read on a wide range of subjects, many of them having to do with political economy.

—I'm pretty radical, she claimed. I'd be a revolutionary if the times were different.

She was vehemently opposed to anything that might diminish her individuality or freedom. She was antagonistic toward authority. They found common ground in that they both disliked *the system*, which they understood as any organized structure, governmental office, or private enterprise that had the potential to trample an individual's rights without the possibility of recourse.

____

11 André Breton, *Nadja* (New York: Grove Press, 1928).

Together they spent a day reading *The Port Huron State-ment* out loud to each other.

—This is my bible, K said after they finished it.

Soon Harold began to miss her when he wasn't with her. Her energy was contagious and she made him feel vibrant and gallant. That she was drawn to him excited him. He had a premonition that sex with K was not out of the question. And while the idea thrilled him right down to his groin, in which, when he thought about sex with her, he felt the nerves tingling, he was also terrified of the thought he might not be up to the act. She was twenty years younger and probably used to a performance level that was likely beyond his capability. He knew his best days as a lover were behind him because no matter how hard he tried during rehearsals with himself, once he was done with the opening act, he couldn't manage to rouse himself to give an encore even using the most outrageous pornography he could find as a stimulus.

Since she didn't like stories, he hadn't told her about his cancer and the damage it had done to him, and the thought of having to bring it up to explain a potentially suboptimal sexual encounter depressed him. So, while he was desperately physically attracted to K, his performance anxiety kept his desire in check. The risk of exposing his frailty and possibly suffering the humiliation of being unable to please her dulled his longing. To prevent his desire from surfacing while he was with her, he drowned it in alcohol, and marijuana, if she had any.

〰

One afternoon the moment Harold had been dreading arrived. K said:

—I don't want to go to a bar. Why don't we go to your house and chill out? I've got some dynamite smoke.

—My place is such a mess. Maybe next time, he said.

—Are you afraid of me? she asked.

—No. Of me, he said, laughing nervously.

—Don't be. I can take care of myself if I have to.

—I'm sure you can, but....

He floundered and switched subjects, without being sure they had been talking about the subject that was on his mind.

—My place is a huge mess, he said, still trying to stall.

—It can't be that bad, she said.

—You'd be surprised, he predicted. It occurred to him that he had neglected to tell her about his project of collecting the mail.

—I don't think so. Not much shocks me. Let's go, she commanded.

When they arrived, K was taken aback at the massive amounts of mail that filled the house. Stacks of it now lined the walls of most of the rooms on the ground floor, the magazines and catalogs attaining heights of up to three or four feet in some places.

—What is all this? she demanded. Are you a hoarder?

—No. It's a project I'm working on. Someday I plan to return it all, or use it to do something outrageous, he said, although up to that moment he had never considered what his ultimate plan for the mail would be.

—Wow. I knew there was something different about you, but who would guess you're that far out there?

She walked around the ground floor, peering into each of the rooms. Buddy followed her at close quarters, sniffing her whenever she stopped to look at a photo on the wall or take in the expanse of empty space.

—He's so nice, she said, reaching down to pet him. What kind of dog is he?

—A friendly dog.

—I mean what breed?

—Well, at the shelter they told us he was half spaniel, half Lab, and half mutt.

K looked at him quizzically. She didn't have a follow-up question.

She walked with as much swagger as the appraiser who had sauntered through the house taking notes to come up with the estimated market value in advance of his divorce.

—A lot of space for one person, she said. But there's hardly any furniture. Pretty bare bones.

—I got sick of it all.

—I don't blame you. Less is more, she said.

When she was done with her inspection, she ignored the couch, sat cross-legged on the living room floor and began rolling a joint. He asked what kind of music she wanted to hear. She said she didn't care, but when he suggested something by Arcade Fire or Radiohead or the Smiths, she said no.

—I'm thinking maybe something by Sleater-Kinney, or anything by Jack White or, wait, I know ... Wild Belle. Yeah, *Giving Up on You* would be cool, she said.

—I don't have any of those, Harold said.

They settled on the Black Keys. He brought out a bottle of Scotch and some glasses, and they took sips between hits off the joint. K marveled at his vast collection of books that lined the shelves surrounding the fireplace.

—I bet you claim you read them all, she said.

—Yes, but that doesn't mean I retained all I read, he said.

They finished the joint and were sitting side by side, contentedly listening to *Psychotic Girl*, when, without any provocation, K stripped off her shirt and slipped out of her jeans. Aside from her shoes, they were the only two articles of clothing she was wearing. She sat before him totally naked. Absolutely nude. There wasn't a follicle of hair anywhere on her body except her head. Her lithe yet luxurious figure looked exactly how he had pictured it. Without the slightest trace of self-consciousness, she stretched out before him like a wild animal. Somehow, naked, she appeared dangerously young. She had the air of an ingénue, like Jean Seberg in *Breathless*.

—How old are you again? he asked.

—I told you before, she said.

—Tell me again.

—Thirty-four, she said. Thirty-five this year. Here....

She dumped her bag upside down, spilling all its many and various contents across the floor.

—My license is in there. She poked at her wallet with her big toe. You can check if you don't believe me.

He checked. She was telling the truth.

After this inquisition, there was some fumbling as they directionally rearranged themselves. The sure sign canoodling was about to commence.

When they kissed, Harold experienced paroxysms of pleasure he hadn't known in years. K's lips were pursed, dry, yet yielding to the touch. The taste of her tongue was delicious. Its texture was smooth and grainy and soft. The warmth of her trembling body pressed against his was divine.

He took her in his arms. His mind was shrieking *no, no, this will end in disaster*, but his body was moving ahead, lusting forward. He pulled off his clothes, and flesh pressed against flesh, and they fell upon each other in a tangle of arms and legs.

Abruptly, K stood up and took him by the hand.

—I like to have sex in a bed when I'm stoned. Let's go to the bedroom, and I'll show you something I learned in a porno movie.

He followed her, watching her sashay down the hall toward the stairs, singing the chorus from The Clash's *Guns of Brixton.*

Somehow, despite his self-doubt, which followed him up the stairs like a malevolent shadow, whether it was the alcohol or the marijuana or her unbridled and uninhibited enthusiasm and encouragement, he managed to pull off a performance at least equal to his pre-cancer days.

⟨∿⟩

Their sexual union a success, they began spending more time together. Toward the middle of the semester, with his financial assistance, K arranged it so that two nights a week she was allowed to leave her son with her grandmother and have a *sleep-away* at his house. She always brought books with her. At various times, she showed up with *Notes from the Underground, Leviathan, The Theatre and Its Double, The Third Body, The Art of War, Either/Or, Ubu Roi, I Love Dick, The Will to Power, The Diary of Che Guevara.* Harold asked her how she made her reading selections. She said she didn't.

—The website picks them. After you purchase a couple of books they show you what other readers read who read the same thing as you. Pretty cool, right?

Harold had no comment.

They would read in bed after sex. When K got tired of reading, she searched the web on her laptop. She often engaged him in a discussion about something that grabbed her interest just as he was trying to go to sleep.

—Listen to this, are you listening?

—No. I'm trying to sleep.

—I'm going to read it anyway.

She would force him into a discussion.

—Nobody seems to know anything anymore, she said one night.

—I'm sure that depends on what you mean by *know*, he said.

—No, it depends on what you mean by a *fact*, she said. Go on the web. On almost every site you visit, in every comment section, someone challenges a fact put forward by someone else, not to mention every so-called *truth* presented by someone. They dispute the evidence. And without evidence you can't know anything.

—No, you can't, he agreed. There's no consensus on what constitutes a reliable source of information anymore. Nor does anyone seem inclined to agree on methods of inquiry that would result in people being able to sift through information and then agree on the *facts*. As far as I can tell, there are no facts anymore, only data.

—That's what I'm talking about. You can't get anybody to agree on anything. Did the Holocaust occur? Did men walk on the moon? Did the CIA blow up the World Trade Center? Is climate change real? Are there Targeted Individuals? Is the New World Order secretly in charge of the government?

—No.

—You say no, but if you look online, plenty of people think the opposite, or they aren't sure, or they think it's likely. It's insane. People come right out and say they have the right to believe at their own risk any hypothesis that tempts them that seems reasonable.

—I think that was William James's thesis,[12] Harold offered.

—Does he have a blog?

—They didn't have blogs back then.

—Well, what I mean is that the lack of belief in facts has made knowing if anything is true impossible.

—Truth does seem to be in short supply, he said. Epistemology has been replaced by Google searches. Which only brings up data aggregated from the web.

—Yeah. That shit keeps me up all night, K claimed. I'm addicted to tracking stuff down. Getting to the bottom of things.

—Except there is no bottom.

—That doesn't stop me from searching.

—Searching is a pleasure because it requires no work. And pleasure under any circumstances is hard to renounce, he said, as he rolled over and tried to sleep.

—I know. I'm a sucker for pleasure. But I'm a nihilist at heart. I want to feel good, and I want everything to disintegrate. I want it to all blow up, so we can start all over. But I don't want to lose you, or my son.

—Thanks.

K kissed him and said:

—See, that's what I love about you. You make me feel smart.

〰

---

12 William James, *The Will to Believe* (New York: Longmans, Green and Co., 1897).

Their conversations went through wild gyrations, sometimes making sense, sometimes veering off into meaningless drivel. Harold didn't care. Here was someone he could talk to about issues and concerns that were near and dear to his heart. And while K held radical beliefs, she also took pleasure in childlike activities, such as running around the house with no clothes on. She was wild and exuberant and excessive and like no one he had ever met, and he loved her for that reason.

〰

It was early November. The leaves had turned colors and hung heavy on the trees, which seemed ready to shed them, tired of carrying their dead weight. Harold spent hours on his bike riding through the surrounding countryside. He rode in the late afternoon, after his class was over, when the temperature had moderated some from the early morning hours and there was less of a chill in the air. After daylight savings time the sun set early. He sometimes stopped riding right as the sun's rays were hitting the leaves at the tops of the trees, gloriously illuminating their multicolored canopies. The wind rushed through them, and they chanted like a chorus.

During these moments, as he stood in contemplation by the side of the road, he was moved by something that was not completely comprehensible. He felt something strange might occur at any moment, maybe a miracle. At any instant he might be enlightened. Someone or something might speak to him.

Nothing happened. The shadows deepened. The cars whizzed by. Twilight caught him off guard, and that transitory unsettling state between light and dark always made him melancholy. So he would head home to shower and call K and she would brighten his spirits.

〰

K went to Connecticut to visit her parents over the Thanksgiving holiday. Jake and Sarah came home. They stayed with Harold. They went to visit Carol twice but didn't volunteer how the visit had gone, and Harold didn't ask.

After graduation, Jake had landed a job working at a startup in Silicon Valley. While home, he spent most of his time texting his girlfriend, who lived in Los Angeles. Sarah, too, had graduated and was working as an intern at a nonprofit foundation in Washington, DC. She was preoccupied with Harold's well-being.

—Why don't you do something that makes you happy?

—Who says I'm not happy?

—Well, you only work part-time. You don't have a girlfriend as far as I can tell. You just hang around the house. And you have to do something with this mail. I mean, it's nutty.

—It's my hobby.

—Why don't you have a girlfriend?

—I go out on dates, he said.

He didn't want to lie. He didn't want to tell the whole truth either, and therefore he declined to specify that the dates were all with the same person. Moreover, though he loved K, he couldn't decide on the exact nature of his love. They saw each other almost every day. He missed her when he wasn't with her. He thought about her all the time, and he felt good when he thought about her. Yet he still wasn't sure how deep his emotions ran, or how committed he was to their relationship. And he didn't want to articulate any of this to his curious daughter.

—Are you dating anybody interesting?

—Absolutely.

—Anybody I should meet?

—No, no. Not yet. I'm still exploring.

—Are you not over her?

—Over who?

—Mom.

—Yes.

—Well then, you have to move on, Sarah admonished. I don't like it that you're by yourself.

—I have Buddy.

—I know you love him, we all do, but he's not a person. You need someone. You should try online dating. There are so many people out there. You can't even imagine. You remember my friend Jessica? Her parents got divorced last year, and her mother met a man online, and they're getting married this spring.

—I don't want to get married again.

—You don't have to marry. You can just meet people.

—I'll consider it.

〰

—We should start a blog, K said one night.

—Why?

—Because, while you come off as being this mild-mannered person, you have a lot of ideas, some of which are pretty radical. I think you might be a badass. I mean, I think I'm pretty badass, and I hate a lot of things, and sometimes I don't even understand why. I'm angry, I guess. You've got reasons for everything.

—I suppose I do. He was noncommittal. And I'm angry, too, Harold admitted.

—We're all angry. A blog will give us an outlet.

—I thought you hated blogs.

—I do. But I like some, she conceded. Anyway, you'll write for it, and I can design it. Maybe I'll write a column too.

—What would you write about?

—I don't know … things I hate.

—That should be easy for you, Harold laughed.

—Maybe, but we have to do it. You told me you wanted to be a writer or an editor or something. This is your chance. I mean, it's not like you've got a million things going on. You've got more time than anybody I know. Now, think of a name.

—A name?

—For the blog. We need a name. What about Castle and Hardscrabble?

—Those are our names.

—We can be like Siskel and Ebert.

—I don't want to be like Siskel and Ebert.

—We can be culture haters. Or culture critics. Or … whatever.

—I don't know, he said.

Then, he blurted out:

—The Apostate.

—The what?

—The Apostate Post.

—What does it mean?

—People who have forsaken their faith.

—Faith in what?

—In everything they were taught to believe in.

—Like a nihilist?

—Yes.

—I like it, she said. It's got religious overtones. See, you can do it. I bet we'll get visits with a name like that.

—Really?

—Sure. It sounds kind of edgy and subversive. I'll buy the name and get going on the design, and you start writing. It'll give you something to do when I'm not here.

—What am I going to write?

—Anything you want.

↜↝

Writing was the last thing on Harold's mind. When he sat down in front of a blank piece of paper, at first all he did was stare at it. Despite all the myriad thoughts that came into his consciousness every day, and the fact that he had, basically, written for a living, he couldn't think of anything to write. It took him days of contemplating before he was able to cobble together some thoughts from tracts he had read in magazines and pulled from the Internet. There was so much rattling around in his head that it took him another week to organize his notes. And then another few days for him to reorganize them and begin to outline something that had some sense of coherence.

What he wrote about was not dissimilar to the ideas he had expressed in his point-of-view papers at his job that had landed him in trouble. However, now that he was free from corporate life he was able to state, in no uncertain terms, his opinions. And once he started writing, he discovered he could continue writing until he couldn't think anymore.

He developed a habit of writing in the morning, editing what he wrote in the afternoon, and revising his edits in the evening. He gave the finished piece to K, who read it out loud:

My Internet Nightmare
The Internet's enslavement of the mind, particularly through social media, is odious. The owners and operators of these media outlets have cloaked themselves in the rhetoric of social righteousness in order to hide this Leviathan's insidious intent. They speak in Orwellian rhetoric. We want to organize the entire world's information. Our mission is to make the world more open and connected. You can make money without doing evil. You can make money by turning chaos into order. They encourage everyone to like them, and they encourage the ones who like them to encourage others to join in liking them. They want their users to share their mission. Like the Messiah, they want followers. Yet these companies have no reason for existence other than to make money from advertising. They are the savviest data gatherers that have appeared on the face of the earth to date. Their tools for identifying you are invisible, but they are watching you as you flit from screen to screen. They know your viewing history and your preferences, your searches, your purchases, your location, your social connections. They know more about you than your employer and your significant other and the government, for whom, in fact, they help gather data. You are perpetually under surveillance. Advertisers are the beneficiaries of the social graph provided by these so-called innovative social innovators. Over one billion people share their experiences and express themselves through one particular network. And each and every one of the users is nothing more than a target for advertisers to home in on and exploit. In fact, the very thing that

is sold as the appeal to the people who participate in these networks—the reach, the relevance, and the social context—is what is sold to advertisers as enhanced opportunities to generate brand awareness and affiliation and the possibility of creating new ways to generate near-term demand for their products from *consumers* likely to have purchase intent.

And there you have it. The C word comes out. Right out of a corporate prospectus of one of these companies. *Consumers.* You, me, your neighbor, *the people*, are not viewed as people. We are consumers in the strategic outlook and balance sheet of these organizations and networks.

These media outlets are totalitarian systems whose sole objective is the manipulation of consumers in the interests of crass corporate commercialism. Everyone knows this. But everyone ignores it and is sucked into the vortex of vapidity that these companies represent. So go ahead: build your standing in the twitterverse. Post all your personal information on your wall. Send your selfies. Share your preferences. Every comment is tracked and its key words logged as metadata. You are tagged and followed as if you were a felon wearing an ankle bracelet. What does it matter? It's the way of the world today. It's the price we have to pay. They say a frog placed in a pot of warm water will not try to jump out immediately, but by the time the temperature becomes hot enough to cook him he has no energy to exit.

—Wow, I knew you had something to say, K said. See, you are a badass. You're my Underground Man.

—The thinking isn't all that original, or radical.

—It's good enough. We just need to get the party started.

—What did you come up with? Harold asked.

—Here, listen:

I hate almost everything. Like shopping. I detest shopping. But sometimes I have to shop. But I can't shop. Because when I walk into a clothing store and see rack upon rack of jackets and coats, shelf after shelf of shoes, and scores of skirts and tables with belts and scarves of every size I can't stay in the store. Even if I need a belt, I can't stay. The overabundance makes me sick. It gives me a headache. The music makes me want to heave.

I walk into a drugstore to buy some ibuprofen. And there is too much of everything in there too: boxes and packages and bottles and cans and jars and containers. I want to vomit. I start reading the descriptions of the ingredients of the painkillers be-cause my head is killing me, but looking down the aisle at all the choices I realize there are more words printed on these packages than all the books in the library. I can't read them all. I'd never get out of the store. I look at the bottles and boxes lining all the shelves, box after box, bottle after bottle, murder-ous Myrmidons arrayed in their self-replenishing rows. And none of them are what I want. I only want one ingredient and they all have more. It's too over-whelming. I get fatigued, exhausted. It's too tiring.

And then because there are so many options star-ing me in the face, taunting me, daring me to pick one, I grab the wrong one. But I don't know it's the wrong one until I get home and realize NO, NO, NO, I didn't want ibuprofen with a decongestant, I only wanted ibuprofen. But the label was so small I couldn't see that there were two ingredients, and the boxes like criminals in a lineup had been insou-ciantly sneering at me, taunting me, and to get it over with I picked one, and it was the wrong fucking one! I hate shopping.

—Sounds just like you, he said.

—Does it sound angry enough?

—I can't tell. It is emphatic. Nice word choices. You must have spent some time with a thesaurus.

—Thanks. Well, I'm going to post them, and we'll see if anyone reads them.

—Do we care?

—That's the whole point, silly. We want comments, so we can build an audience.

~

The blog post received one comment from a reader named ReadytoRoll: *NICE!!!*

—That's how it starts, K said.

—But only one person responded, Harold said, a little disappointed.

—Yes, but more people will read it. What we need is for people to repost it. For now, it doesn't matter. And for this guy, it made a difference. And that's good. It's like the starfish story.

—What story?

—You know, a young guy is walking along a beach on which thousands and thousands of starfish have washed ashore. He sees an old man walking and picking up one starfish after another and tossing them back into the ocean. *Why are you throwing the starfish into the ocean?* the young guy asks. *Because the sun is up and the tide is going out and if I don't throw them in they will die,* the old man says. *You can't possibly save them all. You can't even save a tenth of them. In fact, your effort won't make any difference at all,* the young guy says. The old man listens and then bends down, picks up another starfish and throws it into the sea. *It made a difference to that one,* he says.

—I didn't know you thought about making a difference.

—Well, I think some things should make a difference, like art.

—Is that what we're doing? Art?

—Well, I'd like to think so. I think any time you organize your thoughts in a creative way, that's an attempt at art.

He felt closer to K than he ever had before.

⟨∿⟩

Between his class work and writing for the blog, Harold found himself once again in the world of ideas, a world he hadn't participated in since leaving graduate school. After all the years he had wasted working in a corporation, he thought he was finally moving toward a life that had meaning. He felt he was coming alive.

He worked hard to transmit to his class his enthusiasm about the books he had assigned. He explained the importance of the ideas that were embedded in them. He said all the works he had chosen for the course had protagonists who were lonely displaced souls, people who had walked away from ordinary lives to travel the planet seeking enlightenment and transcendence. These characters dimly understood that we are all spiritual vagabonds doomed to wander under indifferent skies while pondering the meaning of the human condition. They were aware that at any moment they could come face to face with the meaninglessness and absurdity of existence, as did Meursault in *The Stranger*.

⟨∿⟩

—I want to get out of here, K said one night.

—Get out of where?

—Out of New York. Out of this whole East Coast thing.

—And go where?

—California, but Northern California, I think, away from the big cities, but along the coast. I want to see the ocean.

—What will you do?

—I'll find something. Continue going to school. Freelance.

—Sounds kind of sketchy.

—No. It's time for me to move on. My ex is being released from prison soon, and I don't want any contact with him. Why don't you come with me?

—What would I do in California?

—Same thing you're doing here: teach, ride your bike, play chess, write. Come. It'll be an adventure. We'll take a road trip. Road trips are sexy.

—You want to drive out there?

—I'm not flying. I hate flying. Every time I think about flying I hear this big BOOM in my head as the plane disintegrates into a million fragments because of a bomb some idiot sets off. Or I see the plane hurtling toward the ground after sucking some geese into an engine. Or the pilots take it on a joy ride and dump it in the ocean for reasons unknown. I can't stand thinking about it. Why put your life at risk?

—Driving is riskier than flying, he pointed out.

—Maybe.

—And flying takes much less time.

—What difference does time make to us?

—None, I guess.

—Right! You're not doing anything, and neither am I. Don't make me go alone, she pleaded.

—What about your son?

—He'll stay with my grandmother until I get settled, and then he'll join me.

—What about Buddy? I can't leave him.

—Can't he go to a kennel? I mean, if my son can stay with my grandmother, why can't Buddy go to a kennel?

—He's never been to a kennel.

—What did you do with him when you went on family vacations?

—He stayed at my parents'. And my mother passed away, and my father lives in Arizona.

—Well, he could come with us, she said, softening her stance. I don't think he'd like it.

—No, he wouldn't.

—Then put him in a kennel. They have nice ones where they don't keep the animals penned up. He'll be fine. You have to come. I'd be too lonely without you. We can work on the blog while we're on the road.

—I'll have to think about it, he said. Anyway, I can't leave until the semester is over.

—Deal, K said presumptively.

〰

Pondering the implications of accompanying K on her trip, Harold realized that if he went with her, any description of his behavior would most likely include a phrase such as: *He ran off with a student*, or, *he left with a woman he met in his class*. Of course, he wasn't in any sense running away, but the implication would be just that. Moreover, there did seem to be something Humbert-like about taking off on a cross-country jaunt with a woman who was much younger than he was. And that concerned him, since that was what Humbert and Lolita had done. And it hadn't ended well for Humbert.

When he examined K's proposal more closely, however, there didn't seem to be any obvious impropriety about it. K was of age and divorced and he was of age and divorced. Yet while she was of age, she was considerably younger. And while this didn't bother her, he knew that his kids would think it creepy that K was so much younger than he was. Of course, he hadn't revealed anything about K to his kids. Jake never asked him questions about his personal affairs. And while Sarah continually questioned him about his romantic life, he continually prevaricated, if not flat-out lied to her. If he told them what he was thinking about doing, the questions would follow fast and furious. Who was this woman? Why was he going to California? Was he going to come back? Was this a serious relationship?

He didn't want to be interrogated because he didn't know the answers.

He had kept his relationship with K quiet. He had hinted to some of his closer riding friends that he was seeing someone, a woman he had met at school. He didn't give out any details. The little he shared had generated many snide comments. But despite the good-natured ribbing and ongoing probing, he had refused to give up any additional information to anyone, and had lied when necessary to protect his privacy.

He was unhappy that he lied. His inability to talk about K with his kids, or his friends, troubled him. But it was due to his uncertainty about the nature of their relationship, which at first he had assumed would be nothing more than a short-lived fling. Now, after months of dating, it was clear that he and K were serious about each other. Theirs was an uncanny union, but one that brought them both, Harold thought, some sense of serenity and happiness. However, the suddenness with which K had announced her intention to move to California was startling and somewhat scary. He wasn't sure if it was a spontaneous act intended to express her free spirit, or her touch of bipolar speaking out, or some sort of test of his commitment. It unnerved him. In a way, her urge to hit the road was no different from her out-of-nowhere desire to start a blog, a demonstration of her overall approach to living, which was, as she had told him, to do whatever she wanted to do.

⟵∿⟶

Like it or not, Harold had to decide whether or not to accompany K on her trip to California, and he was running out of time. The semester was coming to a close. K had started making preparations and asked him every day if he was preparing to leave. She had mapped out the route and reserved a truck to move her belongings. She said they could make it across the country in five or six days if they drove in shifts. She planned to rent a self-service storage space in the San Francisco Bay Area and dump her furniture and clothes in it. Then she would turn in the truck, rent a car, and take two weeks or so to cruise up the coast, investigating the cities and towns, seeking a place to settle down. He could fly back whenever he wanted, she said.

Harold didn't want to go, and he didn't want K to go. He didn't want anything to interrupt the little world they had built for themselves and in which he felt extremely comfortable. He tried to dissuade her. She remained adamant in her decision.

—I've got to change my life, she said. And a little change wouldn't hurt you either.

He knew if K left and he stayed behind his life would be miserable. The thought of being alone again terrified him. He would never find someone like her again. It was pure dumb luck that had thrown them together in the first place. He was happy when he was with her. He thought: I haven't been this happy in a long time. I really must be in love.

So, after much procrastination, he began looking into kennels for Buddy, and after identifying one he thought satisfactory, he told K he would be ready to leave any time she was. She was ecstatic.

They left town on a Tuesday. The truck K rented had seen better days. It had an uncomfortable bench seat with springs that must have been brutalized over many miles, as they hardly had the strength to support Harold's far-from-bulky body. The air-conditioning produced only moderately chilled air. In no time he began to glisten with moisture, and soon he broke out into a sweat. The cabin stunk of gas and oil and stale French fries from fast-food restaurants. The front wheels had a tendency to wander at the first sign of driver inattention. Despite these shortcomings, K was happy. They were on their way.

The road went on forever. They took turns driving, switching every time they stopped for gas. They flew by farms and fast-food franchises, car dealerships and shopping centers. Big green and white highway signs told of towns Harold had never heard of. There were open fields, cultivated fields, forests of deciduous trees. There was no sense to any of it. Miles and miles and miles of guardrail. They passed through Toledo and Cleveland and Chicago and its endless suburbs. There were more gas stations, fast-food joints, car lots, supermarkets, malls with nationally recognized retailers, clothing stores, liquor stores, hardware stores, card shops, gun shops, shoe stores, drugstores, hair salons, funeral parlors. It looked like someone had strewn the Yellow Pages all over the American countryside. The monotony of it was unbearable.

After a day, they were both road weary. Conversation wore thin. If it weren't for K's phone, which she had spent a week loading with the right music, he would have been terminally bored. K had grouped the songs on her phone together by theme or rhythm or subject or cover artist. She grouped *School Days* with *Another Brick in the Wall*, and *Wonderful World*. She matched *Revolution* with *Volunteers*, *London Calling* with *Gimmie Shelter*. *Baron Saturday* segued into *Monday, Monday* followed by *Friday on My Mind*. And *Life During Wartime* gave way to *Creep*.

—Great classic sets, Harold said. You should have been a DJ.

—My father was a rock-and-roll fanatic. Wait till you hear what's coming up now.

It took him only an instant to recognize Simon and Garfunkel's *All Come to Look for America*.

〰

The truck broke down outside of Grand Island, Nebraska. Since there were no other vehicles available, they had to wait for the necessary part to be ordered and installed. It was going to take a day and a half, they were told. They put up at a seedy motel near the gas station where the repair was being made. Their room was small and shabby. Where the paint wasn't peeling off the walls, mold was eating its way through them. The sink and tub and toilet were stained with rust, and the linoleum on the bathroom floor was curling up at the edges of the walls. The cheap sheets and blankets abraded their skin like sandpaper. Harold was unable to determine whether the unidentifiable odor hanging in the air was from an antiseptic used to clean the room or a toxin used to eliminate vermin.

—It's like that gruesome room Sailor and Lula holed up in while waiting to commit the robbery, K said. Remember, in *Wild at Heart*?

—I do. But the bars on the window remind me more of the room in the final scene of *The Passenger*.

—I never saw that movie. What happens?

—Nothing good.

She gave him a searching look. He didn't elaborate further. Instead he said:

—I should have brought my bike.

—Well, since you don't have it, let's work on the blog. Are you done with your piece?

—No.

—I'm not done with mine either. Let's see if we can finish them and get them posted before we get back on the road.

K sat on the bed and Harold sat on the only chair, and they both wrote. Harold finished his piece first. He read the result of his effort to K:

> I keep thinking about eschatology. I don't know why. Perhaps because I was thinking about climate change because I saw photos of polar bears eating their young since there were no seals for them to catch because the ice cap is melting at an alarming rate, or the fact that water all over the world is being poisoned by chemical runoff from fertilizers

and from the search for and retrieval of hydrocarbons. Which are, by the way, used to make fertilizer. Which is, by the way, extensively used to grow corn, which is, you guessed it, used to fatten the billions of cattle that are slaughtered every year as well as to manufacture the corn syrup that is added to almost all fast-food products that have made more than a third of Americans obese.

I think it is only human to worry about the end of time, whatever that means. I know that time doesn't end. Nothing can happen to time. Nevertheless, I will speak of the end of time, our time. And this is what will happen: Machines will rule the earth. Humans will cease to exist. The teleological end of mankind is machines. It's that simple. And why should it be any other way? Why should the sentient, conscious animals that we are have any say at the end of time? Why should animals like us, who eat other animals, continue to be at the top of the so-called food chain? Why should there be a food chain? Why should animals that join genitals to reproduce and who continue to destroy the earth, rule the earth? That's the question the Doors asked in *When the Music's Over*:

What have they done to the earth?
What have they done to our fair sister?
Ravaged and plundered and ripped her and bit her
Stuck her with knives in the side of the dawn
And tied her with fences
And dragged her down....

I couldn't have said it better myself. From the moment the first blade of a plow cut our fair sister and the ground was seeded, the devastation began. People multiplied. Populations exploded. The bounty of the earth was exploited recklessly, unabashedly, continuously, backed by religious and political ideology. Populations grew ever more adept at multiplying and exploiting the resources needed to keep themselves alive. Our so-called biological imperative to multiply has kept us busy for our entire history on this planet. There are now more than seven billion of us competing for ever scarcer resources to keep us alive. We created machines to help us with our labor, to do what men no longer want to do. We now have machines that can do what men do better than men. Drones drop bombs. Robots build cars and perform operations on humans. Observant software allows for the detection of our health or emotional state from our facial expression. Machines are becoming more and more intelligent.

The techno-optimists see this as a positive step forward in the advance of mankind. The evolution of faster, more intelligent computers and smaller and smaller central processing units will speed up the process of producing self-replicating machines, increase our productivity, and enhance our well-being. The day machines can fully reproduce themselves from raw materials without any help from us will mark the beginning of the end for humans. The machines' first order of business will be to assure their continued reproduction and domination of their environment, just as it was ours. We will be in the way. They will need the same resources that we need to reproduce ourselves, and they will crush all attempts to thwart their advance. They will be stronger and smarter and will gradually oversee our final dissolution back into the organic morass out of which we crawled. They will capture what we call our self-consciousness and evolve it into a shared consciousness that will culminate in an etherealized so-called *mind* distributed over a network of servers that run the machines that will occupy and dominate the earth.

This is the singularity, the idea derived from Schopenhauer,[13] who thought that individual consciousness was only a temporary state of being and that death would release us back to unity with the blind, unconscious will that was the infinitely

---

13 Arthur Schopenhauer, *The World as Will and Representation* (translated by E. F. J. Payne, New York: Dover Publications, Inc., 1966).

creative essence of all existence. The singularity purports that the spark of spirit in a mortal body that makes humans unique and different from the Other will in the future be software uploaded into the cloud. Humans will no longer serve any useful purpose. Or any purpose at all. Humans, we whose essence has been held to be a noncorporeal spark of consciousness in a corporeal body, will disappear into the mists of time. Machines will rule. Humans will vanish. For, why are we here? Simply to increase the order of the world, to extend our knowledge, to provide higher information that fits a purpose? A purpose? I don't think so.

—How do you come up with this shit? I don't know what *eschatology* means, but I think I totally agree. Now we have to listen to the Doors.

—Thanks.

—Did you come up with something? Harold asked.

—Yes. It's nothing like yours. I can't write that much. But here it is:

I hate clutter. I hate the mess in my life and in yours. The accumulated piles of shit we make everywhere we go are disgusting. I look through my neighbors' windows at twilight and see sticky reminder notes on their refrigerators and magnets holding down lists and shopping receipts and laundry tickets and pay stubs and tables covered with old newspapers and stupid snapshots and recipes that never get made and bills that need to be paid. I think: fuck that. I hate keeping track of things. Calendars with daily boxes crossed off make me sick. I go to people's houses and only see the mountains of stuff. Gee-gaws and knickknacks and stuffed animals and shelves stuffed with tchotchkes make me want to puke. Closets filled with clothes and shoes make me think of overabundance, which, as you may re-member, is something else I hate. Everyone is a secret hoarder. Saving stupid things they think they need or can't bear to part with. Then because they don't throw something out it becomes valuable. Protected from the trash. Elevated to the status of a household god that gets worshipped and cleaned and left in its place along with all the other worthless tokens of existence. Domesticity is depressing. I would burn down my house if I didn't have to live in it.

—Wow, said Harold. He was now convinced more than ever that K shared the same sense of awe at the nothingness that surrounded them. I like it, he said.

↞↠

—Look! This time we got a bunch of comments, K said the next day. These have to do with your post.

She read them to him:

—STILLADOPE: *Everybody already knows this you bozo ... We are already automatons fed our instructions by all the electronic gadgets we carry around with us.... * GENESIS1: *The bible says men are masters over every living thing. That means over animals, so we can't be animals.... We are divine.* STILLROCKIN: *Jim Morrison was a genius, you're not.* ISPY: *L Ron Hubbard predicted the same apocalypse....* SAVOIRFAIRE: *You don't mean Ron Hubbard you moron, you mean Joseph Smith. He said people were the spirit-children of god, not animals ... Animals are for eating....* OMG: *You're confused. The Elohim came first and scientifically engineered all the life forms on this earth.* KNOWITALL: *You're wrong. All this is just a remix of Lanier, nothing new here ... boooring.* DODONA: *With a mix of Nostradamus.* ROCKETMAN: *In 1957 a space ship landed in Area 51 and aliens were released in pods and have been infiltrating the human race ever since, encouraging the mixture of races and diminishing the differences between them so soon everyone will be the* *same and when no one can tell the difference between anyone there will be peace on earth and everyone will disarm and then the aliens will return and crush us.... IAMACAMERA: Get your facts right, the spaceship landed in 1953. I have a picture....*

—It goes on. Isn't it amazing, said K, I mean, the way people interpret things.

—It's a little frightening.

What's being said about your post?

—Here.

K read:

—FRUSTRATED: *I know exactly what you mean. I have to keep myself away from the matches and the gas every day. BIG-MAMA: You go girl. WOMAN2: Anything you save becomes a memory, like a picture, objects are worth a thousand words. You can't just throw stuff out. THEBOSS: This woman is obviously bitter and has little empathy for others. HOME1MAKER: If I see anyone staring through my windows I call the police. Everyone is entitled to privacy even in our overexposed world.*

—Fascinating, Harold said.

〜

Now the countryside was empty and flat and endless. They drove for hours, stopping only to use a bathroom, buy nourishment, or fill the truck with gas.

—I need a real meal, K declared. I can't eat anymore junk food or energy bars.

—We'll stop then, Harold said.

It was three in the morning. They were on an empty stretch of Route 80, somewhere between North Platt, Nebraska, and Cheyenne, Wyoming. A billboard advertised Big Ben's: *Dining the Way You Like It*, at the next exit. Fifty miles later, Harold got off the highway and onto a secondary road. Two miles later he pulled into Big Ben's parking lot, which was jam packed with eighteen-wheel semitrailers and pickup trucks.

As soon as they passed through the doors, Harold realized the place was vast, as big as a suburban supermarket. They were in the middle of nowhere, yet the restaurant was bustling with business. Country music was blaring through speakers suspended from the ceiling. There were booths full of people at all the windows. Miles of counter space and stools coiled around the interior of the diner like a giant intestine. Tables filled the spaces between the counters. The atmosphere was cacophonous. The flurry of activity and the intensity of the sound made it seem like they were walking into a riot. As they headed toward the desk, where a sign asked them to please wait to be seated, a hostess greeted them and steered them to a booth. Harold excused himself to go to the bathroom and asked K to order for him.

The bathroom was as busy as the dining room. Every stall was occupied and every urinal taken. Men were washing up at the sink. Others stood before the floor-to-ceiling mirror and raked combs through greasy hair. Everyone was in jeans and T-shirts and cowboy boots.

Harold took his turn at a urinal, then washed his hands and face. Heading back out to the dining room, he ran into something solid and unyielding. Still dazzled from having been behind the wheel of the truck for so long, he at first thought he'd walked into the bathroom door, or the wall, but he was pushed violently backward and verbally reprimanded.

—Watch where you're goin', mothafucker, a man's gruff voice commanded.

Bewildered, Harold didn't answer.

—Asshole, the man yelled at Harold, giving him the finger.

K was halfway through her scrambled eggs and was working on her French fries by the time he sat down. She had a pile of ketchup on her plate and was dipping her fries in it, using them like a spoon to scoop up as much ketchup as she could before she shoved them in her mouth. She was eating with great gusto.

—You won't believe what just happened to me, Harold said.

—Maybe not. First, let me ask you something. Do you think there's a difference between the type of person who eats one French fry at a time, chewing it up completely and swallowing it before taking another one, and the type of person who keeps shoveling them into their mouth one after another and chewing, chewing, chewing?

—Isn't that the difference between a glutton and a gourmand?

—What do you mean?

—Well, a glutton is a gulper, a greedy eater who shovels in the food without regard to its sensuous nature, and has little self-control. And a gourmand extracts all the flavors and textural changes of the food as it's slowly consumed, savoring every sensation for as long as possible.

—So they're both hedonists. They just go about it differently?

—I guess that's one way of looking at it.

—Because I was worried that I'm a little of each, depending on my mood, she said, wiping up the last of the ketchup with a forkful of egg. By the way, the food's okay, she said. Not too greasy. Now, what happened to you?

—This guy bumped into me and then gave me the finger.

—Yeah, it seems like that kind of place. The waitress said this is the biggest truck stop this side of the Rockies.

After coffee and some pecan pie to satisfy their longing for a sweet, Harold paid and they hustled back to the truck. There was a group of men leaning against the side of a van parked next to their vehicle. Each man was bigger than the next, and they were all drunk or drugged or both. As he fished out the keys, one of them pointed to him and said he was the one who hadn't apologized after bumping into him in the bathroom. Harold ignored him and kept walking toward the truck. The man and his friends formed a semicircle around him. Up close and personal, his accuser was keen to learn what his hurry was.

—We just want to get back on the road, Harold explained.

—Why don't you back off so we can get out of here? K interjected.

The man didn't back off. He insisted Harold first be taught some manners.

The situation rapidly deteriorated. Harold tried to push his way past the lummox blocking his path, intending to get to the truck, but he was shoved backward. K intervened and pushed the brute. Someone grabbed her by the hair and threw her to the ground.

—Outta the way, bitch, someone said.

Harold threw his hands up to try to protect himself from the fist he saw coming. It was too late. His head flew backward from the force of the punch before he had time to think. Then a knee came rushing into his groin.

K jumped up and onto the back of the man who punched Harold and dug her nails into his eyes. He began screaming in pain. K was yelling:

—I'll rip your face off, you motherfucker. You piece of shit.

Harold punched the man in the thorax, and he started choking and buckled and fell to the ground with K on top of him. Then the crowd closed in and someone pulled K off and threw her against a car and began slapping her. Harold rushed to help her.

—Leave her the fuck alone, he screamed. Before he could come to her assistance, several of the men grabbed him. He knocked one of them down. Then another one punched him a few times. He fell limp to the ground. He heard K screaming as a few of them continued to kick him.

K's screams brought help, and the men shuffled off, apparently satisfied with their work.

—Local boys, one of the bystanders offered by way of explanation.

One of the people who had gathered to watch the scuffle said they should call the cops.

—No, no cops. We don't want the cops, K said. She explained that they needed to get back on the road. If the cops came, they would get caught up with them and be forced to file a useless report that wouldn't lead to anything. They climbed in the truck and hit the road.

They were both moaning in pain. K said:

—We just got beat up in a parking lot in the middle of fucking nowhere. Wow, wow, wow....

She was hyperventilating and moaning simultaneously.

—Are you okay? Harold asked.

—I don't know. I don't know. How are you?

—I don't know either.

—Well, the main thing is, we fought back, she said. We didn't give in.

—We didn't, he assented. But there were too many of them for us to win.

—You don't have to win. But you do have to fight. You have to fight back. You have to fight. You always have to fight. And we did. We're fighters, she said. That's the main thing. We're fighters, K repeated.

Then K began to cry, and soon the crying gave way to sobbing.

He comforted her, putting his arm around her shoulder, pulling her in next to him. His ribs were killing him. He had trouble controlling the truck.

K was badly scraped up. The side of her face that had hit the pavement was abraded and red with dried blood.

—I think we need to stop and clean up, he said.

—I can't move. I need painkillers, K said.

Harold pulled into the first open gas station. He tried to coax K out of the truck. After inspecting herself in the side mirror, she said she looked too horrible to be seen in public.

In the bathroom, standing at the urinal, Harold began to pee, leaning against the cold chrome flush mechanism of the urinal with one hand for support. He punched the wall. Everything was so arbitrary and absurd. He felt dizzy. His body ached all over. He couldn't think straight.

He looked at himself in the mirror. He was a bloody mess. A massive headache was coming on, or maybe it was a stroke that was making him dizzy and nauseous.

He thought he might faint. He gripped the sink for support. He wished he could climb into bed and sleep for twenty-four hours. He was in agony.

To wake himself up he washed his face with cold tap water. At the counter inside the station he bought five packets of ibuprofen, two packs of Lorna Doones and a couple of Cokes.

Back in the driver's seat, he helped K clean herself up with some antiseptic wipes she had in her backpack. They both downed the pills, ate the cookies and washed it all down with Coke. Then they set back out on the road.

—We came all this way to get beat up in a parking lot, he said. It's crazy.

—America's a crazy place. Anything can happen, K said.

—It's so odd the things that do. I mean, of all the things that might have happened, this happened.

—I guess none of this would have happened if we had taken a plane, K pointed out. She smiled at him wanly. I'm sorry, baby.

—Don't be sorry.

—But if we'd taken a plane, we wouldn't have had much of an adventure, K said.

Harold couldn't keep himself from smiling.

—I love you, K said.

—I love you, too, he said.

He stroked her face affectionately, and she fell asleep.

Roaring down the highway, Harold could barely see, his eye was so swollen. A rib must be broken, he guessed, from the acute pain he felt every time he breathed. On the radio, Bruce was singing *Born to Run* of all things, and at every chord shift Harold punched the accelerator harder and kept going and going, becoming ever more perturbed as he thought about the events that had transpired. Had he come all this way to be a victim of gratuitous violence? Was it the case that in every chance encounter an act of aggression was lurking beneath the surface? What about acts of kindness? How had it come about that the code of civility that governed social intercourse could be suspended at a moment's notice?

He tried to further analyze this social aberration, but he was in too much pain to think. K was sleeping, snoring slightly, her head lolling back and forth as the truck rolled over potholes and cracks in the road.

Dawn was under way. The sky was blackish purple. In the side mirror, he saw the bottoms of the clouds begin to absorb the light thrown up at them from beyond the eastern horizon. Soon, the sky turned to indigo and then to a limpid blue. It was streaked with soft, white, flat clouds. They crossed the Continental Divide and Harold thought he could sense a change in the grade of the road as it began to descend. The horizon in front of him was filling with the dawn's first light, growing larger and expanding and drawing him into it.

⟲⟳

No sooner did they arrive in San Francisco than Harold received a text from the boarding kennel. Buddy was depressed and not eating. The kennel owner told him he should come retrieve his pet, if he could. There's no sense in torturing the old boy, he was told.

He informed K he had to return to New York. She was distraught. She tried to convince him to stay, but he explained he had to leave and rescue Buddy. He couldn't let him continue to suffer.

—I understand, she said.

At the airport, K pulled him to her and hugged him hard. They kissed a long, gentle kiss. She stroked his face and stared into his eyes.

—We've come so far together, she said. We've been through a lot. We could make a go of it, the two of us.

—I think so, too.

—You need someone like me. I need someone like you.

—You're right, he said, trying to keep the tone of their farewell light, although he felt at any moment he might tear up.

—We have to keep writing. You have to keep sending me stuff, and I'll keep writing too.

—I will, he promised.

—You have to come back. We have to be together. I love you.

—And I love you.

He hugged her and held her close, and then they kissed again, and when he let her go she turned and walked away, waving over her shoulder.

〜

Upon arriving in New York, Harold went directly to the boarding kennel. He was shocked at Buddy's appearance. He had lost weight, and his muzzle had grayed.

—It was wise to come back. He wasn't doing well. When they get old like this they don't handle change well, the owner of the kennel told him. It stresses them out. But he should respond to your love and care.

Harold was overcome by guilt. After thirteen years of never having been in a strange environment, being placed in a kennel and left in the care of strangers must have seemed like cruel and unusual punishment to his canine companion.

Back home, Buddy wouldn't let Harold out of his sight. Whenever Harold kneeled down next to him, to nuzzle his face against Buddy's, his pet would emit a low murmur like a cat's purr, replete with sighs of relief and contentment. He interpreted this as a sign he had been forgiven.

〰

Harold's side was still killing him. He was unable to move without pain. His face was still swollen with contusions. Sleep was nearly impossible. He went to see his doctor. An X-ray confirmed that two of his ribs were fractured. His doctor said the best thing to do was rest. He put a butterfly bandage on one of the lacerations by his left eye to keep it from scarring. Then he ushered him into his private office and told him to wait.

Harold settled into a leather-covered smoking chair next to the doctor's old oak desk. The walls of the office were lined with shelves that held medical books and journals. Comfortably ensconced in this quiet space, Harold felt becalmed but weary. This same sensation had overcome him when Doctor Pavani told him the cells in his prostate were running wild and that he had cancer. He had gotten distracted by the photograph of the doctor's family at the beach and hadn't paid attention to what the doctor was telling him about the sequelae of his prostatectomy. This same sensation had occurred in his lawyer's office during his divorce. Surrounded by volumes of law books and mesmerized by the murmur of the HVAC system, he had slipped into a reverie and couldn't focus on the explanation of the proposed terms of his settlement. He had agreed to everything without a fight. In these situations, when he had turned his life over to the care of experts, his will weakened and his defenses dropped and he subsided into docility. His life was out of his control and he could neither fight nor flee. It was, he theorized, why a small animal froze in its tracks at the sight of a large predator.

When the doctor came in, Harold mentioned he had been swallowing handfuls of ibuprofen for the pain. His doctor told him to stop or he would develop an ulcer. He gave him a prescription for a painkiller. Riding his bike was out of the question for the next couple of weeks, he said.

—And keep putting ice on that eye to take down the swelling, he advised.

↜↝

While going through the pile of mail that had accumulated during his absence, Harold found several surprises. First, there was a letter from the IRS notifying him that due to an error in his filing dating back several years, he owed thousands of dollars in additional taxes, penalties, and interest.

Then he opened an envelope that stated in bold letters: **important information concerning your credit**. Inside was a letter from a credit bureau. The bureau was demanding payment for an unpaid hospital bill dating back to the time he had his prostate removed. Apparently, his insurance provider had covered only a portion of the bill, and he was responsible for the difference. The letter stated that the hospital had sent several notices informing him he still had a balance on his account and because he had not responded, the hospital had turned the account over to the credit bureau. The letter went on to say: *Previous attempts to collect the balance of this invoice have been ignored. If payment in full is not received in this office within (10) days, we may take more serious action to settle this account, including referral to a credit bureau. *This is your final notice.**

Harold began searching through his stacks of mail to try to find the previous attempts the hospital had made to contact him. After days of sorting and restacking mail he located such a letter. It had been delivered over a year ago, to judge by the postmark. And he must have read it since it was opened. It did advise him that even after all the fees his insurance policy had paid to the hospital, there was a balance on his account that he was expected to pay.

He then recollected calling the hospital to discuss the matter and being told the invoice was based on a coding error and the amount due would be cleared off his account. He was instructed to ignore the invoice. He had written the name of the service representative who told him this on the letter, along with the representative's telephone number and extension.

Harold called the hospital again. The service representative he had spoken to was no longer there. The new service representative informed Harold that, yes, the previous service representative had resubmitted the claim to the insurance company. However, the insurance company had denied further payment based on the way the hospital had coded the original claim. They maintained they had disbursed as much money as they were required under the policy.

None of this made any sense to Harold. But upon further investigation, in a subsequent conversation with a supervisor, it turned out that while the original claim had been miscoded by the hospital, instead of rectifying the error and resubmitting the paperwork to the insurance company, or accepting the loss of revenue, a billing adjudicator at the hospital had arbitrarily shifted the cost burden to Harold. Hence the invoice. Because he had previously been told to ignore the invoice, he hadn't responded to the other notices sent to him, and because he hadn't responded, the hospital had turned the account over to the credit bureau.

Harold called the credit bureau to explain what had occurred. *We don't accept explanations*, he was told, only credit cards and checks.

While the threat from the credit bureau was upsetting, the letter from the IRS was more menacing since the IRS was a branch of the government with nearly unchecked power. It turned out the IRS was demanding payment—the principle, the penalty, and the interest—for a transaction involving an IRA that was supposed to have been rolled over at the time of his divorce. According to the IRS, they had previously contacted him about this matter, which was not yet resolved. He called the accountant he and Carol had used at the time to seek further clarification. The accountant had retired and moved to Florida. His files had been boxed and sent to storage, and he had no way of easily accessing them or guaranteeing he still had them.

Harold called Carol. Yes, she had taken the duplicate copy of their return for that year with her. But when she moved into her new condo, somehow the box containing many of her personal things, including copies of their tax returns, went missing. She had no interest in helping him split the bill because, as she reminded him, the IRA in question was his, the notice from the IRS had come to him, and the house was in his name.

Harold called the IRS. A recording informed him they were experiencing an extremely high call volume. He was advised to call back later. Then the phone went dead.

After ten days of calling, he managed to reach someone. The person was friendly enough. He informed Harold that unfortunately he was not the right person to investigate his case. He was kind enough to transfer him to the right department, and Harold was assured by an automated voice that he would be connected to the next available representative in that department in the order in which his call had been received. He waited patiently for twenty minutes, and then the connection, after a series of clicks, crackles, and beeps, self-destructed.

Harold wrote a letter explaining the particulars of his case and sent it by certified mail to the address the IRS had supplied.

⟨∿⟩

Not able to ride due to his fractured ribs, Harold passed the time playing chess. He raised his USCF ranking to slightly over twelve hundred. Yet he still somehow managed to lose *won* games, games in which he had a clear positional or material advantage, by frittering away that advantage. Sometimes he was mated in the back rank because he had not pushed forward a pawn several moves earlier, a heartbreaking blunder. More frustrating was achieving a winning advantage and knowing he had the advantage but not knowing how to exploit it. When he played against the computer or listened to the commentary by a grand master as he dissected a famous game, there was always one move that was the most accurate for the position. During some of his games, he sat staring at the pieces on the spaces on the board, paralyzed while the clock was running, lamenting his lack of knowing which move to make. Thus, sometimes he studied rather than played. Using the computer and a book of famous games, he worked out by trial and error different options to thorny strategic problems, hoping to be able to recognize the patterns while he played.

At night he took an oxycodone, washed it down with Scotch, and melted into the couch. Buddy crawled up beside him, and Harold patted his head and scratched behind his ears as they sat staring at the television. He kept the bottle of Scotch near him so he could replenish his glass at will. He and K texted back and forth. During commercials, he surfed the web on his laptop. He watched news feeds or quick videos on chess openings. Sooner or later he succumbed to the distractions in the sidebars or popup news items. The stupid rhetorical questions pulled him in. Did he want to see a killer picture of Scarlett Johansson? Well, yes, yes, he did. He loved Scarlett Johansson.

He knew he was wasting his time, but he couldn't help himself, especially after a Scotch or two. So, he would click on the link, and that's when the self-loathing started. Immediately a luscious picture of Scarlett came up on his screen for his viewing pleasure, framed by ads for travel, bicycles, and insurance. Want to see nude photos of Scarlett Johansson? Well, yes, he had to see those, too. Who wouldn't want to see those?

He clicked, his hormones now agitated in anticipation. He knew he was pathetic, and that at the same time he was trying to satisfy his prurient interest, advertisers were simultaneously trying to satisfy their commercial interests. But every time he clicked on a link a little more adrenaline was released into his system, a few more endorphins kicked in, and his desire for what he was chasing became more and more inflamed. The thrill of the chase overcame him, and he couldn't abandon it without experiencing some of what he wanted. He clicked on *see Scarlett Johansson naked*. It was clickbait. There weren't any photos of her, just the same ads for travel, bicycles, and insurance.

Click here for more photos. He clicked again. Same thing. More ads, but she wasn't there. He had been duped again. But here, look, here was an almost nude photo of her. He clicked. More clickbait. She was fully clothed, only showing some cleavage. Now his self-disgust was overwhelming. He was feverishly following one link to another, each of which had been chosen for him by a set of algorithms that ratted him out every time he clicked. *If you like Scarlett, you should see who we've got on these links: Jennifer Aniston and Julia Louis-Dreyfus nude!*

It took every bit of willpower he had to keep from clicking. He had to close the computer. The entire set of actions was nothing more than a scheme to keep him in the hunt as long as possible until he was finally tricked into clicking on an ad as a substitute for the quarry he had been chasing. Which would remain perpetually out of his reach. Nude photos of Scarlett online would forever elude him, just as if he tried to approach her on the street she would disappear behind a scrim of bodyguards and handlers who would push him away with disdain. He disgusted himself as he imagined these actresses would be disgusted with him if they knew he had clicked on their images, trying to ogle their naked bodies.

〜

Sarah came home unexpectedly for a weekend visit. Harold's bruises hadn't completely healed.

—Oh my god, what happened to you? she demanded to know.

Not wanting to divulge any information about K, he had lied to his daughter about the reason for his recent absence from home. He had told her he was going to a cycling training camp in Colorado. He said his bruises were from falling off his bike.

—How does your face get so messed up falling off a bike? Sarah was curious.

—You hit the ground, he explained.

—You have two black eyes.

—Only one is black. The other one is scraped.

—You have to stop, Sarah said. It's too dangerous.

—Stick to chess, Jake said when he was told.

Harold was touched by their concern. He felt guilty about lying to them. And blaming cycling wasn't smart since from the time he had taken it up they had never been fans of the sport. After his first few minor mishaps, they recognized, as did he, its inherent dangers. And despite the fact that cycling kept him in fine physical shape, they had always condemned it. Now they were more adamant than ever that he cease and desist. He wasn't getting any younger, they pointed out. Which meant his reaction times weren't what they used to be, which in and of itself created a hazard for him. If he loved cycling that much he should take spin classes. They would give him the same amount of exercise without the risk of suffering a debilitating accident, or worse.

It was a reasonable request, and he said he would consider it. But he had no intention of giving up cycling out of doors.

There was no way he was going to relinquish that pleasure to sit on a stationary bike pedaling his heart out and going nowhere in the confines of a safe, dark room. Spinning was exercise, cycling was sport. Sport was adventure. And adventure meant not knowing what was going to occur in any given situation, as he now knew well. The unknown and the unexpected were part of every cycling outing. Implicit in this was the danger that loomed at every turn, and although he would not admit it to his children, this was also part of the attraction. Every ride was potentially your last ride.

—You need something else to distract you, Sarah said. You need a girlfriend.

—Why?

—Because you need someone in your life. It's not good to be alone. You should start seeing somebody. It's time.

—I have you and your brother.

—That's not what I mean, and you know it. You need to go on a dating website and find someone.

—I don't want to.

—How else will you meet someone?

—I don't want to meet someone.

—Yes, you do. Everyone does.

The summer was coming to a close. Harold spent his afternoons sunbathing, reading and writing on the deck. Buddy curled up under the chaise lounge to avoid the sun. The light and the heat produced an insular cocoon that engulfed him and lulled him into a stupor. He couldn't tell if he was asleep or awake or in a dream. He felt transcendent lying out on the deck with the blue jays cawing and the squirrels chattering and the perfume from the wild roses wafting over him. It reminded him of the times he used to visit his grandparents as a child and lie out naked on the rocks by the lake, sensing the connection between himself and all things in the universe. He wanted nothing more than to be enraptured and stay in this close communion with the warm breeze, the hot sun, the blue sky, the white clouds floating overhead. He no longer knew what he was doing with his life, nor what he should be doing, but in the light and heat he felt ebullient rather than anxious. This was all he needed. There was nothing more. Everything else was arbitrary and temporary and false.

〜

K called right after Labor Day to tell Harold she had settled in Bodega Bay, the town in which Hitchcock had filmed *The Birds*.

—It's a beautiful little town, she said.

She and her son were living in a small rental house. She had a view of the Pacific Ocean from her front window.

—The sunsets are ethereal, not to be believed, she said.

The coast, the inland hills and vineyards were spectacular, she said. It was a cyclist's dream. The beauty had inspired her to take up painting again, which had been her intended major in college. She was an artist, after all.

—What are you painting? Harold asked.

—Sunsets. Big color field blocks in the style of Rothko, she elaborated. You have to see them. You have to come. You'll love it here. I miss you.

—I miss you, too.

—Then come.

—I can't right now.

—Is it because of my son? He won't bother you. He doesn't bother me. He's a great little guy. He's very self-sufficient. And he doesn't need a father if that's what you're worried about. He needs an education.

—Your son isn't the issue. I can't leave. I've got some problems with the government, among others.

—Don't fuck with them. When my ex got busted I tried to fight them to keep the house, and they took it and all my money. I'm telling you, I fought the law and the law won.

—Didn't we listen to a song with that name in the truck?

—Yes, by the Bobby Fuller Four. The Clash also covered it. But that's what will happen to you if you try to fight them. They'll win.

—I'm trying to set things right. There's also this credit bureau harassing me.

—Get the fuck out of there and come here. Don't you miss me?

—I do, he said. I really do.

—Okay, then come. In the meantime, we have to keep writing for the blog, she said, switching subjects. We have to keep it fresh. If we keep it up, we can monetize it.

—Monetize it?

—Yes, make money. The only way to make money is to have visitors, she said.

—Our visitors don't like us.

—So what? Some of them do. Over time we'll build up an audience. Then other people will link to us, and when we get enough traffic, advertisers will pay to be on our site.

—I know how it works, Harold said.

—Well, that's how we'll make money. We need to make money, right?

—Yes.

—So get busy.

✺

Despite his doubts that they would make money from the blog, Harold did have a lot of time on his hands. When he got bored, he sat on his deck with his laptop and tried to come up with topics to write about. Much of what he sketched out was based on leftover musings from notes he had made during his working days. He quickly abandoned it. Seeking more stimulus, he sought out his decades-old college course notebooks that were packed away in a box in his closet. He read through his essays and term papers. He found the beginning of a critique of *The Port Huron Statement*. He came across a list of philosophical questions he had never had the time to attempt to answer. He took notes on his notes. He consulted textbooks and dug up the primary sources they referred to.

Finally, he began to write. It wasn't easy for him to find his voice or the right voice for what he wanted to say, but the act of writing was intellectually stimulating in and of itself, and the pleasure it produced was palpable. It cheered him and, importantly, distracted him from the loneliness he felt now that K was no longer with him. When he finished the piece, he sent it to K.

> I sometimes wonder how anyone can lay claim to having a mind of his or her own. I mean, how do we truly know anything about ourselves? Have you

ever *really* thought about yourself? Have you written yourself down? Can you sum yourself up? Who are you? No more than the trivial phrases included on your wall on Facebook? What comprises your personality? Mine? I don't know.

I figured I might feel better if I got to know myself better. So I had a dialogue with myself. I said to myself: Isn't it true that no matter how hard I try to adhere to the Socratic dictum to *know thyself*, the socioeconomic and cultural milieu I belong to will prejudice and predetermine my analysis? And won't *any* analysis be further compromised by the limitations of the universal Kantian categories that make thinking possible while simultaneously making it impossible to know the thing *itself*? Which in this case is *myself*.

Language and its metaphors generate a self-perpetuating aura that hovers over all our speech acts and creates the appearance of freedom while keeping us imprisoned within the rhetoric we use to communicate. Therefore regardless of how acutely aware of this we become, our awareness will not lead us to freedom, or to a cathartic liberation of self, and will not create us as an individual, nor place us outside the system, but will only, at best, put us in another shared category, ad nauseam, ad infinitum. Is there no escape? Is freedom possible? What do we do? Can we ever achieve self-knowledge? Who am I? Who are you?

—I didn't think anyone could ask that many questions. This is heavy stuff. Do you know what it means? K asked.

—I think so.

—It's really good. I mean it. I think you missed your calling. You should have been a philosopher or something.

—Maybe that's what I am, he said, it's just been repressed all these years. Did you write anything?

—Nothing as deep as yours. It's more topical. Here:

> I hate green. Every time I see something with a green recyclable logo, I get pissed. This is another scam for corporations to make more money and take more control over my life. *Please consider the environment before printing.* Why? If I don't print it, I don't have a record. If everything in my life remains digital, I'm shit out of luck if anything goes wrong. Anything stored on the cloud belongs to the owners of the data centers where it's stored because, come on, folks. There is no cloud. That's just language to confuse you.
>
> Everything is stored somewhere, someplace, and if it's not on your computer and you didn't print it or download it and you rent space on the so-called cloud and miss a payment, your access is gone. I say, print everything. The only way to sustain yourself is to ignore digitalization. Without paper, without hard-copy evidence or documentation, who are you? Just another dispossessed person. People without papers are vulnerable. Ready to become victims of the system. Don't let anyone bully you into giving up your hard copies. Hit the print button now.

—Nice.

—Thanks. But I may not contribute much more in writing. I'm going back to painting full-time. You're going to have to carry on alone. So, keep it coming.

〰

Encouraged by K's enthusiasm, Harold tried to organize his thoughts for his next blog entry, but he became increasingly preoccupied by his interactions with the IRS—which were going nowhere. Every time he called he was put on hold, sometimes for as long as fifty minutes. When, and if, an agent came on the line, he or she was sure to say they knew nothing about his case. They transferred him to a different person who, they claimed, would be able to help him. He would be put on hold again, and he would hold and wait and eventually the hold would time out and he would be disconnected, having accomplished nothing.

Then one day he received a letter that gave him hope of resolving his case because it gave him someone's name. He was to contact Mr. Larry Curt between the hours of 3:00 p.m. and 7:30 p.m. if he had any questions or required further information. A telephone number was provided. This was great because Harold believed if he could talk someone through the facts of his case, it would be clear he had done no wrong. However, when he called, a machine answered and informed him that the answering system for Mr. Curt was full and could handle no further messages. Call back at a later date, it said.

He called back at a later date and the phone rang a couple of times. His hopes were raised because he wasn't shunted off into voice mail. The phone rang and rang and rang, and as he waited for Mr. Curt to pick up, Harold imagined him sitting in his cubicle, slouched in his chair, surrounded by other bureaucrats who were also methodically fulfilling the state's duties. Mr. Curt wasn't answering him because he was on the phone blathering away to some other poor sap who was also caught up in the system. His government-issue metal desk dated back to the seventies and was gunmetal gray and paired with a short-backed, heavy metal chair with padded armrests with cracks marbled in them, small fissures like the ones on overdone hard-boiled eggs. He was surrounded by piles of tax returns and manila folders and letters and white Styrofoam coffee cups with dregs of curdled milk at the bottom. Mr. Curt was talking to someone, explaining the law of the land, staring at the flashing light on his other line, the line on which Harold was calling, hypnotized by the steady, insistent, recurrent, flashing reminder that he had another caller, the same way Harold was hypnotized by the steady, insistent, ringing in his ears because Mr. Curt was not answering his call. Harold was loath to hang up because he might be only one ring away from an answer: at any moment Mr. Curt might finish up his conversation and pick up his call. But that didn't happen. And eventually Harold hung up.

In the days that followed, each time Harold dialed the number he either reached the answering machine, which still wasn't taking messages, or he was subjected to the same endless ringing. And because Mr. Curt was obviously insensitive to his plight, Harold came to hate him. Finally, after two weeks of calling daily, his hatred reached such a pitch that Harold thought only of the insults he would hurl and the verbal harm he would inflict upon this unresponsive bureaucrat should he ever reach him. So Harold stopped calling Mr. Curt.

Instead of calling, he went back to writing to the IRS. He succeeded in making epistolary contact with someone. He didn't know who it was, but some functionary acknowledged him by return post. The letter informed Harold that the IRS had previously notified him of his infraction and had sent him a notice outlining the principle, the penalty, and the interest he owed the government. That communication should be in his possession. The letter went on to say that if he had wanted to contest the penalty, he should have sent a written explanation with all necessary information at the time of receipt of his first notification of infraction letter.

Search though he might—and he took days going through stack after stack of envelopes looking for a letter from the IRS—he could not locate the first notice the IRS claimed it sent. He took photos of all the mail in his house and included them in a long, detailed letter to prove he had received no such letter. He demanded the IRS prove they had sent a *first* notice. He wanted a copy of the letter as evidence they were telling the truth.

↜↝

Harold explained his predicament to his cycling group, hopeful someone would offer advice on how to extricate himself from the mess.

—Dude, The Baker said, if you didn't have bad luck, you wouldn't have any luck at all.

—That's not helpful, The Landlord chastised. He's got himself caught in the maw of the machine. It could happen to any of us.

—But how do I get out of the maw? Harold asked.

—There's no way out.

—That's not helpful either, The Baker pointed out.

—You have to get them to buy your story, The Ring said. Keep writing letters. That'll keep 'em at bay.

—Everyone's got a story. Yours is no different from all the other ones they hear. You know what they call stories? Excuses. Just get a lawyer, said The Mope.

—You can, but it'll cost you. And a lawyer won't get you out of it. He'll come up with a way to settle it. And charge you for it.

—But it will save you a lot of aggravation, offered The Baker.

—For twice the cost.

—Pay everybody off and move on, Single-Speed said.

—It's a lot of money, Harold said. Thousands and thousands of dollars.

—Whoa! In that case, wait it out and settle on the dollar.

—The IRS doesn't settle, The Landlord said.

—Agreed. The time factor will work against you.

—I have to fight because it's not fair, Harold said.

—Nobody cares about fair, brother. No one cares about right. It's all about the money.

—I can't just capitulate to the system. Paying is an admission of, if not guilt, then responsibility. That's not morally right. I didn't do anything wrong. What would you do?

Nobody had an answer.

〰

A month later the IRS informed Harold that while he may have responded to their previous notices, they had not received payment, and therefore the issue was not resolved. Because his account still carried an open balance, it had been assigned to the Office for Enforcement Action, which could seize his wages or house or both. Now he had both the government and the credit bureau threatening to dispossess him of his property.

I'm being hounded like a criminal, he thought. He was so furious he had a hard time focusing on anything but his disputes. That he couldn't stop himself from agonizing about how these issues would be resolved distressed him even more. He wanted to go about his life like a normal person. But the uncertainty of the outcome of his battles caused him so much stress that he sometimes woke in the middle of the night drenched in sweat.

The wrongness of it all galled him. The credit bureau was no more than a bunch of thugs and one day they would probably send someone with a baseball bat to teach him a lesson. He could deal with that. He couldn't figure out how to deal with the IRS. They continued to send him letters that opened with the innocuous salutation, *Dear taxpayer*, and then proceeded to threaten him—in their latest communication they outlined the steps by which they would seize his house and put it up for auction—without offering him a forum in which he could present his side of the story. It made him want to scream. That Mr. Curt didn't answer his phone after sending him a letter suggesting that he call was an insult that still rankled.

Anger ate at him. How could this be happening? He was an honest, law-abiding citizen. Perhaps he or Carol or the accountant had made a mistake. Was this any way to proceed? Were these threatening letters necessary? He was being bullied by the government. He, a lone citizen, was locked in a fight with a huge unresponsive system, and he had no recourse available to him. Oh sure, the letters stated he had recourse. One letter included a handout titled *Your Rights as a Taxpayer*. On the front were printed *The Taxpayer Bill of Rights* and *The IRS Mission: Provide America's taxpayers top-quality service by helping them understand and meet their tax responsibilities and enforce the law with integrity and fairness to all.* On the back, it listed ways to appeal and provided tax information and advocate services. This was all bullshit. Lies. Because despite these fine sentiments, in letter after letter, all the IRS did was escalate its threats.

Harold contacted the advocate services and the representatives of his local Democratic and Republican Parties. He sent letters to his congressmen and senators, outlining his case and pleading for help. They all advised that he contact someone different or work out a payment plan with the IRS, which would, one politician assured him, accommodate his financial situation. They were much more flexible these days, he was told. No one was interested in coming to his assistance.

❦

Sarah kept nagging him to date. She e-mailed him. She texted him. She called him.

—You have to be lonely, she said.

—Not everyone who lives alone is lonely. And I've got plenty to keep me busy.

—You can't become a hermit, she said.

He considered telling her about his relationship with K, but the thought of having to recount the history of how they met, and how long they had been seeing each other, and how he felt about K, which his daughter would be sure to want to know, dissuaded him. He couldn't bear the thought of bringing up his trip to California. Which would require admitting he had lied about his whereabouts, and the cause of his injuries. And if he weren't careful he might also wind up divulging that he had promised K he would move to California. About which he was still ambivalent.

Finally, rather than continue to ignore his daughter's request, he submitted. Nothing would come of it, he was sure.

It would be a harmless distraction. And he needed to be distracted.

↜↝

Sarah was delighted with his decision.

—Seeing someone is exactly what you need to pull yourself out of your funk, she said. You can't spend all day fighting with the government and some silly credit bureau, she said.

—I have to do something, Harold said. I've told you, they're not going away.

—You'll figure it out, I'm sure. I have faith in you. In the meantime, you need company. There are so many people online, you're sure to meet someone you like.

Maybe my daughter is right, he thought. For a moment, he fantasized about meeting a woman who would know how to solve all his problems. He would be so grateful he would reward her with love. That he could envision loving someone other than K perturbed him. It made him wonder whether he did actually love her. How deeply was he committed to her? He wasn't sure. She was far away. Maybe agreeing to sign up for the dating site was the sign that he was looking for a way out of his alliance with her. Because if he met someone he liked, and the feeling was mutual, sex would be sure to follow. And that would destroy the sanctity of their committed relationship. Which he was pretty certain he didn't want to do. He was emotionally confused, and no longer knew what he wanted. Why did K have to move to California? They had been so happy. There was no chance of finding anyone else like her, even with the vast powers of the Internet dating site that would be at his disposal. He didn't want to lose K. He wanted her by his side. Did he want her badly enough to uproot his life and move to California to be with her? He wasn't sure. But every day he didn't leave to join her made it harder for him to see how he ever would.

↜∿↝

Sarah sent him the link for the site she wanted him to use. He could start looking at women's profiles immediately, she said. But first he was going to have to answer questions about himself, providing sufficient information to give a potential date an idea why she should respond to his profile. And he was going to have to provide a description of himself, *in your own words*, as the site put it. The final step to complete his profile required that he upload a photo. Harold agreed to answer all the questions asked of him, but he balked at providing a photo.

—You have to, his daughter declared. You wouldn't bother to read the profile of a woman who didn't have a photo, she said. Well, it's the same thing for women. They want to see what they're getting.

—What if someone recognizes me?

—Someone who?

—I don't know. Anyone.

Although it wasn't anyone he was worried about. What if K discovered he was on a dating website?

—I'd be embarrassed if someone recognized me, he said.

—You'd be embarrassed you were looking for a date? Why? Do you think it makes you seem desperate? What's the difference between searching online and going to a bar or a party, or lurking in the frozen foods section in the grocery store or sitting in Starbucks in the hopes of meeting someone? I'm telling you, everyone does this.

—Do you?

—No.

—Then everyone doesn't do it.

—I don't have to do it. I have a lot of friends. I meet people through them and through work. You sit in the house all day. Please, make up your mind you're going to do it. And do it.

Under duress, Harold conceded. He chose what he thought was an appropriate photograph of himself and sent it to Sarah for her approval.

—You're going to post a photo of yourself sitting on your bike, in spandex shorts, wearing your helmet and sunglasses?

—Yes.

—Good luck with that.

—They'll see I'm athletic and have nice legs, and that I'm in terrific shape.

—It's like you're wearing a costume. They'll think you're hiding something. I think you need to go on the site and see what people write and what kinds of photos they put up. After that, you can create a blub for yourself, and you'll be good to go.

↢∿↣

Harold visited the site. To get a sense of what to say about himself, he first read what the men wrote. He discovered they wrote very little, and when they wrote more than very little, it was bad and boring. Even the fellows who were trying to be humorous, or different, or appear sensitive, which they did by saying they were sensitive, were horrible communicators. Most of them were only capable of throwing out sound bites that involved their love of sports or travel. The divorced were eager to get on with their lives, put their past behind them, use the lessons they learned to create a better future without drama. In many of the blurbs the men evaded writing anything about themselves by claiming *it* was all about chemistry or *I'll tell you when we meet*, because, as they admitted, they were unable to communicate their feelings in writing. Which was strange, he thought. Because if these men couldn't put their feelings into words and write them down, why should a potential date think they would be able to articulate the words verbally when they were together? Words were words. You either had them or you didn't.

And why did so many of the single men have photos of themselves without their shirts on?

Uncommunicative or loutish was how most of them came off. If there was one thing most of them shared, however, both the never-married and the previously married, it was that they were *fun-loving*. They were easygoing and fun-loving men, and they were seeking fun-loving women.

—It must be a code word for sex older people use, Sarah guessed, claiming she didn't know anyone who was fun-loving.

Tired of scouting men for instructional purposes, he turned his attention to women, the object of his quest. They were much more effusive and florid in their efforts to portray themselves. If the men were reticent and selfish about what they revealed, the women were oversharers, uninhibited exhibitionists by comparison. On his very first foray into the search for a match, he came upon a forty-five-year-old woman in a town near him who was looking for a companion to accompany her through her next stage in life. She called herself *TimeTested*, and she wrote:

I was born in Texas and raised in Oklahoma by my grandparents after my parents abandoned me. Well, it was actually my mother who abandoned me after my father was shot to death in an attempted stick-up of a liquor store where he was trying to steal money to buy heroin. My grandparents were nice people and made sure I went to church where I learned to overcome my adversities and find my faith. Despite my challenging childhood I have learned to live life to the fullest. I want to be around happy people though I am frequently sad probably due to my early life experiences. I enjoy being real and honest. I enjoy being in nature, but city life is really better. I've been told I'm real, earthy and have a heart, whatever that means. I'm true to me and what matters to me. I went to college in my home state and pledged a nice sorority, and I still see my sisters. I married right out of college, but it didn't work out so well since my husband turned out to like men more than me, so I took my son and after many trials and tribulations I landed in the New York burbs. I was involved with a nice man who taught me a lot about the finer things in life, but all he did was give me money and wouldn't marry me, so after a few years, when his wife cut off his allowance, we stopped seeing each other. I'm curious, always thinking and constantly learning and growing. Things I like: Cohen Brothers, Bruce Lee, Led Zeppelin, Rolling Stones, the Black Keys, Katy Perry, Celine Dion, Queen, Klimt, Nietzsche, Chagall, Picasso, Calder, Eames, Kim K, Chanel, Linen, Levi's, BMWs, Triumphs, Mercedes, Edward Said, Gregory Peck, Clint Eastwood, Glen Beck, Steve McQueen, organic food ... to name a few. I like art. I like shopping. I also like to be around very creative people with a joie de vivre attitude, though I am very conservative both politically and religiously. I enjoy the ocean and small animals, but birds frighten me. I like intimate spots with great food, although I always worry about food poisoning in non-chain restaurants. I would like to travel to Asia, but do not like to fly. I like to hang at the beach with my son and my dog, yet I do not like the water. I also like parks with views of the mountains, but I am afraid of heights. I would like to meet someone with similar tastes and hopes.

Harold was flabbergasted. Why did this woman start by recounting a crime? Did a potential suitor need to know her father died at the bad end of a gun barrel? Wouldn't that scare everyone off? Then, *I like art.* The ramifications of this banality made him cringe. And, Edward Said? Really? What were the chances of that? However, the rest of her description was thrilling with its rhetorical flourishes and balanced clauses. What answer could there possibly be to the dialectical opposites she posited? While it was hard for him to see why anyone would respond to a description like this, from his years in marketing he knew that broadcast advertising, which was what a dating site was, generally generated a one to three percent response rate, so at some point, someone would respond. She was an attractive woman, in decent physical shape to judge by the photographs, and sooner or later someone would see something in her description that he didn't. Someone would focus on one point: *yeah, I like to look at water but not get wet.* Or, someone might sympathize with her fallen father, be seduced by the romance and the woman's rise from unfortunate circumstances, send her a wink, and they'd be off and running.

⌁

After much procrastination, Harold came up with a profile for himself that he thought avoided both oversharing and sounding like a sap. He sent it to Sarah.

White. Male. Tall. Thin. Handsome. Friendly. Occasionally funny. Fleetingly optimistic. Socially skilled. Religiously athletic. Aesthetically motivated. Politically liberal. Cycling fanatic. Women who are intellectually inclined and physically fit and slim preferred. Knowledge of chess a plus.

—I didn't want to use a pronoun, he explained, defending his word choices although she hadn't yet commented. It's different, he continued. It's thoughtful, and it's as articulate as any of the descriptions I saw, maybe more so. Does including *handsome* make me sound conceited?

—It's like a bad obituary, she opined.

—You don't like it?

—Dad, she whined. I'm trying to help you. And you're not helping yourself.

—What do you mean?

—You plan to upload a photo of you in your bike getup along with this description?

—What's wrong with that? I don't want a lot of responses.

—You're purposefully undermining the whole effort.

—No, I'm not, he said, although he knew she was right.

—Yes, you are. Why don't you take a selfie? I'll write something for you, then we'll upload it, and you'll be good to go.

—No.

—Okay, she said. Good luck.

↜↝

Harold posted his picture and profile on the site. He exercised self-control and didn't check to see if anyone had viewed him for twenty-four hours. Then, curious as to the type of woman he would attract, he logged on and looked.

Not a single woman had viewed his profile. He checked again the following morning. Still no viewers. He waited a few hours, and after lunch, because he had nothing to do, he looked again. He was being ignored. He checked that night before he went to bed, and in the morning when he woke up. No one had looked at him. Soon, he couldn't restrain himself from checking his account whenever he opened his computer. After three days, still no one had viewed him. Perhaps the women on the site didn't like his looks, or his personality. Or maybe his daughter was right, he thought. His *getup*, as she had called it, and his description of himself, were off-putting.

Finally, a woman viewed his profile. Harold reciprocated and looked at hers. She wasn't his type. A few days later, several additional women viewed him, but didn't contact him. Which was fine with Harold, because when he viewed their profiles he found them unappealing. Anyway, why did he care? Meeting someone would only further complicate his life.

In the meantime, he became obsessed with looking at women's pictures and profiles on the site. He spent hours trolling through what the site claimed could be potential matches for him by constantly changing the parameters of his search. Every time he altered the age range, the distance from his current location, and the height, weight or ethnicity of a potential date, he gained access to a different population of thousands of women. He clicked on one photo or another, almost randomly. Then he read their stories.

The women he bracketed for his search were between forty and fifty. For the most part, their stories were profoundly boring. They talked about how they had gotten over the negativity of their divorce or separation or last relationship and how they were now more positive and grounded, how they were intent on moving on, becoming balanced, how they needed and wanted and deserved *me time*. Invariably their tales were accompanied by long lists of trivial things they liked, punctuated by sloppy sentimental effusiveness about the love they were looking for, the ideal companion and friend they needed on this next part of their journey through life, and the chemistry that had to ignite the spark if it was going to work. Or their stories were deeply biographical or psychological— some almost phantasmagorical—outpourings of longing and suppressed and stifled emotion, of dashed hopes and dead dreams, stories of women seeking redemption through companionship and love, the love they had lost or never known.

No matter how badly expressed, however, the deep, existential longing and need for love he read in these profiles touched him and made him sad. He, too, was lonely. With K in California, he was bereft of the emotional support that had made him feel alive when they were together. He felt an ache in his heart when he thought of her.

〰

One day, *Hothalfbreed* turned up in one of his searches. Her photos were fantastic, wildly suggestive. Just as her genetic heritage was mixed, her photos showed her to be a cross between a vampy, glitzy Victoria's Secret model and the girl next door. She had posted a dozen photographs, many of which did not show her, but tranquil Japanese gardens and melancholic, misty shorelines, presumably to demonstrate her sensitive side, which was in sharp contradistinction to her words about herself:

I'm a Thai Jewish chick, the spawn of miscegenation. You better look it up if you don't know what it means! There will be a test! LOL. I was raised as a Christian on a coin toss, but now practice Buddhism. I have beautiful smooth silky skin and dark hair that you'll go gaga for. I am in FANTASTIC shape. Those pictures aren't retouched, I promise you. I am devastatingly beautiful but also a psycho bitch from hell! You know what I'm talking about? I'm only half educated. I'll leave it up to you to figure out which half. LOL. I don't have kids, or want kids or like kids. I was never a kid. But you will definitely like me! That is me in that bikini. All kidding aside (I intended that pun), I'm only a little kinky, but it's truly a tragedy that we need such websites here on earth to find a match made in heaven. Are you tracking? I mean, where have we gone as a society? That's what makes me psycho. I don't know what makes me a bitch. LOL. What happened to meeting someone by chance? Walking, and bumping into someone at the grocery or the post office? Or a café, for god's sake, now that there's a billion of them! I never go to the grocery BTW. I only eat fast food. I'm not hoping for much from this site, but I thought I'd give it a shot. There is such a thing as luck, you know. Even a blind squirrel eventually finds a nut. But you must respect my profile: geography, age, body type ... and weight and HAIR requirements. Otherwise don't respond!

After reading so many banal and conventional descriptions, Harold thought this approach refreshing and charming. He liked her language. It was simple and direct and crafted to express her vision of the world. It was not a silly, simplistic list of likes and dislikes. Nor did she invoke long walks on a beach or in a park. Or mention the songs on her smartphone. Or that she wanted to travel or was well traveled. Someone who wrote this kind of truth was seeking a similar soul, hoping by her loopy aggressive tone to scare off the timid, the meek, and the conventional. He imagined it was something K would have written.

He favorited her, and when he checked back a few days later, mainly to look at her photos, which were truly magnificent, some almost pornographic, she had updated her description:

> Okay, so doesn't anybody read anymore? Has everybody forgotten how to comprehend? This is what's wrong with our education system. Are you too caught up in your stupid video games? Put down SimCity and Angry Birds and pay attention you idiots because after 10,000 emails, okay, maybe 1,000, I didn't count them goddamn it, I can't help but wonder why someone from Anchorage, Dallas, Miami and Philadelphia would email me. I live in Brooklyn, you ignoramuses. It says that in my profile. BROOKLYN, New York, is in NEW YORK, for those of you geographically challenged. And if you don't live in New York you don't qualify. I was pretty plain in explaining that in my profile. Under no circumstances am I going where you are. I don't care how much better the weather is. LOL. And BTW, why does a 72-year-old man repeatedly reach out to me when I put a cap on 50? Why can't a short, BALD, fat Italian man take no for an answer? I'm not being mean, but let's be realistic. I have a lot to offer, and I'm not giving it away. I've got standards and I'm not compromising them for you! Yes, you're so fantastic you think I'll make an exception for you. Travel to Miami? I don't care if you buy the ticket, I'm not coming. Doesn't anyone have any respect for my wishes? I mean, really. Yes, you think your kids are the cutest thing on the planet, but I don't. I told you I didn't like kids, no matter what age they are. What part of that declaration didn't you understand? I don't have them for a reason. Okay, got the picture? Now, let's all try to concentrate really, really hard and give it another shot.

This was a fantastic follow-up, he thought. Even though she didn't correctly identify the problem, or the entire problem. Because *Hothalfbreed* came up for her pursuers just as she came up for him: female, forty-four, single, no kids, fit, etc. The men pursuing her had come across her the same way he had discovered her. But they didn't pay attention to what she wanted, as she noted. They paid attention to what they wanted. They saw her hot, exotic body and they wanted her. Her image obliterated every stipulation she had set forth in her profile. While lack of comprehension might partially account for the lack of qualified candidates, what was skewing her responses was that her potential matches had *got the picture*: the images of her were so powerful they overrode the reading. Because when photos like hers were flashed in front of you, the words accompanying them became invisible. Once a man made up his mind that she was hot, nothing else mattered. Every man believed he met the specifications she was looking for, or some of the specifications, no matter how far off from the truth he was. All the arguments language could muster could not convince her suitors to stop trying to have her for this simple reason: desire erases language.

❧

Many more women viewed Harold's profile over the next two weeks, but he didn't receive one wink, nod, like, or query. No one favorited him. His daughter begged him to change both his photo and what he had written in his *in my own words* section, but he refused. They have to accept me for me, he told her.

〰

K was anxious for Harold to write another piece for their blog.

—We need to keep the conversation alive, she said. Give me something more personal, she instructed. People seem to like that.

—Like what?

—Something with you in it. Personal.

—What are you going to write?

—I'm not. I'm painting now, and I think what I'll do is start posting photos of my work, with accompanying commentary. Kind of like a conceptual piece.

She then inquired when he was going to join her.

—After the semester is over, he said.

—I think you should come now. I really miss you. Don't you want to come?

—I do, he said, wondering if he had been emphatic enough. But I have to settle things here first. I have to clear up this mess with the IRS and the credit people.

—Is that an excuse? Is there something you're not telling me? You have to tell me. Be honest. You know I am, always.

—I know. He then pivoted, away from her imperative to tell her the truth about his emotional state of mind, and voiced a different truth: It's really a bad mess I'm in with these credit people and the IRS. You have to believe me.

—I do. But I'm telling you, don't do anything stupid, you promise?

—I won't.

Every day thereafter she sent him a photo of the sunset from her studio window. *Look what you're missing*, she wrote. *Tell me you'll be here soon*, she implored.

Harold continued to put off making a decision. Sometimes he thought about simply packing up, paying off the IRS and the credit bureau, and joining K. But even if he paid off his tormentors, and took off for California, what would he say to his kids? It would be embarrassing to have to confess that all this time he had been secretly involved with a woman and had been lying about it. And once they got past the lying, they would be sure to ask what he meant by *involved*. Was it serious? Why hadn't he told them? Did he love her? Well, maybe it wasn't love. *Be honest*, K had exhorted him. But how could he be honest with her when he wasn't sure he was honest with himself? After all, why was he fascinated by the women on the dating site? What was he looking for? Was it natural to still be so curious about other women when he was supposed to be in love with K? Or was it his frustrated libido that was leading him to look at profile after profile. How did his life get to be such a mess? He couldn't figure out what to do.

Overcome by guilt, Harold went back to his computer to write for K. He wanted to create something she would like. Something that would make her happy. After days of struggling to come up with an idea, he wrote her: I hope this is what you're looking for. It's more jeremiad than screed:

> I was thinking. Something about culture and its function and its relationship to the Internet. Culture, as I understand it, is supposed to broaden and deepen the appreciation of life, bring a greater understanding and sentiment to experience. Culture helps us develop a more acute perceptual filter. Reading and thinking and experiencing art add layers of neuronal

sensitivity to our brains. Exposure to the separate reality that is art may allow us to see meaning in arrangements of things where someone uncultured only sees the things. It may be what Paul Éluard was referring to when he said ... *there is another world, but it is inside this one.*[14]

I often wonder what will happen when the cultural canon of knowledge shared by many of my generation falls into disuse. I often ponder how many more years it will be until this dwindling tribe becomes extinct or totally inconsequential, or before they raise their voices to rebel in one last hurrah against the ever-increasing ignorance of the past that continues to accelerate, aided and abetted by our electronic gadgets.

I may have outlived my time or usefulness or both, but I am going to continue for a word or two. What do we lose if we do not know of the suffering of Job, or feel the emotion and pain of Oedipus? And what if what Donne speculated is true: that *all mankind is of one author, and is one volume?*[15] What if we finally stop reading? What if we devolve to the level of expressing ourselves in emoticons? What happens to a person who is bereft of the knowledge of the heroes of literature, of literature itself? Do you feel differently if you have not heard in your mind the terrifying *cri de coeur* of characters trapped in irresolvable moral dilemmas that crush even the most indomitable spirits? What if one has never had an engagement with James or Woolf or Faulkner? What of the archetypes that have come down through the ages and whose stories have informed us of what it means to be heroic, just, magnanimous ... evil? Where do we learn what a miscarriage of justice feels like, or the jubilation of the triumph of will that overcomes all odds? Where, if we are not reading literature, is the

---

14 Paul Éluard, *Oeuvres Complètes* [Collected Works] (Paris: Gallimard).
15 John Donne, "Meditation XVII," *Devotions Upon Emergent Occasion* (Montreal: McGill-Queen's University Press, 1975).

guide to help us learn how to translate our experiences into feelings that can be shared?

If, as it has been said, *aesthetics is the mother of ethics*,[16] when we lose the connection to the great chain of being of universal consciousness that is the mythic and artistic exploration of the depth of the human soul, do we not become shallower? Do we not lose some of what it is that makes us human? Yes, *It is difficult/to get the news from poems/yet men die miserably every day/for lack/of what is found there*.[17] So are we not diminished in our capacity for feeling, or worse, our understanding of feeling, or worse yet, our ability to empathize with others' feelings? The spectrum of emotions and the arc of their intensities are learned responses, not inherited traits. They are diminished if they are not reinforced and can become unavailable as responses to events, leaving us feeling frustrated and forlorn and empty. If it turns out in future days that the deepest we can plumb our souls is only to a level that relates to a character in *Call of Duty* or *Grand Theft Auto*, do we not become caricatures of what it used to mean to be human?

—Nice job, K said. Just what I was looking for. Especially since it sounds like you.

—Thanks. I think since I started teaching, something has come alive inside me. When I write, I feel better, somehow. And more radical.

—Harold, this is great stuff. I should read more so I can understand it better. I'm going to look up some of these authors, and jeremiad and screed.

—Good idea.

—Okay, Mr. Professor. I'll do my homework. You keep writing.

---

16 Joseph Brodsky (Nobel Lecture, 1987).
17 William Carlos Williams, "Asphodel, That Greeny Flower," in *Asphodel, That Greeny Flower and Other Love Poems* (New York: New Directions [1962] 1994).

The credit bureau was unrelenting in its pursuit of the money they claimed Harold owed them. Letters arrived on a regular basis. Phone calls came at all hours.

Desperate to tell his story to someone in person, and to present the facts that proved his innocence, Harold went to the hospital, the original creditor, and insisted upon meeting with a credit representative. He brought his file of correspondence, including all the bills and all his notes from his many telephone conversations. He had a list of the names of the persons to whom he had spoken and the dates of contact and summaries of his discussions. For easier comprehension, he had incorporated everything into a PowerPoint slide presentation on his laptop, and this is what he showed the representative.

On one slide, he pointed to the spot on a flowchart where the miscoding that resulted in his being held liable for the balance of the amount due had occurred. In a copy of the billing code book he had bought online, he showed the representative how the burden of the cost had been arbitrarily shifted to him due to a clerical error. The credit representative was very polite and listened attentively to his story and was appreciative of his presentation and his substantiating evidence. After checking a few inputs on her computer and having a cryptic phone conversation with some other colleague, she said:

—I'm sorry, your account is no longer active with us.

—But it should be with you.

—I don't know anything about *should*, sir. All I know is it's not.

—You can't help me?

—No, sir.

—Can anybody help me?

—I don't know, sir.

〰

Neither the credit bureau nor the IRS would buy his story. Everything he wrote was rejected out of hand. Morose and out of sorts much of the time now, Harold's riding suffered. His cycling group told him to pay up and move on.

—You're not going to get out of this, Single-Speed said.

—What do you mean? Harold asked.

—He means, said The Ring, that one of those papers you signed at the admissions desk in the hospital constituted an obligation to pay. When you don't pay within the given time frame, the debt becomes a liability on someone's books. When whoever owns the liability wants to get rid of it, they sell it for as many cents on the dollar as they can get. The credit bureau they sell it to will attempt to collect the whole amount and make a profit on the marginal difference: the larger the amount, the more persistent their efforts to collect. If they can't collect it, they bundle it with other debt and sell it to an investor group that specializes in knowing what percentage is collectible. In any bundle, there's one or two large debts. If they collect them, it'll pay for the rest and produce a profit. If you're one of the big ones, they'll keep hounding you until you cough up the dough.

—What do I do?

—There's nothing to do. At the end of the day, all these guys want is the money. It's all about the money.

—But it's all based on mistakes.

—They don't give a shit.

—Maybe I should get a lawyer.

—I've told you before, you'll pay the lawyer, and he'll end up telling you to pay them.

—How is it that there's nothing to do?

—It's the system, my friend. And these credit people will use it to fuck you up. They'll destroy your credit rating, put a lien against your property, and get the sheriff to take it. They're unscrupulous.

—What about the IRS?

—They're just as bad. Government-sanctioned thuggery.

⬱

One morning a notice in his e-mail in-box announced: *Girlygurl looked at your profile and sent you a wink. Why not contact her today?* Curious to read about the first person who had responded positively to his profile, Harold clicked on hers. She was forty-five, lived in the next town, and was looking for a man between fifty and sixty. She wrote of herself:

> You must be able to enjoy a woman with spirit and intellect. You should have friendships and family ties, and actively maintain them. You should enjoy time alone and being with your buddies and don't think about breaking your exercise routine on my account. I will happily be the girl waiting to see you when you're done. I am a passionate and creative creature and loyal and more likely to stick up for others than myself. A happy demeanor and sense of perspective mean I find joy in simple pleasures. I like my humor and martinis very dry and my Scotch on the rocks but my relationships straight up!

Confident and physically expressive, autonomous and attentive, emotionally articulate, affectionate but never smothering, I understand the importance of chemistry in a relationship.... I like to explore it fully with the person I am passionate about. Life is a journey and I am looking for someone who yearns for adventure. Quick wit and deadpan delivery give me the appearance of a nonstick, but I am empathetic and tender and tactile. I want a partner in paradise and offer a port in a storm. I am rough and tough but feminine to the core and a lady at all costs. I love to dress up but can also dress down, and have gone barefoot on the subway platforms late at night and walked barefoot in the East Village in the early morning.

From bedroom to boardroom, I am easily adaptable, like a chameleon. I have a memory like an elephant with all too great knowledge of *The Hobbit*, '80s pop music, and '90s Duke lacrosse stats. I am interested in men who are unafraid of the unknown, open to possibility and greet change along with the occasional catastrophe it brings. Attractive, articulate, and humorous would be a fabulous foundation. Integrity, intellectual curiosity, and loyalty are appreciated. If you share all these thoughts, maybe we can share something together.

Girlygurl had posted ten photos of herself in various outfits ranging from a business suit to a bikini. In each of them, she appeared stiff and uncomfortable and as lifeless as a mannequin in a store window display, though she was theoretically supposed to be having fun. Some of the photos had captions under them. *On the beach in Barbados. Me at the museum. Relaxing at the day spa.* There was something distant and cool and old school and glamorous about her. She reminded him of movie stars from the fifties. She had big, acrobatic hair and alabaster skin and dressed in stylish outfits.

While he thought her attractive, it was disappointing that after reading the 325 words of her profile, he didn't have an inkling of who she was. Who said things like *from bedroom to boardroom*? What did that mean? That she knew how to behave appropriately in both? What would *appropriate* mean? Why would she join in a clause two places, one private and one public, and tease a prospective suitor with the idea she wouldn't disappoint in either? What did this dialectic suggest? That she had attended board meetings and/or knew members of boards? That her scope of emotional and sexual manners was matched by her knowledge of the parliamentarian rules by which board meetings were run? Would anyone reading this ever have thought of taking her to both? Or did this all boil down to: I am an animal in the bedroom and won't embarrass you in public. And if that were the case, then why the pretention? Why not speak plainly like *Hothalfbreed* and set down the facts of your life as they were? Why such calculated, ostentatious use of language? Or, maybe *Girlygurl* was employing the same strategy he had chosen. She wanted to scare away all but the self-selected few who got the joke.

The gamesmanship involved in the dating enterprise suddenly depressed him. He would never know if he were reading someone correctly. The problem was that the self was comprised of multitudinous facts gradually accumulated over the years. Despite the required exhaustive interrogatories one was subjected to about one's interests, hobbies, habits, height, weight, education, religion, and politics, etc. at bottom, Harold decided, the whole online dating process—including the favoriting, the winks, the quick notes—was nothing more than an exercise in subverting time. Which was why people agreed to check off the reductive descriptions that pertained to them on the questionnaires that organized their lives into discrete categories. It was why they supplemented the answers to the questions with a blurb about themselves in their own words. They wanted to increase the probability of having someone get to know them without putting in the time to make themselves known. Time they didn't have. Everyone answered the questions. Just as he had done. Everyone wrote a couple of paragraphs *in their own words*, uploaded a photo, and hit the send button thinking that because they had answered all those questions and written all those words, they had reached deep into the dark pool that was their personality, whereas the image they projected was as shallow as a reflection in a mirror.

He shared *Girlygurl's* description with Sarah.

—I don't think it's that bad, she said.

—Really?

—I mean, it's not really bad. I think she's trying to be cute.

—See. I'll never understand, Harold said. You don't find it pretentious?

—Oh, and you're not pretentious? she huffed.

—Am I pretentious?

—You can be.

—I have high standards. There's a difference.

—You're too critical. She writes well. I would contact her.

↜∿↝

Harold couldn't bring himself to contact her. He returned to look at the woman's photos several times. She was attractive. He wondered what her voice sounded like. He imagined it to be smoky and sensual. But he couldn't overcome his distaste for her writing. Its preachy tone and admonitory form of address were, he was certain, signals that said: *beware, I am a bitch.*

A few days later there was another notice from the dating site. This one announced: *Truthsayer looked at your profile and sent you a wink. Contacting her today might lead to something big!* The dating business was picking up. *Truthsayer* was thirty-seven, lived two towns over, and was looking for a sophisticated, older man.

Her photos showed her to be dark and brooding in appearance, and attractive in an unassuming kind of way. She was, as she admitted, on the verge of looking frumpy. But she had been pretty at some point, he imagined, and with a little willpower she should be able to pull herself back together. She wrote about herself:

> I am not going to lie. Many people, including my former husband and my children, find me annoying. I talk too loud. I am jealous and suspicious since while I consider myself attractive, athletic and fit, obviously there are other women who have better figures and are more attractive. I hate being with men who look at other women while they are with me. Please bear that in mind. I can be very forgetful and that can be fun the first five times I lock myself out of my car, then you'll get tired of it. I leave the dishes in the sink too long. I frequently don't flush the toilet, which is related to my forgetfulness, I think. I love to eat out but constantly complain that what I am eating is not as tasty as it was in the last restaurant I ate in. I also tend to overeat when I eat out since the food is generally much better than what I can cook, but I will blame you for taking me out for the nice meal that led to my overeating. I don't like taking responsibility for my weaknesses. I watch more TV than I should. I am addicted to the Internet and will not put down my iPhone for you even if you beg me, though

I think the Internet is bogus and a plot to control our minds. I don't read enough which is surprising since I am highly educated and pride myself on my erudition. I have moved down market in my friends and acquaintances over the last few years because while I am highly educated and have great taste I am inveterately lazy. I am holding on to my job by the skin of my teeth. I spend more money than I make, but I don't know on what. Like most Americans I have plans to make it big one day. I may have low self-esteem. I need someone to inspire me since I can't do it myself. I rarely pay my taxes on time. I like going to concerts and movies but hate the people who are in the audience and it is not out of the question that I will have an altercation with someone. That someone is usually an elderly cranky man or woman who thinks they are entitled to special treatment because they are elderly. However, it can also be a smartass black or Hispanic who thinks they are in their own living room and carry on accordingly. You may have to defend me. My hair is often dirty, but I will wash it if you point it out to me. Like most women who are not so young anymore I take several medications to ensure I am always in fine working order, but sometimes I forget and then it can get ugly. But I have a sense of humor—after all, I have to put up with myself. I'm absolutely not pretentious. I'm quite gregarious, really, once you get to know me. I'm not one for long walks on the beach unless I'm stranded there and have to go a long way to get back. I'm not implying that I'm not romantic, I consider myself very romantic. I think that whole moonlit beach walking bit is tiresome. I have not done everything by the book. I've had my ups and downs. I'm looking for someone who can appreciate that, someone with his own story. Ultimately, I would like my story to have a happy ending. I'm looking for that special someone to help me write it. Is it you? It might be, but I do have a few deal breakers. You can't be Jewish or Black or Hispanic or Asian or Arabian and must be a Christian. I was raised that way. No drunks, no aging frat boys more addicted to video games than I am to the Internet. No drug users. No separated or married guys. Please don't be gay. I need a clean cut, sophisticated older man with good habits and innocuous hobbies who works every day and wants to make me happy and can deal with my two children. I will try my best to reciprocate.

Harold guessed this woman was on the verge of hysteria. Which was the same ledge he was standing on. She had to be experiencing an ongoing emotional emergency, the urgency of which she couldn't convey to anyone. The only way out of her situation was to write what she wrote, absolutely annihilating her personality by completely enumerating her faults. Which she had laid out in solid, straightforward prose. He looked back at her photos and saw melancholy in her eyes. In them, he read her acknowledgment of desolation and depression. A wave of empathy washed over him. He responded to her wink.

After some innocuous and uninformative back-and-forth messaging, they arranged to meet for drinks.

Harold thought he recognized his date from her photos. She was sitting at the bar. She had described herself as athletic and fit. However, from where he stood—he was still at the front door of the establishment seeing her through a crush of people—he could see something was wrong. The woman at the bar could not be the woman he had agreed to meet. She could not be the woman whose photos had intrigued and beguiled him. But she began waving at him, so there was no mistake. Yet, there had to be an error, he kept telling himself as he approached her. There had to be. There was no way he had agreed to meet someone who had described herself as fit and trim but who in reality was, well, quite robust. She probably weighs more than I do, Harold guessed.

As he drew nearer, he realized all he had ever seen of her was a three-quarters photo of her above the waist. Evidently, she had made use of cropping, and chiaroscuro, to obfuscate the truth, and that truth was now sitting on the stool before him, daintily waving at him.

When he was standing next to her, he saw some aspects of her appearance were true to her pictures. Her breasts were ample, and she was showing the same degree of tantalizing cleavage he had found alluring in one of her profile photos. Her hair was deep chestnut brown with red highlights and was thick and lustrous. Her face was attractive. Her eyes sparkled and seduced. Her skin was flawless.

He took the stool next to her and they began a peripatetic conversation. Her voice was deep and sexy and becalming. He fell instantly under its trance. For a moment, he forgot the physical betrayal of her body. While they were talking, he kept trying to size her up, shifting in his seat, attempting to take in her full measure. She thwarted him at every turn. She kept his gaze above her waist and focused it on her face by locking her eyes onto his, moving her head when he moved his, tracking and capturing his eyes and forcing them to stare into hers. Perhaps, to hypnotize me, he thought. As close as he was to her, he couldn't get a good look at her.

And she wouldn't stop talking. She was making chitter-chatter. Or small talk, which as trivial as it is, serves a purposeful role in communication. In this case, Harold surmised, it was her determined effort to keep him from approaching the issue, a weighty one, that should be put on the table. Because she owed him an explanation about the disjunction between her actual size and the photos and her physical characteristics that she had listed on the site. He thought he was due this explanation because he had showered, shaved, perfumed himself, and dressed in anticipation of meeting someone who fit the description listed on the site, not someone whom, had he sat next to her at the bar because there were no other seats available, he would have largely ignored after a polite hello and a word or two.

For the moment, however, he was stuck listening to her ramble on about the weather, the level of noise in the restaurant, how tough parking had been. At some point he ordered a drink. After a few mouthfuls, he was considerably calmer, still disappointed, but less agitated. Despite her plus size, she was a very high-energy woman. An aura of activity emanated from her every pore. It was surprising she didn't weigh less, with all the calories she must be burning to fuel her frothy personality.

While Harold sat idly, stealing glances now and again at the flat-screen TV above the bar, his date kept up the talk with practically no input from him. She moved with great agility from topic to topic, none of which held the least interest for him, but he was afraid to change the subject and have the burden of carrying on the conversation shift to him. She gesticulated as she spoke, emphasizing her words with hand or body movements, all of which at some point violated his personal space. She allowed herself the liberty of trespassing upon his body, touching his hand or arm or knee for emphasis.

While her talk carried no code other than misdirection, these tactile gestures signified unabashed flirting. She was attempting to gauge his receptivity to her advances. She was spinning a web designed to capture and keep him next to her for as long as she could. She didn't want him to go. She didn't want to go. She was in no hurry to return to her lonely home with two sleeping kids who would, she said, awaken upon her return, before she paid the babysitter, and demand she pay attention to them. They would exhaust her before they fell back asleep, leaving her with no energy but to collapse on the couch in front of the television with her computer on her lap, and sitting there she would snack as she scrolled through the channels and trolled through the profiles of men on the dating site where she had come across him.

Harold was ready to decamp. He felt bad about leaving Buddy home alone. His canine companion had followed his preparations for departure with lugubrious attention, trailing behind him through every room, hoping against hope up until the very last moment, when Harold gently shooed him away from the door and closed it behind, that he might be invited to accompany him.

His date ordered them another round of drinks. He hadn't planned on having more than one drink if he decided his prospective companion was unattractive. You have to have one drink no matter what, his daughter had forewarned him. It's the polite thing to do. And now that he had had one drink he wanted another one. If he went home, he would continue to drink by himself and fret over his battles with the collection agency and the IRS and lament how lazy and useless he was and incapable of writing anything more for the blog because he was too distracted.

Harold asked about appetizers as he didn't want to imbibe more than one drink on an empty stomach. Celia, his date, began reading him the choices, which were written on a chalkboard above the bar.

All of a sudden his presence in this restaurant, sitting on a bar stool next to a woman he had met online, seemed wrong. What was he doing here? Why had he come? Then he remembered: he had come to give and receive comfort. And that was impossible. Because while he thought he had familiarized himself with Celia by viewing her photos, almost daily, and had fastidiously analyzed her *in your own words* section, and fantasized about different aspects of her personality, she had misled him. She was not who she had portrayed herself to be. She was nothing more than a stranger. The idea that he could share his anxieties with her, and talk about his troubles with the credit bureau and the IRS, both of which were closing in on him, was out of the question. Nor could he entertain the idea of helping her unburden herself. He no longer cared. All the hopes he'd had for this rendezvous died the instant he glimpsed her.

Celia was still reading from the list of appetizers. Each time she finished describing a dish, she added her own commentary and waited for Harold's approval, staring expectantly into his eyes. He had read somewhere that if two people stared into each other's eyes at the right moment, at the right intensity, then, similar to the suddenness of a *coup de foudre*, they could see a glimpse of the soul. He wasn't sure if this was true, and if true, whether it would be a glimpse of one's own soul or the other's. In either case, this evening he didn't want to experience any revelations beyond the petty exchange of data he and his date were having.

Harold determined that it was his reticence that caused Celia to take it upon herself to avoid any awkward silences. That was why she kept commenting on every item she read from the menu. Whether it was the mussels in white wine sauce or the tuna tartare, she had eaten it somewhere prepared in this fashion or that, with these friends or those, and it had been good or bad, or she made it better at home. Operating on the assumption that the way to a man's heart was through his stomach, she now and again interrupted her discourse to ask him questions. *Do you like shellfish? Which kind of sauce do you prefer, red or white? How do you react to garlic? Are you familiar with estragon?* She was, he thought, information gathering: the first step in any research project. She wanted to get to know him and seemed to be aware that people came to know other people little by little. That was a positive sign. For it was only little by little that you learned what a new friend or potential lover liked and disliked. You learned their fears and hopes, desires and dreams, their habits and foibles over time. Some of them would be irritating, some ingratiating, but when two people ended up as a couple, it was chiefly because they had been exposed to each other's personality incrementally.

The conjoining of personalities into a couple was a slow and insidious process that gathered its own momentum. It might take months or years before you could consciously admit that there were traits or quirks of personality that drove you crazy about your lover. And not in a good way. Even if at the beginning of your relationship you sensed deep differences that indicated *this will never work*, you likely kept telling yourself, *well, we can overcome that, we can be compatible. She'll change. I'll adapt.* That was how people compromised their way into an untenable relationship. Harold knew this firsthand from his experience with Carol. They had built their life together around all sorts of tenuous and questionable suppositions, most only half true, at best. Over time, the emotional recognition of their incompatibility insinuated itself into their relationship, creating an unspoken but damaging psychological burden. Since their differences were irreconcilable, nothing could be done to ameliorate them. The only way to salvation was for one of them to walk out the door. That was the road Carol had taken. Despite the heartbreak she had caused him, he knew he should be grateful that Carol had had the strength to do what he never could have done.

Celia was still reading from the chalkboard. Every time she stopped, she stared at him so hard he couldn't think. He had to lift his glass and take a sip from his drink to break eye contact. She was hungry for information about him. And soon, anesthetized by the alcohol, Harold painlessly gave up the names and ages of his children and his former wife and how long he had been divorced. He let it slip that he was basically unemployed and trying, perhaps struggling was a better word, to figure out what to do with his life. He revealed his enthusiasm for cycling and his fondness of chess.

Celia shared the names of her children and described her job. She was an auditor or actuary in some firm in the city, and it was boring work, and she wanted to get out of it. She had won a very nice settlement from her ex-husband, who was a bum, really, a rat who had run out on her but left her very well off, but if she left her job she would have nothing to do, unless, of course, she had a partner in crime, which was why she had joined the dating site.

She began to go into detail about everything she mentioned. When she talked about her son, Harold had to know, she said, that while he hadn't met him yet, he had beautiful chestnut hair, like hers, and exquisite fingernails, though he didn't like people to notice them, and he was a gaming enthusiast and comic book collector, though he had trouble reading because he was dyslexic. Next, she wandered into the sticky morass of her emotional life and the disappointment that her marriage had been, which was the cause of the sad state of her current physical condition since she was too depressed to exercise and eating came easier as a way to release her pent-up emotions. Not to worry, she said, once she was happy again she would shed the excess pounds and be her old slim self in no time. Harold had surely figured that out, she guessed, because he was such a nice man, so kind and thoughtful, so unlike many of the jerks she had met through the site. He was quite a bit older than she was, which she liked, because she felt she needed a mature man. He was obviously sophisticated, and she liked that, too, because she thought of herself as being sophisticated. She was an old soul in many ways, she said. She was sure he was as well.

She was stuffing him with compliments, trying, Harold suspected, to get him to fill her up with the same, or at least to prevent him from saying anything even vaguely critical. The alcohol made it easy for him to swallow everything that came pouring out of her. It was strange, because while the tone of her online profile had been harsh, if not abrasive, and certainly self-critical, she exhibited none of those qualities in her discourse here at the bar. He had been prepared to meet someone more edgy, someone with a sarcastic bite who would proffer acute, insightful observations. She brought none of that to the table. Aside from her size, she was completely normal.

It occurred to him that he had been duped twice, for she was neither visually nor verbally the person she had portrayed herself to be. Were it not for the fact that he was, almost against his will, enjoying himself, he would have been angry at her for her misrepresentation. But the buzz at the bar was pleasant. The clink and clank of the dishes, the constant movement of the patrons shifting seats in and out, and the televisions on the wall behind the bar created a warm and lively atmosphere that lifted his spirits. Celia's voice had a mesmerizing effect on him. It almost made him wish he reciprocated her evident feelings for him. But despite her rich, breathy voice and her lustrous dark hair, deep soulful eyes and obvious interest in him, he could not overlook her weight.

At some point, they each acknowledged they had to drive home somewhat sober and therefore needed to call it a night. Celia insisted there was still one question she still had to ask.

—Okay, Harold acquiesced, reluctantly.

She was staring into his eyes.

—Well, I mean, she hesitated. I was wondering…. She stopped. I mean, she started. I think I was pretty accurate in how I described myself in my profile, don't you?

For the first time, she looked away from him, freeing his eyes, allowing them to take in the vision before him that was Celia. She leaned back on her stool, posing magisterially, permitting him to envelop the full spectacle of her corpulent and bountiful body.

Harold was speechless.

—I mean, I may not look it, but I'm still in excellent shape. Touch my thigh, she commanded, taking his hand and placing it there.

She flexed her muscle. He felt it faintly beneath the adipose tissue as it tried to exert itself. He smiled at this demonstration of fitness, and she smiled back at him, again locking her eyes to his.

He was trapped. There was no way he could give her any other answer than the one she had provided. He couldn't contradict her. He was being coerced into corroborating her vision of herself as compact and fit. His will weakened by alcohol and his ego flattered by her keen interest in him, he could do nothing to cause her distress, nothing to correct her misperception of herself. It would serve no purpose and only lead into an area of discussion where he did not want to go. Go home was what he wanted to do. So, while he felt guilty for not being honest, all he could do was assent to her vision of herself.

—Very strong, he said, withdrawing his hand from her thigh.

—Because I sometimes worry I'm misleading people, she said. But you don't think so.

—No, he lied, categorically closing off any further discussion.

He stood to indicate their time together had come to an end. She stood, too, and let him know she needed to use the ladies room before leaving. She leaned into him and gave him a light kiss on the cheek. He returned the gesture.

—I had a nice time. I hope to hear from you, she said.

↞∿↠

When Harold turned onto his street, he saw two police cars with their lights flashing parked in front of his house. There was also a police SUV in his driveway, preventing him from turning into it. He parked on his front lawn and jumped out of his car.

—What's going on? he demanded of the officer standing on his front lawn.

—You live here?

—Yes.

—Your alarm went off.

The cop let him pass.

Harold made his way to the back of the house. Through the window in the mud room, he saw police milling about in the kitchen. As soon as he entered, he noticed Buddy sprawled out on the floor in the middle of the action.

—Buddy, he called.

Buddy didn't budge.

Harold called him again, encouragingly, but with more emphasis in case Buddy hadn't heard him.

—Buddy, he called, his voice rising because of a premonition of pain.

—Sir.

—Buddy, Harold called, crouching, his knees almost to the ground. He called out his pet's name again, but gently, like a supplication.

The room was suddenly silent.

—Buddy?

—He's dead, sir.

—He's dead? What do you mean he's dead? He shook Buddy gently. What do you mean he's dead?

—He charged at us, sir.

Harold knew this wasn't true. Just then he became aware of the blood soaking Buddy's coat, darkening his fur.

—You shot him?

—Sir, he charged at us.

—He doesn't charge, Harold contradicted the cop. He can't charge. He's fourteen. He's old and decrepit and can hardly walk.

—Sir, I am reporting the situation as it occurred.

—No, you're not.

It was only now sinking in: Buddy was dead. Murdered.

—You killed my dog!

Harold was now screaming.

The two officers in charge stonewalled.

—It was self-defense, said one.

—We were responding to a possible crime scene, said the other, larger one who had a tribal tattoo peeking out from under his shirt collar.

—And was there a crime?

—Not as far as we could tell, sir. Probably an alarm malfunction.

—Then why did you kill my dog?

—The dog was threatening me, said the officer, whose name was Molloy.

—He doesn't threaten. You could look at him and see he's not threatening. He can barely get around by himself. Harold was hollering at the top of his lungs.

—Sir, I advise you to calm down. You've been drinking.

—I'm not calming down until you tell me what happened.

—I explained what happened, sir. He charged at us.

—That's not what happened.

—Are you calling me a liar? Molloy asked. He moved threateningly close to Harold. His partner sidled up behind Harold. He was sandwiched between the two men. They were both smirking.

—Yes! I'm calling you a liar. A fucking liar, Harold screamed. You came into my house and shot my dog.

—The alarm you installed summoned us, sir. We were responding to a possible crime scene, and the dog interfered with police business and had to be neutralized.

—And on the fucking alarm registration form I've filled out every year and mailed in with a check for twenty-five dollars, it says in big letters: *Harmless dog in house. Does not bite! Do not harm!* Can't you read? And you shot him!

Harold and Molloy were now standing chest to chest, breathing into each other's faces. Harold wasn't backing down.

—You committed a crime. You're a fucking criminal, Harold yelled.

—Sir....

—What are you going to do, shoot me too? Fuck you.

Harold didn't know what he was saying. The cop began threatening him with arrest and jabbering about his interfering with a police investigation, threatening him with a summons for disorderly conduct in his own house.

It was unbelievable. These fucking blue shirts with their bulging muscles and jack boots and guns were traipsing through his house after killing his dog. They were mocking his powerlessness. They wanted to silence him with the threat of incarceration. He, an ordinary, law-abiding citizen, was being threatened with jail because they had ignobly killed his dog in his own house. What was the world coming to?

Suddenly, one of the cops threw a blanket over Buddy, scooped him up and carried him away. The room emptied. And where there had been activity and noise it was now still and silent. It was a terrible, horrifying silence, an emptiness that broke Harold's heart. Alone, he sat at the kitchen table and sobbed.

⌇

In the days following Buddy's burial, many of Harold's friends stopped by to say how sorry they were. Everyone expressed a mix of sympathy and outrage. Harold told and retold the story to each person who inquired. Someone would take him aside and in a hushed voice ask, *what happened?* Harold didn't tire of telling the tale. Each time he recounted the event, the telling brought back the vision of that evening and all its attendant horror and sadness. And rather than diminish the memory's intensity, the repetition of the story further increased his sense of loss and the guilt he felt about having left Buddy alone to go out on a blind date, of all things. A blind date when he shouldn't have been out on any date. He was in a relationship, for god's sake. Maybe this was his punishment. Why hadn't he left after one drink? Why had he stayed at the bar with a woman he knew he had no intention of ever seeing again? He was overcome by remorse. And the greater his guilt became, the more his hatred of the police increased.

Most of Harold's cycling group stopped by to pay their respects. They were outraged at the cops' callous and extreme behavior. Some of them suggested suing. Others counseled him to file a complaint with the town and see that the officers were reprimanded. A few worried that any action at all would bring down upon him the wrath of the entire police force. They warned him that the brotherhood of blue would band together and make his life miserable. The police are militarized and dangerous, they said.

—I won't be intimidated, Harold said.

—You have to let it go, said The Ring.

—I'm not going to let it go, Harold said. I can't.

Jake and Sarah came home to console him. Carol sent a sympathy card. K spent hours on the phone with him, listening to him rant and rave about all the years of love and tenderness that had been terminated prematurely by a bullet. With the help of too much alcohol, he wailed about the years of love that had been gunned down by some stupid, stupid fucking cops. Buddy had been taken from him by violence that was unimaginable. In his own home. Not hit by a car. Not felled by a disease. Not crippled by age-inflicted infirmities and pain that might, just might, have required his being put out of his misery in a humane and theoretically painless procedure. But killed by insensitive thugs.

No fan of the police, K further incited him, offering him her own critique of the abuse of power by the state. The cops were cowards and perverts and bedwetters, she said.

—Come to California, she pleaded. You have nothing to keep you there now.

—I don't know what to do. I'm too confused, he confessed.

—You have to come, now. I'll take care of you.

—I know, he said. Let me settle everything here first.

—I understand, she said. I'm here for you. I love you.

—I love you too, he said.

↜〜↝

The house didn't seem quite so lonely while Jake and Sarah were there to fill the void created by their departed pet. Sitting together in the kitchen, they reminisced about Buddy's exploits and looked at pictures of him in the family photo album. Harold poured himself glass after glass of Scotch while the children gingerly imbibed the wine he poured for them.

—They didn't even say they were sorry, Harold said.

—They can't. It makes them liable.

—I'm going to sue.

—I don't think you can.

—Of course I can. This is America. Anybody can sue anybody.

—But it won't work.

—Why are there so many things that don't work? Why is there so much that I can't do anything about?

His children glanced at each other but said nothing.

Tears welled up in Harold's eyes. He didn't want to cry. He wanted to know why he had been made to suffer. He wanted to know how putting in an alarm to protect his family had led to the protectors of the peace shooting his dog in his own home. Nothing made any sense. Carol leaving him. His cancer. Getting fired. His inability to control the media that preyed upon him. His fight with the IRS and the credit bureau. Why was everything so fucked up?

—They murdered our dog, your pet.... He was a good dog. An old dog. He didn't deserve to die like that.

〰

Jake returned to California, where he was studying for his MBA at night while working for a tech startup during the day. Sarah had taken a full-time job at a nonprofit women's rights organization in New York. She stayed at the house, trying to persuade Harold to sell it and move back to the city. While he appreciated her emotional ministrations and filial devotion, he was too distraught to hold a meaningful conversation with her. The moment didn't seem right to tell her he did plan on selling the house, nor did he have the emotional strength to tell her he also planned on moving to California, not New York.

—You need to get counseling, Sarah said, trying to be helpful.

—I need to think things through, he said.

He loved his daughter deeply, but he was relieved when she returned to her apartment in the city.

〰

Harold needed to be alone. He tried to think his way through this tragedy, but he couldn't. Instead, he sat in his chair at his desk during the day and did nothing but stare catatonically into space. His study was filled with light as bright as fire on clear days, soft as thistledown on cloudy days. The only sound came from the atmospheric pressure pushing against his eardrums, an eerie, high-pitched, electrical screaming. Sometimes he heard his pulse pounding. Other times it went silent. Then he felt cadaverous and empty and cold. The creaking and cracking of the house that sometimes made him anxious at night was oddly silent during the day. Randomly, he would get up and move through the rooms of the house without making a sound. And the sound he yearned to hear, the *click, click, click* of Buddy's nails on the wooden floor as he followed behind him, was lacking.

It all seemed like a dream. The events that had occurred had to be unreal. Because it couldn't be the case that the police had entered his home, neutralized his pet, as they euphemistically referred to it, and then dismissed his complaint against them, acting as if they had done nothing more than peaceably put Buddy to sleep.

For days Harold sat in his chair, staring into space, living in a trancelike state. At times he was unable to tell if he was at one with everything or totally dissociated from everything. Through the window, he watched the birds hunting food and the squirrels dashing back and forth across the yard, darting up and down the trees, running in circles. He did nothing. He tried to come up with a topic for the blog, but he was too weary to write. He wanted nothing more than to sleep. But he couldn't sleep and suffered through long restless nights.

〰

Nobody would help him pursue his cause for justice for Buddy. The emails and letters he sent demanding restitution were met with bureaucratic indifference. As soon as they could, the officials to whom he addressed himself receded into the anonymous, impenetrable power structure that was the government. No one would take his calls or answer his written correspondence. Nobody cared that the cops had cavalierly killed his pet without suffering any consequences. Harold contacted his local city council members. No one was interested in him or his dog. No one would listen. They had bigger fish to fry, he was told. It happened more often than he thought, they explained. He was advised to stop trying to rub the police department's nose in it.

Harold wouldn't stop. He believed the violence committed against him was wrong and gratuitously wicked. He hired a lawyer to help him. After filing numerous petitions and lawsuits, which were all dismissed, the lawyer said there was nothing more to do. Yes, he acknowledged, it was a miscarriage of justice, but spending more time and money on it wouldn't be productive. Fighting the cops and the county prosecutor and city hall would only lead to trouble. He quit the case.

❧

Harold pressed on alone. That autumn, he began protesting in the street. Several days a week he donned a big sandwich board with a photo of Buddy on it. The words *Justice for Buddy* framed the top and bottom of the boards. For hours at a time he paced back and forth, first in front of the police station, then in front of the borough's administration building. He handed out copies of a small brochure outlining the crime committed against him and Buddy and his grievance against the state. Everyone who stopped and listened to his story was sympathetic to his cause. Some promised they would write a letter in support of him. Some donated money.

❧

The cops weren't happy with Harold's attempts to keep their crime in the public eye and began to harass him. No sooner did he pull out of his driveway and head up the street than a police car pulled up behind him. Sometimes the car followed him to his destination and then sped away. Sometimes a cop pulled him over and demanded to see his license, registration, and insurance, took the documents with him to his car, and after an interminable delay issued Harold a ticket for a dirty license plate or careless driving. Or he was ticketed for failure to use his turn signal even though he had used it, or for speeding, although he hadn't been speeding, or failure to come to a complete stop at an intersection when he had come to a complete stop. He noticed a correlation between the number of days he marched in front of the police station and the number of times he was pulled over during the week.

—If you get too many points for moving violations, your driver's license will be suspended, The Mope informed him.

—They're trying to shut you down, The Landlord said.

—Just stop it, The Ring warned.

—There's nothing you can do. The whole system is corrupt. The cops, the prosecutors, the judges, the local authorities, they're like a fraternity. They all protect each other, said Einstein. You can't win. Hell, they kill innocent people every day and go unpunished.

—No one wants you to give in, but you have to be sensible, The Landlord said.

Harold would not be dissuaded from seeking some sort of justice, even if it meant he would receive only an apology.

The letters from the IRS and the credit bureau became of secondary importance to him. He no longer cared about their threats. His focus was on obtaining some sort of acknowledgment that a crime had been committed against him and his pet.

He wrote a scathing article: *Your Local Police: Protectors of the Peace or Band of Bullies?* In it, he documented the murder of his pet and his harassment by the police. He named names. He fingered the perpetrators. The local newspaper wouldn't publish his article, calling it inflammatory and calculated to cause disharmony in the community. He printed copies and distributed them while he was out protesting. He posted the article on the blog. It received more positive comments than any other entry. Some of the people who commented provided links to other sites where victims of pet murder also tried to raise awareness and seek justice for the crime committed against them. It was to no avail.

Returning home from a bike ride one day, a car with blacked-out windows pulled up next to him and kept pace as he pedaled along. Harold was riding on the shoulder of a two-lane road. The car began pushing him closer and closer to the ditch that ran alongside the road. It moved away, allowing him a safe margin. Then closed in on him again. When he slowed, the car slowed, playing a sinister game of cat and mouse.

The car window rolled down. There sat Molloy, the cop who shot Buddy. His partner was driving the car.

—Hey, buddy, Molloy yelled out the window, causing his partner to begin laughing hysterically. How's my buddy doing?

Both cops howled uncontrollably at the pun.

—Keeping fit there, buddy boy?

They continued to amuse themselves at his expense.

Harold didn't answer. He kept pedaling. Now and again he turned to stare at them. Since he was wearing sunglasses, the cops were unable to see the hate Harold directed at them. He thought about spitting on Molloy. But his position on the bike was too precarious. A sudden turn of the car would cause him to crash. He held his tongue and listened to their litany of insults and shameless references to his pet that they threw out the car at him.

Then Molloy said:

—Hey buddy boy, if I was you, I'd be real careful on that bike. We'd hate to see you get in an accident.

Both cops laughed uproariously.

—Listen, Molloy said, stop being so fucking stupid. Or one day, you'll be out on the road alone ... and hard to tell what could happen....

The window rolled up, and the car sped away.

Shortly thereafter, in the supermarket parking lot, Harold had a chance encounter with the town mayor. He informed him of the harassment and threats, including the latest incident. The mayor listened politely.

—I'm sure they didn't mean anything by it, he said. They're all good men. I'll look into it. I can't promise much if you keep pushing their buttons, he warned.

—They threatened me because I want to see justice done, Harold said.

—Everyone wants justice. The reality of the situation is that the law will always protect the officers of the peace because it's assumed they act in accordance with the law in the line of duty.

—So you're saying these guys are going to get away with this crime and be allowed to continue to mock and intimidate me. Where's the justice in that?

—You can't keep rubbing their noses in it. Nothing good will come of it.

—Something has to come of it, Harold said.

—My advice is to let it go, the mayor said. I'll talk to them, he repeated.

Harold had no way of knowing whether the mayor talked to the officers, or their superiors. In either case, the harassment continued.

⌇

K wrote:

> Harold, I know you are suffering, and I feel so awful for you. I am suffering for you. Please tell me what you're going to do. I needed somebody in my life when I met you, and while you may not think so, you need somebody now. I want you with me here, by my side. I can't be by myself for very much longer without going bonkers. And neither can you. We are essentially lonely people and we need each other. Please come join me before something terrible happens to you.

He called her and said he would join her. K was ecstatic.

—You're going to love it, she said. You're going to love it here.

〜

Harold felt better having made a commitment to K. He had to leave this place. He couldn't stay any longer. He figured he'd pay off the credit bureau so he could sell the house. The IRS hadn't made a move against him yet. He would deal with them in due course.

He hired movers and began to pack.

He didn't know what to do with the all the mail.

Or what he would tell his kids.

〜

Two weeks after his talk with the mayor, while heading home on his bike, Harold sensed the ominous presence of a car trailing behind him. It was the same dark-gray, black-windowed car in which Molloy and his partner had accosted him.

The car sidled up next to his back wheel. Harold kept pedaling as he didn't want to stop and chance a confrontation. The car inched closer. Harold tried to go faster, but he was tired. He was at the end of a long ride and didn't have any energy left. Anyway, it was futile to try to outpace a car. He wanted to make it home without an incident. Now, exhausted, he slowed down even more. The car slowed, too, keeping right beside him. Then, without warning, it turned into him, its bumper hitting his rear wheel. Harold felt himself losing control of the bike. He gripped the handlebars and tried to keep the front wheel steady, but the impact of the car made this impossible and forced him to veer onto the gravel shoulder. As his bike careened out of control he must have blacked out because upon opening his eyes, he found himself at the bottom of a ditch filled with water and mud and bramble and gravel. Soaking wet, Harold got up and shook himself off. The rear wheel of his bike was broken and he would have to walk the rest of the way home. Aside from tearing his bib and some minor scrapes and contusions, he was all right. But his hatred of the police settled in a deep, dark place inside him.

↜↝

Over the next several days, every time Harold thought about what had happened to him, the more outraged he became. The police had killed Buddy and gotten away with it. Now they were trying to kill him because he wouldn't remain silent about their reckless abuse of power. Their attempt on his life cried out for retaliation. But how? Where could he turn for help? The State wasn't going to intervene on his behalf. The mayor had been pretty clear about that. Harold felt isolated and impotent. Which was, he realized suddenly, the intent of the constant harassment to which he was being subjected. He had survived cancer, divorce, and dismissal from his job. He'd suffered those physical and emotional insults with quiet fortitude. But between the ongoing persecution by the IRS and the credit bureau, and now the police.... How much could a man take? How could he live with the humiliation of not standing up for himself when there was no one else to stand up for him? For the rest of his life he would live in shame if he didn't take some action. He couldn't cower and run. He couldn't take off for California and let the police think they'd won. He had to teach them a lesson. A lesson they deserved. And the more Harold thought about it, an extreme action appeared to be the only way to teach them a lesson and free himself from the ignominy in which they were forcing him to live. Extremism in the defense of liberty[18] *was* acceptable. The cops had taken the law into their own hands. Why couldn't he? He was entitled to stand up for himself. He knew how to fight. He had fought the brutes who had attacked him and K in the parking lot in Wyoming. K said he was a fighter. So, he would fight. What choice did he have? Sometimes in the course of human events it was necessary for a person to dissolve the political bonds that connected him with society and to assume the separate and equal station to which the laws of nature entitled him.[19]

⌁

---

18 Barry Goldwater: 1964 Republican National Convention speech upon accepting the nomination for President.
19 U.S. Declaration of Independence.

Harold formulated a simple plan. He told his children he was going to California for a vacation. I need to clear my head, he said, by way of explanation. They both thought it was an excellent idea.

The next day he rented a box truck. Using a wheelbarrow, he loaded the truck with the postcards, letters, manila envelopes, magazines, newspapers, catalogs, and fliers—all the unwanted mail he had been bombarded with for years on end. It took him three days. The labor left him exhausted. But for the first time in a long time, each night he fell into a deep, dreamless sleep.

After the truck was loaded, he spent a day researching online how to make a slow-burning fuse. He settled upon a method that used potassium nitrate and sugar, and purchased the necessary materials. The instructions required him to mix the potassium nitrate and sugar in a pan of boiling water. When the water evaporated and the mixture thickened, he stirred in about six feet of yarn, making sure the entire length of it was saturated. After taking it out, he dried the yarn on newspaper and then cut it in thirds, making three fuses. His scheme had a bit of Rube Goldberg about it, as he planned on using the fuses to ignite a bundle of matches that would, in turn, ignite a flare that would subsequently ignite the shredded paper he would use for tinder, and once this got going, the flames would ignite the gas in the cans and start the conflagration. At the local gas station, he filled the three polyethylene plastic canisters he had bought with high-octane gas and loaded them into the truck. Back home, he drilled holes in the roof and sides of the truck to make sure there would be sufficient oxygen to feed the flames and vent the smoke.

The next morning Harold went down in the basement and unpacked the guns his father had left him when he moved to Arizona. He took out his Winchester rifle and a box of .223 Remington cartridges. He chose a 9mm Beretta for a sidearm. He loaded four clips with full metal jacket, 124-grain bullets, slid one into the pistol's magazine, cocked it, put the safety on, and then stuffed the other three clips in his pockets. He took the box of 9mm bullets as well. He unpacked the shoulder holster and put it on and tucked in the Beretta. Back upstairs, he got his coat and backpack. He printed his ticket for California, checked the boarding time, and put it in his pocket. Then he put the rifle in a double 50-gallon black garbage bag, along with all the ammo and the scope, and carried everything out to the truck.

From his surveillance missions, he knew Officer Molloy and his sidekick should be leaving police headquarters to go on patrol in about sixty minutes. This would give him enough time to park, light the fuses and get up the stairs to the roof of the building across the street from the station.

No sooner was he on his way than his stomach began to growl. He hadn't eaten. He was tempted to stop for a coffee and a bagel, but it was absurd to be thinking about food at a time like this. Moreover, he had seen too many movies in which the protagonist's slight deviation from a planned set of actions, due to some physical necessity or uncontrollable psychological urge, foiled the entire operation. And while a diversion caused by a character flaw was acceptable on screen to create dramatic tension, he didn't want anything to foil his plot. He didn't want any drama other than the one he was going to cause.

He was stopped at a light, turning the dial on the radio, when he heard:

Spring was never waiting for us, girl
It ran one step ahead
As we followed in the dance....

It took him only a moment to realize he was listening to Richard Harris belt out *MacArthur Park*, a song he hadn't heard in at least a decade, if not longer. The song's shifting tempos and overwrought lyrics oscillated from melancholy to outright bathos. He had loved this song when it came out. It corresponded to some deep unknown yearning within him, capturing the emotion of loss and beauty and sadness and hope. While it was sappy, it never failed to stir him. Now it seemed all wrong. All wrong for the mayhem he was about to create. He needed to hear something more militant, something more obstreperous. Something apocalyptical. Like the Doors' *The End*. Or better, the second half of *The Soft Parade*, with its increasing, insistent, sinister organ and rolling drums and rising level of threat as Morrison's voice became ever more gut-tural and ominous *callin' in the dogs, callin' all the dogs, callin' on the gods*. These didn't seem like the kind of thoughts he should be having in light of what he had planned, but he didn't know what kind of thoughts he should be having. And he had no time to think about thinking anymore because he was in front of the police station, and all he wanted to do was focus on the plan, which called for finding a parking place. It was early enough that there were two contiguous spaces a little north of his target, and he fit the truck neatly into them, just two car lengths from the entrance of the police station.

Harold exited and went around to the back of the truck. Setting the garbage bag next to him, he unlocked the gate.

After making certain no one was watching, he climbed inside. He unscrewed the caps of the gasoline cans and splashed some gas around. He arranged the bundle of matches and the flare. He set the fuses in place. Then he lit the paper. He waited until the fire got going, then he exited the truck, shut the gate, and locked it.

The building he had chosen from which to wage his war was across the street. It was a four-story walk-up. The door to the fire escape was at the back of the lobby. No one was at the front desk. He bounded up the steps. Once on the roof, he propped the door open with a pencil. He made his way to the parapet and looked down at the street, where smoke was starting to escape from the truck. At the other end of the block he saw his car sitting in the municipal lot, waiting for him to make his getaway. Everything was going according to plan.

Harold sat down and took the rifle, the scope, and the ammunition out of the bag. He attached the scope. Then he loaded the rifle magazine and pulled back the bolt, chambering a cartridge. Getting up on his knees he looked over the edge of the parapet. He saw he could improve his sight angle if he moved down toward the south corner of the building, which would put him opposite the police station. By this time, smoke was pouring out of the truck. He ripped the cover off the box of cartridges for easy access.

He heard raised voices in the street below. People were congregating near the truck, obviously concerned about the evolving situation.

Harold checked his watch. It was 7:50. Officer Molloy should be walking out the front door of the station at any moment. And sure enough, right on schedule, there he was, standing outside the threshold of the door, staring at the smoke, nonchalantly chatting with some other cop standing next to him, suspecting nothing. Harold was down on one knee now, the rifle barrel resting on the parapet. He found Molloy in the crosshairs of the scope. Just then Buddy's murderer turned abruptly and headed back inside. Harold placed the crosshairs right on the back of his neck, right above where his stupid tribal tattoo peeked out from under his collar, and as Molloy pulled open the door, Harold attempted to pull the trigger, but the muscles in his finger went slack. He was paralyzed. Out of nowhere, he heard the words of long ago in his head: *don't let him get away, pull the trigger, pull the trigger slowly, son, breathe in as you pull so you don't move the barrel*, and he breathed in and pulled the trigger. Molloy crumpled on the ground. With the fire blazing and sirens wailing, it was hard for those near the downed officer to figure out what had happened.

No one ran and ducked for cover. Molloy's snarky partner came out to see what all the commotion was about. He knelt down next to Molloy and felt his pulse, then drew his sidearm. In the blink of an eye Harold chambered another cartridge and shot him through the temple. He fell on top of Molloy. *There now*, he heard a voice whisper in his head.

Harold was packing up, preparing to flee, when the wind, which had been steady but faint, started to pick up. He watched as a sudden gust pushed open the rooftop door, and the pencil that had been preventing it from closing fell to the ground. The door slammed shut. He dropped the rifle and ran to the door. It was locked from the inside. There was no handle on the outside.

He stood motionless, in shock, shaking his head in disbelief. Then he ran around the perimeter of the roof, looking for another way out. There wasn't one.

He began laughing hysterically.

Meanwhile, he heard increasing activity on the ground below, voices yelling and people running. He glanced over the parapet. Smoke was billowing out of the holes in the roof of the truck. Flames were licking the side panels. Any minute, the gas tank was likely to blow. The street was deserted. The bodies of his victims were gone. The fire truck sat idling, lights flashing. He was preparing to shoot his way through the door to make his escape when a voice announced:

—You're completely surrounded. There's no way out. Give yourself up now, the voice commanded.

He cautiously peered over the edge of the parapet. He spotted a cop behind a tree with a bullhorn. There were other cops crouched behind cars and behind the brick wall in front of the police station. They all had their guns out. The cop was right. There was no way out. There was nothing to do. Just as in chess, he was trapped in a back-rank debacle. He was done for.

He sat down. He had been mad, but now he was sorry. His anger had dissolved in the shots he fired. He felt empty, aching and tired, very tired. He had hated the cops who killed Buddy and who had tried to kill him, but now that they were dead, he realized it was wrong to have killed them. Of course, it was too late to repent. Everything was always too late. He heard a helicopter. As it came into view, he made out the police decal. He was sure it had come to take him out. He didn't want to die. They were going to try to neutralize him from the air before risking sending men up the stairs. He threw himself on his back, pulled out his Beretta and took the safety off. There were eighteen shots in the clip and he had three more clips. Aiming in the direction of the chopper, he fired, emptying the magazine. The pilot must have seen the muzzle flash because the chopper rapidly lifted and cut away.

Harold reloaded the Beretta and chambered another cartridge in the Winchester. It was too bad it had come to this. But he had run out of options. Just how he had ended up on a roof with a rifle, taking revenge, or rather, seeking retribution that had been denied him through every other means, mystified him. What had come over him? He shouldn't be here. This wasn't supposed to happen. Not to him. But here he was. And down there were two dead cops. And that door slamming shut had sealed his fate. Like the cop with the bullhorn had said: there was no way out. He wanted to call K and tell her he wouldn't be coming to California. But the conversation would be too heart-wrenching.

He realized that he hadn't even left a note. Or any sort of explanation. Of course, anyone would be able to see his behavior constituted a statement of protest. A manifesto of sorts. Surely anyone who took the time to investigate his life would see today's outcome was the reasonable resolution of everything he had suffered. The logic was irrefutable. Or was it?

Maybe the authorities would be too stupid to understand what had happened here. He was tempted for a moment to lay down his guns, throw up his hands, surrender, and explain himself. Capitulation would yield him his fifteen seconds of fame. In the spotlight, he might be able to get his story out. It wouldn't help. And he wasn't sure he could explain what had occurred. The media would swallow him and spit him out and then rapidly move on to the next tragedy, and he would be left a prisoner in a jail cell while the gears of the system ground on to their inevitable conclusion about his fate. Being held captive by the government, interrogated, and ultimately, doubtlessly, punished for his actions, which he knew were wrong but rational, was out of the question. He had been dealing with idiotic, unresponsive, insensitive institutions with no good results for too long, and to continue the same behavior and expect a different outcome from those he had received on previous occasions was the very definition of insanity. And he wasn't insane. He had fought the law. He had taken retribution against the system. He was sorry he had killed those men. He wanted to say he was sorry. He wanted to see his kids and tell them he was sorry for what he had done. He wanted to tell K he was sorry. But there was no chance he was going to turn himself in and get brutalized in the maze of the justice system. The state didn't have a clue what justice was. Otherwise, they would have punished those cops. It was all a bad joke.

The helicopter came back for another go at him, but the pilot must have seen him raise the rifle and veered off. Before long, the police would come crashing through the rooftop door.

Enervated, he could do nothing to prepare for the onslaught to come. He didn't want any more trouble.

Sitting in the sunshine, he was at peace. The light warmed him and calmed him and made him feel, as it always had, at one with everything around him. For a moment, his mind went blank. Or he fell asleep. He was so tired.

He watched the smoke from the truck rising into the sky, higher and higher. The gas tank ignited, and there was a thunderous explosion. Without thinking, he raised himself to take a look at what he had wrought, and the instant he showed himself something hit him in the chest and flipped him around. He stumbled and fell over the parapet, and

before he could think, before one more word came into his
mind, everything went black.

❧ ❧ ❧

www.ingramcontent.com/pod-product-compliance
Lightning Source LLC
Chambersburg PA
CBHW031022120726

47905CB00007B/2010